POOR BOY ROAD

James L. Weaver

Poor Boy Road

First Published by Lakewater Press 2016

Cover Design by Emma Wicker

ISBN-13: 978-0-9944511-3-2

BOOKS IN THE JAKE CALDWELL SERIES

POOR BOY ROAD

ARES ROAD

BLACKBIRD ROAD

ASYLUM ROAD

To my amazing wife, Becky,
and my two awesome kids, Madison and Max.

Your support and daily inspiration made this book possible.
I love you all more than you know.

CHAPTER ONE

The apartment door was a cheap, brown, six-panel hollow core with a grimy peephole and colorfully articulated graffiti—enough to make a priest blush. But Jake Caldwell was no priest. The door would splinter off its hinges with a swift kick from his boot like the previous dozen he'd blasted in over the years. But bashing in doors was noisy and drew the wrong kind of attention. It'd be easier if Carlos simply opened it, so Jake knocked—again.

He waited, listening for sounds of movement over barking dogs and crying babies in the units behind him. He felt conspicuous in the littered hallway with the Glock at his side, the sun shining on his head through a hole in the building's roof like a spotlight. Even in this shitty neighborhood, a guy his size with a gun would warrant an eventual call to the cops. Shadows flickered across the bottom of the door—Carlos staring out the peephole. A stupid move. If Jake was here to whack the guy, he could shoot him through the door. The worst he planned to do was break Carlos' kneecaps.

"Open the door, Carlos," Jake said, pounding the door twice. No answer, but the shadow wavered as if its owner was uncertain if it should stay or run.

Jake sighed and stepped back. With his good leg, he exploded forward, driving his heel above the knob. The lock assembly collapsed against the splintered wood and the door burst open. Carlos cried out as the door cracked his face, his wiry frame

1

collapsing to the floor. He landed on his ass, holding his nose. Blood poured through his fingers and on to his stained, white T-shirt. Jake entered the apartment to the stench of cigarettes and fried onions, and shut the remains of the door behind him. Carlos pushed back toward a kitchen stacked with crusted plates and glasses, his wide eyes fearful.

With the gun trained on Carlos, Jake strode to the kitchen, grabbed a grungy dish towel and dropped it in the bleeding man's lap. Carlos whimpered as he pressed the towel against his shattered nose. The late morning sun peeked through the blinds, highlighting his greasy hair that dangled across sunken cheeks. Jake tucked the Glock in his waistband and picked up a dented baseball bat leaning against a bookcase covered with dead plants. He held it with both hands, testing the weight. Thirty-two ounce aluminum fat barrel. He walked to Carlos and tapped him on the leg with it.

"Where's your daughter?" Jake asked. The last thing he wanted was a little girl to run in screaming. It happened before.

"Hospital."

"Still?"

Carlos nodded. "They can't figure out what's wrong."

"Sorry to hear it," Jake said. He didn't wish that kind of heartache on anyone, but Keats wasn't paying him to be a shoulder to cry on. "The two grand. Where is it?"

"Ain't got it. No insurance and the damn hospital's sucking me dry."

The bat burned in Jake's hands. He didn't want to, but his orders were to liberally apply a blunt object to Carlos' legs if he didn't have the money. There would be hell to pay otherwise. He raised the bat, white knuckling the handle.

"Please, Jake," Carlos pleaded, tears rolling down his weathered cheeks. "It's my little girl, man."

The brief howl of air and hollow thunk of metal meeting bone echoed in his head, a ghostly sound from long ago. The excruciating pain would rip through the man's body, so intense he would shred his vocal cords from the screams. He knew because he dealt this punishment too many times in the past. He could feel it because he was once on the receiving end. As the bat barrel wavered and Carlos sobbed, Jake's cell phone vibrated for the fifth time in twenty minutes. Like the previous four times, he silenced it.

He glimpsed a picture on the kitchen counter of Carlos and his daughter. Eight years old, cute as hell in a white dress with a daisy in her thick, black hair. What would happen to her if Jake broke her daddy's legs? What would Keats do to him if he didn't? His cell vibrated again.

Jake tossed the bat on the floor. It clanked toward the busted front door and he yanked the cell from his pocket, checking the number. 660 area code. Home, if there was such a place. He needed to think, and the call provided as good a distraction as any. Jake answered with his left hand and pulled the gun out with his right, aiming it at Carlos.

"Dad's dying," Janey said. His sister's first words to him in a year. Like he was supposed to give a shit. Jake said nothing.

"You there, Jakey?" she asked. "I've been calling all morning."

Carlos crab-walked across the threadbare carpet toward a darkened corner of the Kansas City apartment. Jake kicked Carlos on the leg. The bloodied face looked up and Jake held the Glock palm out, gesturing him to stay like a dog.

"This isn't the best time, Janey."

"Is there ever a good time for you?"

He pictured her in the kitchen at the old house in Warsaw, tapping a pink-slippered foot on the black and white checkered linoleum. The long, curly phone cord snaked around her bony arm.

He stepped back and sunk his two hundred and twenty pound frame into an ancient brown recliner. He glanced at the coffee table to his left, to a tower of overdue bills from Children's Mercy Hospital and a half-empty pack of Marlboros. He set the gun on his lap and threw Carlos the cigarettes. Carlos fished a lighter out of his pocket and lit one with shaky hands.

A full minute of silence. Jake clicked the old, gold ring against the butt of the Glock, counting off the seconds until he couldn't take it.

"What do you want me to say?" he asked.

"Say you're coming home and helping me take care of him. I can't do this anymore by myself."

"So phone a friend."

"Yeah, right. Like anyone else would help him. Please. I need you."

The old man's hardened face sprang forward. Sharp nose, sharper tongue. Face cracked like an old baseball glove from too much time in the sun and too many Camel unfiltereds. Wispy remnants of dull red hair drooping from his long skull like some creepy circus clown. The white leather belt swinging and that goddamn gold ring. He rubbed his tired eyes. There were a million things he'd rather do than return to his central Missouri hometown. But, he owed his little sister.

"Okay, Janey. I'm on my way."

Jake hung up without waiting for a response. He leaned forward, staring at the photo of Carlos and his daughter across the room, picturing her lying in a lonely hospital bed. Carlos may be shitty with his finances, but he was a decent father. There would be no bone breaking today. Then again, he probably knew that the second he raised the bat.

"It's your lucky day, Carlos." Jake stood and pulled the man to his feet. Carlos winced as he wiped his shattered nose on his shirt.

"You broke my nose."

"You didn't answer the door when I politely knocked."

"I was sleeping," Carlos said.

"Bullshit. You were hiding."

Carlos paused. "No bat?"

"I'm giving you another week."

4

"Keats never gives nobody more time."

"I'm giving you the week, not Keats. Like I said, your lucky day. Go buy a lottery ticket." Jake pressed the gun barrel into Carlos' cheek. "Two grand, seven days or your nose won't be the only thing that's broken. Comprende, amigo?"

Jake tucked the Glock away and walked through the broken apartment door, down the narrow stairs and out to his truck. He climbed in and stilled, inhaling and exhaling measured breaths. Dad's dying. Janey's words hung in the air like a cartoon balloon. He let the adrenaline fade and replaced thoughts of his father with wonders about what Keats would do to him for not breaking Carlos into a million pieces.

Twenty minutes later inside his apartment, Jake pulled the dented, gold ring from his finger and set it on the counter. He grabbed a beer from the refrigerator, staring across the kitchen to the wall calendar sent courtesy of the Warsaw Chamber of Commerce. August featured a white board sign with peeling, green letters welcoming you to Warsaw, Missouri, population 1,654. The battered sign blocked the day's blazing sun and was probably supposed to evoke some warm and fuzzy feeling of the dawn of a new day. Instead, it summed up home in an instant—chipped, shitty and falling apart.

He'd managed to avoid his father for sixteen years. Fucking Stony. Jake had to meet his boss first and, if he made it out of there alive, make the trek southeast to the home he swore he'd never return to. He took another drink from the bottle and poured the rest down the drain. He should've let Janey's repeated calls go to voicemail. She always wore rose-colored glasses when it came to their father. She didn't have the scars he did.

CHAPTER TWO

The patrons who recognized Shane Langston moved out of sight when his muscular frame filled the door of the dimly lit Danny's Bar and Grill, finding the sudden urge to go to the bathroom or check out the songs on the broken juke box. He liked that respect. The foursome at the pool table didn't know Shane and openly admired the busty red head on his arm, her pink spandex jogging suit leaving little to the imagination. Shane eyed them as he walked up to the bar, then ticked his head to his trailing bodyguard. Antonio moved his mountainous black frame toward the men who got the hint and returned to their pool game.

"Where's my brother?" Shane asked the bartender.

"Back office," the bartender replied. "He ain't in a good mood."

"Neither am I." He kissed the red head on the cheek. "Stay here with Antonio, sweetheart. Have a drink."

"My shift starts in an hour," she said.

"This won't take long. You'll be swinging from your pole in no time."

He sauntered the length of the mahogany bar, and past the bathrooms to a door marked "Private." He threw it open without knocking and found his older brother, hands to his head, staring through thick-framed glasses at a computer monitor on his paper covered desk. His brother stiffened and pushed away from the desk when Shane entered, his breathing ragged.

"Thought you were going to Warsaw," his brother said, a tremble in his voice.

"I am," Shane said. He dug his fingernails into his palms as he crossed the room and towered over his brother, looking into his red eyes, pupils dilated. High as a kite. Not surprising, but disappointing, a clean six months down the drain. Danny had the willpower of a gnat.

"Where's the product, Danny? Or did you smoke it all?"

"It's coming. There was…a slight hiccup in the delivery."

Shane shot his palm out and smacked the side of Danny's head, sending his glasses flying against the wall. With his teeth clenched, Shane leaned in. "You call my shipment getting hijacked and two of my men killed a fucking hiccup?"

Danny rolled his chair against the wall, pressing a pasty palm to his head. "I'm sorry, Shane. There was nothing I could do."

Shane raised his hand again, fist white with tension. Danny was always the weak one. Why are you surprised he screwed this up? Shane closed his eyes and breathed through his nose, willing his fist to lower. He walked around the desk and sat in the opposite chair. Danny smoothed back his thinning hair and picked up his glasses from the floor. He sat upright, fidgeting, unable to figure out what to do with his hands.

"What happened?" Shane asked.

"Four guys broke into the office. Shot Dom and Marco in the head and took everything."

"We know who it was?"

Danny shook his head. "Surveillance video didn't help. All dressed in black with masks."

"How'd they know where the office was?"

Danny shrugged and pulled himself back to the desk, flicking his eyes to the computer monitor. "Beats the shit outta me. I switched the location like you told me, never in the same place more than a coupla times. I did it just like you told me."

Shane leaned forward and turned the monitor. A balance sheet for Danny's Bar and Grill lit up the screen. He scanned to the bottom and regarded the large, red figure at the base.

"Seems your bottom line isn't getting any better," Shane said.

"There was the big check you had me cut to that children's agency that hit this month."

"My helping find homeless kids a bed isn't affecting your operational costs."

"I'm doing everything I can. Power & Light District is killing me," Danny said, referring to the bar and restaurant complex across from the Sprint Center arena a couple of blocks south in Kansas City's downtown. A hot spot for sure, but the bar shouldn't be hemorrhaging money. Danny picked at a scab on his arm.

"How much did we lose in your little fuck up?"

Danny's eyes darted around as if looking to the ceiling for the answer he didn't want to give. "About a hundred grand."

"A hundred twenty-five, to be exact. Would just about cover the hole you're in, wouldn't it?"

Danny raised his hands, eyes wide. "Whoa. You suggesting I set this up?"

That's exactly what he suggested. Shane sat back in his chair, searching his brother's wide set eyes.

"Did you?"

"Jesus Christ, Shane. Why would I do that?"

"That's not a denial."

"You're my brother, man."

His brother. One of three. The two oldest six feet under, killed in a shootout with the Chicago police when Shane and Danny were teenagers. Shane's heroes who taught him it was better to be at the top end of the food chain, and not the low end consumer. Danny was never a hero to anyone. Just a stupid, useless addict.

"When did you start using again?"

"I'm not," Danny said.

"Don't bullshit me. You're wired tight as a drum right now. I sell the shit, big brother. I know what it looks like."

"It was just a taste."

Shane sighed. "I'm working hard to get a foothold in this town. If I'm going to take it over, I need you. That asshole Keats isn't just going to roll over and let me have his territory."

"But why mess with Keats? Don't we have enough?"

"That's your problem, Danny. You always were short sighted. You can never have enough. Even Keats won't be enough, but it's a start."

"You really think Keats hit us?"

Drug addicts were notorious liars. Danny was no exception. Shane plucked a letter opener off the desk and cleaned his nails with the tip. "I have no doubt it was him. I just have questions about how he found out about the office location."

"Keats has ears everywhere. He could've heard about it from any of your guys."

Shane stared at the eight inch letter opener he bought for Danny when he gave him the bar business. A gift to his big brother for his six months of sobriety. That was two relapses ago. This time, he actually thought he'd make it. He jumped back years to Mickey and Ian showing him the ropes while Danny stayed home to read comic books. Danny who refused to come to their funeral because it would "be too hard." Danny who spun the revolving door in and out of rehab. Danny who screwed up everything he touched, no matter how many chances he was given. He was weak, and a chain was only as strong as its weakest link.

Shane stood, and paused behind Danny's chair, the letter opener still in hand. Danny tried to push away, but Shane shoved the chair forward and pinned him to the desk.

"I have ears everywhere too, Danny. And I know you told Keats about the office location for a cut of the loot. Didn't you?"

"No. No way, man." Tears choked his voice.

Shane stuck the point of the letter opener under Danny's chin, pressing up and forcing his head back so he could see into Shane's eyes. Shane placed a hand on his brother's sweat-covered forehead. Tears rolled from Danny's bloodshot eyes and over his cheeks.

"I have big plans for Kansas City. You were supposed to come along for the ride. We were going to make it a family business."

"Shane, please," Danny blubbered. "I'm sorry. I didn't think he'd kill Dom and Marco. It wasn't supposed to go down like that."

"It's okay, big brother. I forgive you." With a quick thrust, Shane shoved the letter opener into Danny's throat, holding his convulsing body as the blood spilled down his last brother's shirt. Danny's red eyes bulged, then grew dim. The twitching stopped and Shane stepped back, dropping the letter opener into the pooling blood on the floor.

In the office bathroom Shane washed his hands, then smoothed his hair in the mirror. He took one last look at his brother and walked out the door, pulling it shut behind him.

Antonio hung up his cell phone as Shane strode across the bar toward him.

"Dexter is all set with the supplies. It's going to be a very lucrative load," Antonio said. The red head sipped her drink and flipped through a magazine.

"Good. Send him to Warsaw."

"How'd things go with Danny?"

Shane shrugged. "My brother has decided not to continue with the family business. He left a little mess in his office on his way out."

Antonio looked over his shoulder at the closed office door. "I'll take care of it."

"I'll take her to the strip club. Call me when you're done and we'll head to Warsaw. Keats needs a message."

"What kind of message?"

Shane glanced to the red head, leaned in and whispered into Antonio's ear. Antonio drew back, eyes widening for a split second before resuming his normal stone faced appearance.

Shane's lip curled. "Keats just started a war he's going to wish he never even thought of."

CHAPTER THREE

Jake wove his black F150 to the River Market north of downtown Kansas City, through streets bordered with squat red brick buildings hosting bars, shops and offices. He turned down an asphalt drive and parked in front of the warehouse, its parking lot cracked like a broken mirror, determined weeds rising through the slits. He grabbed the envelope containing the two grand Carlos owed. Taking the cash from his diminishing personal stash was easier than going to his boss empty handed.

The stairs to Keats' office creaked under Jake's reluctant footsteps. He hated meeting with his boss. During his last visit, he tried not to squirm as Keats turned a guy's knuckles to powder with a nutcracker. Jake could still hear the man screaming, like his cries were embedded in the wood-paneled walls.

"Jake," Jason Keats said as if greeting an old friend. The room reeked of earthy-toned cigar smoke. Keats pulled his black-suited frame from a leather recliner. His skin was cold and clammy as they shook hands. His peppered hair slicked back with too much gel. "How's things?"

"Been better. I need to bail for a few days. My old man's dying and my sister needs me back home."

"Sorry to hear it. You close with your dad?"

"No."

"Any particular reason?"

"He's an asshole." He handed Keats the envelope. "Two grand from Carlos."

"He had it, eh?"

"Yeah, shocked me, too."

Keats thumbed through the money in the envelope and raised it to his scarred nose, sniffing.

"Doesn't smell like Carlos. Smells like you."

Jake shrugged. "Smells like two Gs."

Keats smacked Jake on the chest with the envelope. His inviting mood dissolved. "What am I gonna do with you, Caldwell?"

"In terms of what?"

"In terms of you not doing what I fucking tell you to do."

"I got your money, Jason. Count it."

"I know it's there." Keats tossed the envelope on the mahogany desktop. "I told you to break this guy's kneecaps. You going to float every piece of shit I send you to collect on?"

"Isn't breaking kneecaps kind of a stereotype?"

"It's effective."

"Guy can't work if he can't walk."

Keats sighed. "Are you trying to piss me off?"

"Look, his daughter's in the hospital and he's got a pile of bills that would choke a horse."

"I'm not running a goddamn charity. Carlos didn't use the money he borrowed for medical bills. He bet on a dog-shit horse and lost. Again. What's really going on?"

"Nothing," Jake said, slumping in the chair in front of Keats' desk.

"Bullshit. How long you worked for me?"

"I don't know. Five years?"

"Six if you count Oklahoma," Keats said. "You were a dark soul who didn't mind dishing it out."

"I still dish it out."

"Carlos is the third fuckin' guy you've spotted this month. I got no use for someone who can't follow simple orders."

There was no reason for Jake to lie. "It's getting hard to sleep at night," he said, focusing on his bad knee, avoiding Keats' stare.

"You want out?"

There it was, laid out for him. Leaving the life had dominated his thoughts for the last few months. But it would be a tricky extraction, maybe fatal. "No. Maybe. Hell, I don't know."

Keats eyeballed him. "See, you know a lot about what I do. Guys with less knowledge than you have disappeared."

"I'm no rat. You know that."

"An enforcer with a conscious isn't worth shit to me. You want out?" Keats asked again.

Jake twirled the ring on his finger. Echoes of screams. Bones snapping. "Yeah, I want out. This is turning me into someone I swore I'd never become."

Keats hoisted himself from the desk and walked to a wet bar. He poured two fingers of Scotch from a crystal decanter into two glasses, adding a single ice cube to each. He handed one to Jake. Keats took a slug and leaned his steely frame against his desk. Jake stared at his drink. He hated Scotch.

"Your old man's down in Warsaw, right?" Keats said. "Dying from what?"

"Probably cancer. He smoked like a chimney."

Keats watched him, calculating. Jake figured he had a fifty-fifty shot at staying alive to the end of the day.

After a minute, Keats spoke. "Tell you what. You handle a problem for me, and I'll let you go free and clear."

"What's the problem?"

"You heard about Big Teddy?"

"Who hasn't?" Jake said. Teddy Garrett, Keats' rival in Kansas City. The Feds swept up Teddy and his crew last week in a drug raid in nearby Independence.

"With Teddy out of the picture, the roaches are coming out of the woodwork. There's one roach keeping me up at night."

"What's it got to do with me?"

"This roach operates in your old neck of the woods," Keats said. "Has all of Benton County under his thumb, but he's eyeballing expansion into KC. He's an ambitious little turd who I want permanently squashed. You're the boot that's gonna do the squashing. Plus, there's a nice going away present for your years of service."

"I take care of the guy and you just let me go?"

Keats nodded. "You bury this guy and your old man. Two birds with one trip. Then you can ride off into the sunset and do whatever the fuck you want."

Jake narrowed his eyes. Here was his lifeline and he wouldn't have to spend the rest of his days looking over his shoulder. Keats wrote on a slip of paper and slid it across the table.

Jake lifted it and read the name. "If I don't want the job?"

Keats swallowed the rest of the Scotch and chuckled. "I think you know the answer to that question."

Chapter Four

Willie Banks angle parked at the entrance to Casey's convenience store west of Warsaw's downtown. He ran his hand along the rusted side of his truck—its primary color best described as primer—tracking the lunchtime crowd. He waited for three things: the phone call; his partner Bub to finish taking a crap; and for sweet Halle.

A red flash of guilt rolled through Willie as Halle strolled out the front door, but it didn't stop him watching her across the parking lot. He may not have finished high school, but even his limited twenty-three-year-old intellect was well aware that sixteen-year-old Halle represented statutory rape. But he could look and fantasize. Perfectly round, little ass in tight jean shorts, bronze quads popping with each stride. Long, blonde hair flowing down the middle of her tanned back. A brilliant smile that stopped his heart every time he saw it. She was the full package and he loved her, not that he'd ever let anyone know. He licked his chapped lips as his partner Bub lumbered out the door behind her, a missile-lock stare on her swinging back end. A stare so hard he stumbled off the curb and dropped his pizza box; but only giving up when Halle climbed into her mom's car.

"Goddamn," Bub said as he hefted himself into the truck with an acrid wave of body odor, like he had dozens of rotting rodents stuffed in his pockets. He scratched the sparse stubble on his cheeks, the fat folds on his neck bunching up as he craned to watch the car drive away. "That Halle gets any hotter and I'll just have to take my chances with the Old Bear."

"He'd skin your fat ass alive, Bub." The car headed east up the hill toward downtown and out of sight.

"I ain't scared of big bad Sheriff Bear."

"Then you're a fuckin' idiot."

"Wish he'd back off us," Bub said, balancing the greasy pizza box on his lap as he got situated. "We gotta make a living, right?"

They waited in silence while the Lake of the Ozark weekend tourists mixed with the locals around them. Bub finished off the pizza slices, downed the forty-ounce can of Budweiser and scrubbed his mouth with the back of his meaty forearm. He belched loud enough to shake the flakes of rust from the side of the truck.

"So what the hell are we sitting here for?" he asked, tossing the empty box to the floor and wiping his greasy fingers on his overalls.

"We're waiting," Willie said.

"Duh. For what?"

"For Shane to call."

Bub huffed and lit a cigarette from a white generic pack.

A rail-thin woman with stringy, black hair that looked as if it hadn't been washed in a month walked out of Casey's, a bottle of soda in her hand and two dirty, snot-nosed kids at her feet. Delilah Warner. She stopped when she spotted Willie's truck. She jerked her head around checking out the area for cops, trying to appear casual—and doing a piss poor job of it.

"Get a load of Delilah," Bub said.

"She looks like she got hit by a truck. You got anything on you?"

"Yeah, a little bit."

"Good, 'cause she's heading our way."

Delilah slid over to Bub's side of the truck, dropping a twenty in his hand. He handed over a plastic bag and she disappeared around the corner of the store.

"Right in front of her fucking kids, man," Willie said.

"So?"

"So? That doesn't bother you?"

"Why would it? Cash is cash. When we getting another shipment?" Bub asked, stuffing the twenty in his pocket. "We're runnin' low. Down to pebbles."

"Supposed to be next week."

"Mexicans hauling it again?"

Willie nodded. "Monday, I think."

Bub belched again. "I hate dealin' with those greaseballs. Puffin' their chests and flashin' their guns. Assholes."

"Got no choice, Bub. Bear has a vapor lock on supplies. We can't make any quantity worth a damn on our own."

"Well, Shane's still making a fat ass roll off it. What about us?"

Willie didn't answer. The economy sucked and people were strapped, which cut into Willie's margins. Of course, Shane got his cut. Shane Langston always got his cut.

"Shane oughta say something to those guys," Bub continued. "That last package sucked. Might as well been selling rocks of baby powder. You try it?"

Willie shook his head. He didn't touch the product. Never do what you deal. Especially when what you're dealing ain't yours in the first place. He'd seen firsthand what meth did to people—his mom, the poster child. Lank hair, black gums, cadaver face; like someone sucked the life essence from her and left nothing but a shell. Too consumed with the poison to even think about actually being a mother. He also saw what Shane did to dealers who dipped into their supply and got sloppy. Willie liked having all his fingers attached.

"I still think we should take the Mexicans out," Bub said. Willie rolled his eyes. "A truckload of drugs and wads of cash. One score, that's all we need. Hightail it out of Benton County and disappear."

"You got a death wish, my friend," Willie said.

"Not if we do it right." Bub took a deep drag and flicked the cigarette butt out the open window.

"There ain't no doing it right. They got Uzis in those trucks and those crazy wetbacks would carve the Mexican flag on your fat, dead belly. Even if you got away with it at the time, they'd find you. Where you gonna go? Mexico?"

"Maybe Canada," Bub offered. "My momma says I got some Frenchy in my blood."

"You're as French as a Mickey D's fry," Willie said. "If the Mexicans didn't get you, Shane sure as hell would. Dude's got mad reach."

"Still worth thinking about, man. Better than this nickel and dime shit we're making now."

Willie couldn't argue with his logic. They used to make a decent living passing meth to the County's downtrodden. Until Sheriff Bear squeezed the trade, shut down the labs, and the mass distribution of meth in Benton County came to a screeching halt. Now that the Mexicans were moving product north, a chance of getting back in the game reared up. There certainly wasn't much else to do for a living for the likes of him in Warsaw.

"We need some bank," Bub said. "Get us on the good side of Poor Boy."

Willie nodded, thinking about his trailer back in the deep woods off Poor Boy Road. Out of sight, out of mind. A stranger venturing off Highway 7 or Old Highway 65 heading toward Fristoe on double-lettered roads like MM or NN might find some seriously nice lakefront homes owned by people in real estate or banking. The stranger had an equally good chance of wishing he never made the turn off the highway, and would be happy to get out of there unscathed. Crumbling wood-framed homes and shacks, some so run down that hanging laundry provided the only clue someone actually lived there. Every town, every city had their economic dividing line between the haves and the have-nots. Poor Boy Road was their line.

Willie fantasized about moving far away plenty over the last year. Fly away with the little bankroll he stashed away in his momma's old music box behind a loose brick at his trailer. Drop the meth dealing and live cheap as he made his way somewhere warmer. Maybe go to Colorado and hook up with his little brother. Avery said it was good money. Anywhere else would be fine as long as it was far from the rotting meth mouths pleading for more and the vice grip of Shane Langston.

Just as Willie was a hair's width from kicking Bub's ass out of the truck and peeling away in a cloud of dust with a hearty Hi-Yo Silver, his burner cell phone rang. Willie answered, listened, and the thoughts blazing down the road disappeared. Sixty seconds later, he grunted and hung up.

"So what's the plan?" Bub asked.

"Shane wants to meet."

"Here?"

"My place. We gotta get Howie and Bennett."

"What the hell is it about?" Bub asked.

"Didn't say. I didn't ask."

"He sound okay?"

"He sounded pissed. Someone's ass is in a sling."

"Hope it ain't mine."

"You and me both, man."

Willie started the truck, backed up and sputtered out of the parking lot to Main Street. He hung a left and paused at the intersection at Highway 7. The empty stretch of road invited him to head west out of town. Willie's instincts screamed at him to turn that way. Instead, he turned east toward home. A knot balled in his gut. When Shane was pissed, things tended to get bloody.

CHAPTER FIVE

How the hell had he got himself twisted in this mess? Jake sighed as he cruised south on US 71 Highway out of Kansas City, through the city of Grandview and on to places less populated. Take care of his dying old man and kill a rival drug lord for his boss. What a clusterfuck homecoming.

Hard to believe he'd been doing this shit for Keats for six years. He used to lie to himself and think of collecting as just a job like someone working in a bank or flipping burgers. He'd tell himself those he collected from were degenerate scumbags who rolled the dice the second they took a dime from a man like Jason Keats.

The douche bags were the easy ones. The ones to whom the world owed a favor. Nothing was ever their fault. The fuckin' Jets blew the spread by allowing that last meaningless touchdown. The asshole boss fired them, not because they couldn't show up to work either on time or sober, but because they didn't like their ethnic heritage, whether black, Hispanic, Italian or White Trash. These people always blamed someone else for their crappy lives and Jake had no qualms putting a few lumps on their skulls with a blackjack to collect what they owed.

The problem was they weren't all douche bags. Sometimes they were friends. Sometimes the sound of a friend's thumb snapping like a twig echoed in his dreams. Sometimes the howling winter winds outside his window in the dark of night sounded like the screams of a child walking in as he punched their daddy to a bloody pulp. Sometimes he had to get up and scrub his hands raw under scalding-hot water to get at the blood that would never wash out. Sometimes he stared in the mirror at hollow eyes, seeing the face of a man who hid in the shadows, a man he swore he'd never become. Sometimes.

He rolled past Harrisonville and exited US 71 on to Highway 7, his stomach knotting tighter as he closed in on his hometown. Thirty minutes later, he drove into Clinton and stopped at Wendy's to take a leak and grab a late lunch before pressing on.

Jake could almost smell the oil and grease from the Clinton junkyard where the old man used to take them on the weekends. Jake and Nicky crammed together in their dad's ancient heap, listening to him cuss the wasted truck's very existence in between puffs of Camels lit one after the other in an unending chain. Stony placed Nicky in charge of keeping upward pressure on the eight-track cassette in the dash, so "He Stopped Loving Her Today" would play without warbling. Any deviation to the tone of George Jones would earn Nick a smack to the back of the head. Ever since Mama died, Stony would listen to almost nothing else in his truck but that eight-track. The premise itself made for a stupid country song.

The roads curved and the hills deepened the further Jake got from Clinton, like the road itself didn't want to go to Warsaw either. He took a pull from his water bottle and turned on the radio, tired of the silence. He sang along and agreed with Kenny Chesney; he should indeed sit and have another beer in Mexico. Mexico sounded good. Warm sun, fine sand beaches, clear blue water and Pacifico beers lined up in front of him. Find a big-breasted señorita with a happy disposition. Maybe after this trip. Maybe after Stony finally kicked the bucket and he fulfilled his obligation to Keats.

The town of Coal swam up, so small that if you sneezed, you'd miss it entirely. Jake slowed without thinking and pulled into the dirt lot of The Coal Bin. He dropped his six-foot two-inch frame out from the truck and ran his hands over his cropped hair, pushing his muscular arms into his back. The vertebrae clicked and crunched.

As he leaned on the warm hood, smelling a mix of manure and exhaust fumes, a dark-haired boy darted out the front door of the white-washed general store and jumped off the step. The boy looked just like Nicky. Mop head and deep dimples the girls giggled over. Nicky. It was hard not to remember their last trip here.

They'd had a particularly good junkyard hunt, Dad finding a needed part to some contraption he was fixing. Old Stony feeling generous, actually hugging his two boys as they went inside, the non-violent physical contact a rarity. Jake peered into the pop cooler while Nicky perused the candy rack. Stony's thin, steely arm draped around Jake's neck.

"You always had a sweet tooth for that orange fizzy shit, Jakey." He stroked the back of Jake's head. "Why don't you get one of them Orange Crushes?"

"Just wondering if I should try somethin' new," Jake said, liking the feel of his dad stroking his ten-year-old head despite the cold band of the ring on Stony's finger.

"Nothing good comes outta new things, boy," Stony said. "Stick with what ya know and you'll never be disappointed. Come on, pick something. We got shit to do today."

Jake grabbed the can of Orange Crush and set it on the counter next to Nicky's Hershey bar. Stony added three packs of Camel shorts to the haul, which would last him the rest of the day and into tomorrow afternoon at best. Depending on how much he drank.

Jake and Nicky grinned ear to ear as they strolled out of The Coal Bin. Janey would whine she didn't get anything, but for now, the brothers were kings. Kings until Nicky tripped over a pothole on his way to the pickup sending his unwrapped candy bar flying through the air, dumping with a puff on the thick dirt in front of the gas pumps. Tears welled up in his eyes as he stared at his lost treasure.

"Pick it up," Stony said after a moment, dark storm clouds rumbling to the east with his clipped cadence. Stony's mood could turn on a dime. Dust covered Nicky's candy bar along with a dark liquid. Probably oil leaked from some junk

heap. A glop of bird shit rested on the edge, already blending in as the summer sun blast melted the chocolate.

"Pick it up," Stony repeated, each word a menacing statement. Jake tightened his grip on the Orange Crush can.

"But, Daddy," Nicky protested. Stony took a step toward them and leaned forward, his bared, yellow teeth inches from Nicky's face.

"Boy, I paid a quarter for that candy bar and you will pick it up in the next two seconds or you will be one sorry little son of a bitch."

Nicky picked up the candy bar by the end, holding it in front of him between his thumb and index finger, like a dead rat he held by the tail. He shook it. Some of the dust fell away, but the dab of bird shit clung to the end of the bar, white with black speckles.

"Eat it!"

Nicky looked at Jake in horror, desperate for some support. Jake dropped his gaze to his wiggling big toe sticking out of his hand-me-down tennis shoes. There was nothing he could do.

"Eat it," Stony repeated.

"But it has bird poop and dirt on it," Nicky said, his voice the high-pitched whine that set their father off every time. Jake cast a quick glance to the old man's wry smile.

"I don't give a damn what it's covered in, boy. I give you a treat and you throw it on the ground like we got money coming out our asses. Now, eat it. And if you try to wipe off anything from that candy bar before it goes into your whiny fucking mouth, I'll beat your little ass until you can't sit for a week."

Tears rolled down Nicky's face as he brought the shit-covered chocolate bar to his mouth. Jake held out his Orange Crush for Nicky to wash down his punishment. Stony's hand shot out like a striking snake and knocked it from his hand. His soda fizzed in the dirt before Jake scrambled to grab the can. He hurried to the pickup, away from his brother and Stony. He faced the truck and raised his head to the cloudless sky. Nicky began to cry.

The slam of the front door to The Coal Bin scattered the echoes of Nicky's cries. A farmer emerged from the store with a pack of cigarettes in his hand. Jake climbed into his truck. He'd thought about going inside for old time's sake, but remembered the old times weren't so good. As he rolled back on to Highway 7, he remembered after that trip, Nicky never ate chocolate again.

CHAPTER SIX

Shadow and light danced as Jake cruised the tree-lined highway, the outskirts of Warsaw looming ahead. Three years ago he'd made it this far, only to chicken out and take the long way around to the cemetery so he didn't have to set foot in town. How much had the place changed in his sixteen year absence? The sign declaring the town's motto of "Striving to Be Drug Free" was gone. He guessed they eventually gave up.

Casey's hunkered in a depression on his right, the lot full of trucks and boats gassing up for a day's adventure on Truman Lake. The lake and the associated reservoir covered over fifty-five thousand acres, featuring great crappie and bass fishing waters bounded by jagged bluffs. Thousands of tourists flocked to the area for weekend getaways or national fishing tournaments. It appeared the town's big source of income hadn't changed.

His sister Janey would be waiting at the house. The thought of the homestead tightened the knot in his stomach and an overwhelming urge to head back to Kansas City rippled through him. But that would mean a return to a life with Keats. If he wanted out, he had to press on. He turned off the highway and on to Main Street, Bob Seger ironically playing a song of the same name on the radio.

As he crested the hill, all three blocks of downtown Warsaw rose up. Hole in the wall restaurants, corner bars, and the small town standards of an attorney, drug store and bank. A side street dipped toward the lake, empty trailers perched on the asphalt while the boats flashed back and forth on the water.

The road declined past a muffler shop, and squatty houses cropped up on either side, alternating between well maintained and borderline abandoned. He wheeled to the right at a fork and the ranch houses gave way to a used car lot, gas stations and a strip mall housing half a dozen businesses. The old Pizza Hut still operated in a bowl below the road. He'd managed to work there for a brief three days before the old man came in drunk looking for free pizza. When he didn't get any, Stony broke a stack of plates along with the jaw of the store manager who promptly fired Jake through a mouthful of bloody teeth.

Jake rolled down the window to evacuate the memory and gunned the truck south to the White Branch exit. He stopped at the T-junction across from the Headwaters Motel looking down the hill to some of Dad's favorite watering holes. Memories flashed like lightning—his first kiss, his first slug of Jack Daniels in misty rain, the first time he found the value of a pool cue as both a money making tool and a weapon. The Roadhouse Bar where he learned in a muddy parking lot how much pain he could both dish out and endure.

He turned right heading past the Lake Hills Motel and the high school where Jake met the only girl he ever loved. After a series of twists and turns, Poor Boy Road lay ahead. Stony said someone named the road after a combination gas station liquor store ran by Howard and Madge Gardner in the fifties called Poor Boy Store. A Poor Boy Garage came and went next door, ran by one of his dad's drinking buddies. Jake guessed the name just stuck.

He turned, cruising slowly all the way to Turkey Creek Cemetery, where generations of Ozark families were buried. He stopped at the entrance to the tiny cemetery, waiting for some feeling, any feeling to take hold. Instead, stone-cold silence. He drove through the empty lot and parked by the gate. As he climbed out the truck, a flash of brown nabbed his attention across the road. A beautiful auburn horse with a jagged white splotch on its forehead focused bowling-ball eyes on Jake over the top of a white fence. Nicky loved horses.

Jake plodded through the gate and down the cracked, asphalt pathway. Ancient, pitted cemetery headstones mixed in with freshly covered graves. Born in 1827, died in 1866. Born in 1979, died in 2013. Side by side, the recent and the historic. Generations of families laying together forever.

Jake walked a hundred yards to the back of the cemetery before stepping off the path through the mix of grass and thistles, past headstones gaudy and plain. He stopped before the simple black, granite tombstone of Margaret Anne Caldwell—died June 5, 1985. Nicky was ten, Jake eight and Janey five when their mother dropped dead of a heart attack in the family kitchen while making dinner. He didn't remember much of her. Just a haze of a long-haired woman who loved him.

Next to her marker was another that brought a flood of memories, not hazy this time but high-definition sharp. Flashes of laughs and screams, fists and fights. Tears burned inside Jake's face, aching to be released. He choked back the pain. Caldwells didn't cry. Heading back toward the truck, the plain, black, block letters etched into a generic, white granite marker burned in his retinas. Nicholas Caldwell. Born November 3, 1975. Died February 7, 2012.

Jake had watched Nicky's funeral from the safety of his truck, far down the road. There'd be too many questions he didn't want to answer, and the anger still boiled toward his father—an emotionless robot by the graveside. Janey's shoulders heaved with sorrow under a midnight black dress that belonged to their mother. He saw all the familiar faces and though part of him wanted nothing more than to go over, the shame for abandoning them pressed his foot on the gas as Nicky's coffin was lowered into the earth.

He stared at the tombstone a moment longer, checked his watch and headed back to the truck. His cell rang as he reached for the door handle. Keats.

"Where are you?" Keats demanded.

"Heading to the house to see my dad."

"What about Langston?"

"I just got to town, Jason. Haven't exactly had the chance to do any detective work."

His boss's heavy breathing cracked the cell phone. "I want that motherfucker dead. I don't care how you do it, just do it now."

"What happened?"

"A box with a dripping head just showed up on my desk, that's what. The head of his fucking brother."

Jake leaned against the truck and blew out a breath. "Jesus."

"Yeah, Jesus. That's exactly who that crazy little son of a bitch is going to need before I'm through with him."

"Why'd he kill his brother?"

Keats paused. "Don't worry about it. You worry about putting him in a body bag. I know what you're going through so I'm going to be generous. You got two days."

Jake stood, gripping the phone tight. "Two days? I don't have a clue where this guy is and don't even know what's going on with my dad yet."

"Two days, Jake. Or I'll send someone else to do it and they'll be coming home with two body bags."

The line clicked and Keats was gone. He pressed his lips together and resisted the urge to throw the phone across the parking lot. He stared across the road to the horse.

"What the hell are you looking at?"

Jake climbed in his truck and headed toward home, the forty-eight hour clock in his head ticking away.

CHAPTER SEVEN

Willie drummed his fingers on the steering wheel, waiting for Howie in the clearing where the Skaggs' trailer slumped. Shane wanted to meet at four o'clock and they only had five minutes to make it. He eyed the disarray around him. A rusted Coleman grill next to a makeshift fire pit holding the blackened aluminum shells of dozens of Old Milwaukee cans. Sonic and McDonald's wrappers spilled from ripped and scattered trash bags, cardboard beer cases and empty cartons of cigarettes resting in front of the trailer where they were thrown.

Howie Skaggs, skinny with auburn hair he probably cut himself using rusty scissors and no mirror, stumbled toward Willie's truck, his hangover apparent as he squinted against the descending afternoon sun. He stuffed his lucky Green Lantern T-shirt into the front of his jeans before climbing into the back of the truck. Bennett, Howie's brother and trailer mate, waited in the truck bed, chain smoking generic cigarettes and flicking his zippo lighter open and closed. A third character named Artie Thomas sat next to Bennett. Willie went to high school with Artie and occasionally used him, but he wasn't a regular crew member. Willie didn't trust the shifty-eyed asshat, but sometimes they needed a body for grunt work.

Willie headed deeper into the country down Poor Boy Road. The wet winter had taken its toll on already marginal roads, and he bounced off familiar ruts for a few miles. They crossed Miller's Creek with a splash, and darted along a partially hidden path marked by a rusted blue, fifty-five gallon barrel hiding in the weeds. Fifty yards of winding, narrow path led to Willie's trailer. The double-wide slunk back in the trees behind a dirt expanse adorned with a red picnic table on one end, and a rusted, steel A-frame swing from the sixties on the other. Worn chains without seats dangling in the breeze. Trash Willie had yet to burn neatly piled in bags next to a scorched drum.

A new Lincoln Navigator waited for them, shiny and black save for streaked mud splashes on the lower frame. Willie parked under the shade of a gnarled oak. Shane came around the trailer by the picnic table, zipping up the fly of his black slacks. His biceps and pecs bulged through a thin, gray shirt two sizes too small. A used car salesman's smile blazed through his black goatee and dark sunglasses. Willie put the truck in park and climbed out as Shane's giant bodyguard, Antonio, emerged from the Navigator. Shane was a compact ball of muscle, like a pitbull. In comparison, Antonio was a black mountain who scared people into submission just being there.

"Willie," Shane said, offering a solitary, bone-crunching pump. Shane sat at the picnic table. Willie and Bub joined him as the three other mopes headed inside the trailer. Shane lit a cigarette, took off his sunglasses and set them on the flaking wood.

"How you been?" Willie asked.

"Good. Business is picking up a bit, money rolling back in as you know."

"Not as fast as I'd like."

"Not as fast as any of us would like, Willie. Patience."

"You must be doing better than us," Bub said. "Nice Navigator."

Shane's thick eyebrows drew together and he inclined his head slightly toward Bub. Willie's lips tightened.

"Was I talking to you, Bub?"

"No," Bub whined, like a six year old who got his hand caught in the cookie jar.

"Then keep your mouth shut until I ask you something. Nod that fat fucking skull if you get me."

Bub nodded and scratched at the table with a yellowed thumb nail, red faced and abashed. Shane's clenched jaw released.

"I got two things," he continued. "One is the deal I mentioned. The other is a loose end we need to deal with."

At the mention of a loose end, Willie tensed, his asshole puckering shut like a time lock vault at the bank. Bub's hand gripped the edge of the table. Willie and Bub had both witnessed the bloody way Shane dealt with loose ends.

"Relax," Shane said. "It's not either of you. First though, the deal. We have an opportunity to supplement our product supply. Get back in the manufacturing business instead of playing middleman to the Mexicans."

"How?" Willie asked.

"Got a connection out of St. Louis. He scored some bulk supplies we can use to make a ton of product."

Bub's hand released and he raised it to ask a question, like a third grader in class. "What about Bear?"

"Don't worry about Bear." Shane stubbed out his cigarette in a clay pot. "This is a finite supply we'll set up in a temporary lab. We'll cook it quick in a secluded area, and have the stuff bagged and ready for distribution. I take half of the haul for my other dealers, you get to keep half since you're my biggest base of users anyway."

"Who cooks?" Willie asked. Willie could cook decent meth in small batches, but it wasn't the quality of Shane's chefs.

"I bring up my guy from Kansas City. You, Bub and the Skaggs' boys assist. My cook brings me my half, you guys sell the rest and I take my usual cut minus five percent."

"Minus five?"

"Yeah," Shane said. "You've been doing good work here, Willie. Times have been tight, but you stayed the course and didn't bitch. Thought I'd give you a little bonus for this batch as a thank you."

"Appreciate it, Shane," Willie said, allowing a smile to appear. "Where's the cook going to be?"

"Got an old house picked out on Poor Boy Road. Saw it on a helicopter tour over the area last month. Antonio checked it out a couple weeks ago and says it looks good. Even has a back door trail outta there in case shit goes bad."

Willie was pretty familiar with the inhabitants of Poor Boy Road and couldn't think of any abandoned house. It had to be hidden pretty well. Much needed dollar signs flashed. If it was a big enough haul, he could get the hell out of this racket and Warsaw.

"Sounds good," Willie said. "When?"

"Tomorrow," Shane said. "We get the lab set up, and cook all day and night. My guy bails by Thursday night and you're set with product for a while. We use the Mexican product to build up a little surplus so the demand doesn't outrun the supply."

"Sounds like a plan." Willie took a deep breath. "And the other thing?"

Shane's piercing black eyes bored into Willie's soul. Made it like every thought he ever had was laid out on the table; one reason Willie never played poker with the man. That and Shane was the world's worst loser.

"You got somebody who can't keep his mouth shut," Shane said. "My insider says he's feeding info to the narcotics task force Bear set up."

"That group's done," Bub said. "Cleared out last fall."

"You don't know shit about shit, Bub. The task force didn't go away. They're just lying in the weeds, waiting to pounce."

"You trust your insider?" Willie asked.

Shane pursed his lips. "More than most. I got a pretty deep hook in. Your guy is negotiating. He hasn't given them names yet, but it's close."

Willie considered his crew. Bub wouldn't say anything to anybody. Howie and Bennett would be loyal up until the point where they got seriously squeezed by the cops and neither had shown a sign of that. There were a couple of guys who worked with them last summer, but one got locked up for stealing cars and the other moved out west somewhere. The one guy left with knowledge about anything was the one he never fully trusted.

"Artie," Willie said.

Shane winked. "I knew you were smart, Willie."

"Shit."

"That's exactly what he is right now," Shane said. "He's mine."

Bub shrugged off the demise of one of his cohorts, the fat rolls of his neck bulging out with the effort. Artie was a douche bag. If he disappeared, the machine would keep running. Willie didn't want to think about Artie's fate, but it wasn't like he could do anything to stop it.

"Fine," Willie said. "He's all yours. We can manage with the four of us. Gives us a bigger cut anyway."

Shane winked and stood. He brushed the dirt from the seat of his black slacks and pointed to Antonio, who opened the trailer door and disappeared inside. There were shouts and a rock of the trailer as someone smashed against the wall. A terrified Artie spilled out the front door and crashed to the dirt with a face full of blood. Shane bent over him and spoke in a low voice. Artie shrank back and screamed "no" over and over, scrambling away from Shane. He backed into Antonio who boxed his ears and slapped a dark bag over his head. He secured the bag in place with a couple wraps of duct tape. Antonio hauled Artie up by the arm pits and carried him to the back of the Navigator, throwing him inside like a sack of potatoes.

"So, you start the cook tomorrow. Go get the place ready." Shane wiped his hands with a handkerchief, then handed Willie a local map with directions to the cook house. "I'll call you to make sure everything's set and we'll be ready to roll."

Shane and Antonio climbed into the Navigator. They rolled out of the clearing and out of sight. Bub headed to the trailer leaving Willie by himself wondering how many pieces they would cut poor Artie into.

CHAPTER EIGHT

Jake turned off Poor Boy Road and up the lane to the house. He ignored the old mailbox stuffed with envelopes and fliers and rolled up the tree-canopied drive, wincing as overgrown branches scraped along the roof of his truck.

The old homestead was a snapshot of when he left at eighteen. The brown ranch still needed paint and still gave off a "go the fuck away" vibe. Curtains drawn on the windows, porch light clinging for life by the wires, and a screen door hanging askew by the top hinge. The front door stood open, but it was dark inside. Jake parked behind a maroon Taurus, probably Janey's, and got out.

A late afternoon breeze rustled through the trees and across the face of the house, sucking the air from inside. A dead leaves smell of death and decay. Probably why Janey had the front door open. He climbed the cracked concrete steps to the door, stopping short of the last one. He still had time to get back into his truck and bust ass out of town before he got wrapped up with his father's situation. But, even then, Keats' two day deadline wasn't going away.

Janey emerged through the door, a freshly lit cigarette in hand, as if she read his thoughts of bolting. Coming out to lasso him inside. She looked thin, even for her, in blue jeans and a white T-shirt under a red plaid button down. A pang of guilt stabbed his gut. His baby sister looked ten years older than he did. Her face brightened. She hopped off the front porch and threw her arms around his neck, burying her face in his chest.

"I'm so glad you're here." She stepped back, taking him in. "You look good, big brother."

"Thanks…" Jake said. He started to say "you too," one of those automatic programmed responses people gave, but he didn't want to start the reunion with a bald-faced lie so he stuck with the truth. "It's good to see you, Janey."

"It's been awhile." She dropped the cigarette and stubbed it out with a scuffed brown shoe. Jake last spoke to her a year ago, a few awkward moments at best when the tax bill on the family property was due. They used to be close before he split and left her stuck in that shithole.

"Still working at the sheriff's office?"

"Still," she said. "A monkey could do my job, but it pays the bills."

"And Luther?"

"Same. Getting fatter," she said. "They took him off the loading dock and stuck him in the office at the lumber yard. Assistant manager. A little better pay and hours. Gives him more time to make the rounds at the bars."

The arduous chores of taking care of her father and bailing Nicky out of trouble locked her fate in place at too young an age. Janey ended up marrying Luther Tully, a pot-bellied lug of marginal intelligence who managed to hold a regular job at the lumber yard in town. Luther hated to bathe as much as he hated to shave. They had a couple of snot-nosed little delinquents running around town: Eli and Willis. Jake couldn't tell his nephews apart since he'd only seen their pictures from Janey's sporadic Christmas cards. Though Janey could've done better than Luther, she also could've done worse.

Janey used to be pretty. Not like she would ever grace the cover of Cosmo, but she was a natural beauty. Straight, white teeth and bouncy natural, red curls that compressed and released with every stride like dozens of little springs. In the wee small hours in his

Kansas City apartment when he lay in bed counting the headlights from passing cars flashing across the bedroom wall, his thoughts would drift to her. The guilt of leaving his little sister behind with Stony lay across him like a suffocating blanket he couldn't shrug off.

Their names ran along those lines of hard living etched in her face. Luther, Nicky, Eli, Willis, Stony, Warsaw, Jake. The curl had disappeared from her bouncing mane over the years, like the hair straightened on its own from the weight of despair, the weight of knowing she would never leave Warsaw.

"So how is he?" Jake asked.

Janey pondered the question. Her eyes were dark and heavy, once full of life, now full of something else. She kicked the cigarette butt into the overgrown grass.

"Cancer is eating him alive," she said. "We keep pumping him with drugs to deal with the pain, but he moans when he's awake and groans when he's asleep. Every third day or so he actually knows what the hell is going on. Ain't any way for anyone to go."

"Some would say he deserves every ounce of pain he's in." Janey cringed as if he slapped her. Damn it. Why did he say that out loud?

"Some would say that. I wouldn't," she said.

Janey saw some of the shit he and Nicky had gone through, but didn't experience it herself, which must have made it easier to fudge the memory and forgive. Stony didn't necessarily like having a girl. Bitched about it all the time. But through the bitching and moaning, he treated her more humanely than his sons.

"Where is he?"

"In his chair in front of the TV. He seems to like having it on, like it gives him something to focus on besides the pain in his gut. I just need some help."

"Why don't Gramma and Grandpa haul their ass up from Louisiana and help?" Jake asked.

"They died years ago. I left you a message."

"Ahh, sorry," he said. Asshole. "I don't know anything about what to do."

"There's a nurse who comes in the mornings, monitors his meds, changes him. Gives him a sponge bath every few days."

Jake sniffed the air wafting through the front door.

"Doesn't smell like she's done it in a while."

Janey shifted, a hint of controlled impatience. He had no idea what she'd been through the last few years, and especially the last few months. He didn't want to know then and was pretty damn sure he didn't want to know now.

"He's dying, Jake," she said. "He's past the point where the home nurse and I can do much more for him. Maybe he needs to go somewhere. One of those Hospice Houses? Then again, I have trouble seeing him in one of those places on his last days. Hell, I don't know. He doesn't have much time."

"How much longer?"

"The doctors won't say. Anywhere from a few days to a couple of weeks."

Jake leaned his head inside, then took a step back at the powerful smell. A musty mix of looming death and antiseptic cleaner. Maybe a hint of some lilac air freshener, its sweetness only adding to the nausea factor. He stepped inside and scanned the living room, memories washing over him. The fireplace where he and Nicky used to sit playing with their action figures, battling to the death on the brick mantle. The rocking chair where Mom would sit, sipping her tea, reading the Westerns she loved so much, occasionally knitting doilies that would adorn the coffee tables of her friends. Her brown eyes flitting between what she worked on and the front door. Waiting for Stony to come home from whatever bender he was on. She might sit for days at a time. Stony disappeared like that. He'd go to town on some errand and disappear for a week.

The old man's tool belt, covered in dust bunnies, lay abandoned in the corner by the fireplace. Stony used to build houses, the one thing at which he excelled other than drinking—and beating his wife and

39

kids. Jake still had a scar on his temple from the ring. His tenth birthday when he had the gall to wear Stony's tool belt for a school project. Most fathers would actually help their kids build a bird house, maybe swell in pride at the sight of their son wearing the tools of their trade. Most fathers.

Jake resisted the overwhelming urge to run again. He didn't need to be here, didn't want to be here. To hell with the old rotting bastard. That wasn't his father in there, Jake never had one as far as he was concerned. The feeling coursed through his veins, screaming and lighting his brain on fire, the same urge that raged through him at eighteen. He might have bolted had Janey not stroked the back of his arm, anchoring him. Besides, even if he bailed on Stony, he still had to fill his obligation to Keats.

In the far corner of the living room rested the old brown recliner, the Styrofoam stuffing peeking through the worn armrests. Dad's chair that nobody but him could sit in. You might manage a spell in it while he was gone, but he'd know. The second he dropped his bony ass in his chair he'd sense some change in the cushion or smell something funny. His eyes would fire up and dart from family member to family member until he found the guilty party. He'd give a tight-lipped smile, and nod, a bobblehead on a tight spring. He wouldn't do anything then, but he would remember.

An old floor lamp cast a glow on to the yellowed skeleton in the chair. The legs and torso covered with a thick afghan blanket, howling, white timberwolves on it. One of those blankets spied in a thrift shop with wonders of why the hell anyone would buy something like that. The hands twitched on the armrests, scratching at the emerging stuffing; mere bones covered by paper-thin skin. His thick, red hair replaced with white wisps hanging limply against a sunken face. His once lively eyes cast a dull, uninterested gaze toward the television sitting in its usual place against the wall. The five o'clock news from Kansas City on the tube with no sound.

The shock of his father in this helpless condition pulled Jake across the threshold. Janey placed her hands on either side of the doorjamb as he approached. With each deliberate step, the old man's labored breathing grew louder, a rattling sound as the air bounced off his mucus-lined lungs. His jaw hitched open and shut, lips pulled in against toothless gums. Jake stopped at the chair and squatted, unsure what to do.

The memory movie rolled, flashes of times long ago. Over the years he only focused on the bad times, the beatings and the verbal rants. Lashes with the belt, a tree switch, or whatever else his father could get his hands on. As he took in what remained of his father, other things surfaced. Helping Stony fix the car of a couple with a young baby who couldn't afford to get it towed to town. Playing catch with Jake and Nicky in the back yard, showing them how to throw a curveball. Patiently helping Jake thread a worm on a hook when they went fishing at the pond, not even getting angry at Jake's squirms as the worm drew back on itself when pierced with the hook. A high five and a rare hug when Jake shot his first deer. Another one when Jake broke the school record for touchdowns in a single season in high school.

His father struggled to breathe and Jake's mind drifted to the comic books he had as a kid. One of Batman's arch enemies. A split personality. One side of the villain's face was the dashing district attorney do-gooder Harvey Dent. The other side, the scarred and crazed villain Two Face. You could look at Harvey Dent and try to justify the things Two Face did. Stony had his share of Harvey Dent moments, but his Two Face moments greatly tipped the scales. The bad always outweighed the good. In the end, the bad was all that mattered.

Stony's head stirred, shaking almost imperceptibly from side to side. A few rapid blinks over the vacant eyes. They moved to his lap and slowly to Jake. Jake's heart beat fast as those eyes pulled focus and saw him, really saw him there. His father's thick, eyebrows furrowed together and recognition flickered. Jake was unsure if he wanted to reach out and touch his hand, or walk out and drive back home. Maybe he had a little Two Face in him as well.

"Hey, Stony," he said at last, hands clenched tightly together on top of his knees. What else could he say?

Stony grunted and whatever electrical circuits fired in his brain to bring him briefly to life clicked off and the vacant gaze returned. His head rested back against the tattered recliner and the rattled breathing started up again.

"I gotta get to work, Jake," Janey said behind him. "There's food in the fridge and he shouldn't need any medication for a while. I wrote the meds down on a list on the table. I'll swing back on my dinner break to check on you."

Jake focused on the howling wolves on the blanket covering his dad's legs.

"Call if you need anything," Janey said.

It wasn't until her car started and crunched over gravel did the tears roll down Jake's face.

CHAPTER NINE

The cook house was a shit-heap that passed the state of condemned two decades ago. Willie took in the sagging, rotting front porch of weather beaten wood, forming a creepy grin under a pair of broken windows. Gray paint peeled off in long strips like flayed skin. Overgrown trees and thick bushes on the side hugged the tiny ranch like the place would collapse if you cut them away.

Bub climbed out of the truck. "What a creep hole."

"Yup," Willie said. "The location's perfect, but I got a feeling we're gonna get dirty as hell trying to clean it out to get ready to cook."

"Place looks haunted."

"Ain't no such things as ghosts, Bub. Shane picked the place. We might as well get busy gettin' it ready. Be hell to pay if it isn't."

Willie moved to the porch, testing the wood before putting his full weight on it. He kicked away empty beer cans and cigarette butts. Someone had been using the place as a hangout. Probably local kids doing some daytime drinking. Willie sure wouldn't come out here at night. If Shane worried about any foot traffic, he wouldn't have picked the site in the first place.

Shane was dead on about the location. The house sat a quarter mile down a rutted lane off Poor Boy Road. A rusted, four-railed, green gate overgrown with foliage guarded the entrance. They drove by twice before finding it. A footpath ran along the side of the house and disappeared into the woods. Willie didn't know where the footpath led, but would scout it himself tomorrow.

He touched the rusty front door knob, afraid it would crumble in his hand. The door resisted but eventually gave in with a ghostly groan. The movement kicked up a thick layer of dust that Willie let settle before he moved inside. Something squealed and scurried away in the darkness.

"This place makes my trailer look like the Taj Mahal," Willie said.

"What the hell is the Taj Mahal?" Bub asked behind him. Willie rolled his eyes and stepped in.

An old dust-covered sofa with rat-eaten cushions occupied most of the space in the tiny living room. A couple of folding chairs sat around a beat-up coffee table, littered with beer cans and an overflowing ash tray. An old console television with half a red brick protruding from the broken screen rested in the corner. A floor lamp stood in the other corner with a yellowing pile of the *Benton County Enterprise* at its base. Willie checked the dates on the newspaper. Two and a half years old.

A narrow dining room with a cheap card table surrounded by four mismatched chairs lay across from the living room. An old china hutch towered behind it, empty except for a few chipped plates and a black and white picture of a rail-thin man in a ragged shirt and a fat woman in an awful diamond-patterned dress, both wearing expressions of equal misery. Willie picked up the picture, wiping the dust layer away with the side of his hand.

"Who is it?" Bub asked from the doorway.

"Royce Weathers," he said. "Always wondered where the old asshole lived."

"Royce? He's been dead for years."

"Gotta be at least five. He used to tear it up with my old man. Wonder what happened to the wife? Can't remember her name."

"Mable, I think," Bub said, the wood floors creaking under his weight as he stepped inside. "She bailed town two seconds after they threw the first shovel of dirt on his coffin. Used to see her around, but haven't seen hide or hair of her in a couple years."

"Can you blame her? I wouldn't want to come back to this shithole, either."

Willie tossed the picture back on the hutch and walked the short hall leading to the kitchen. A few black-crusted dishes lay abandoned in a sink covered with mold. Next to it, a grimy, white refrigerator Willie vowed not to open. He returned to the kitchen and flicked a light switch up and down a few times with no effect.

"Gonna have to get some lights up here. Only a couple hours till dark," Willie said, inwardly groaning at the prospect of hefting the bulky generator. He worked the faucet handle at the sink, getting nothing but a shudder of pipes and no water. He pulled out a notepad, making a list of supplies they'd need, and handed it to Bub.

"Go to Walmart and pick these up." He reached into his pocket and peeled off a few twenties. "Pick up Howie and Bennett on your way back. It's gonna be a long, dirty night getting this place ready."

Bub trudged like a little kid asked to clean his room, but had to figure driving back to town would be better than hanging out there. Willie followed him out to the truck and grabbed a few brooms and trash bags he brought with him. Bub wedged himself behind the wheel, fired up the truck and took off toward town. A breeze rustled through the trees, branches scraping the old shingled roof. Thinking about the money, Willie got busy.

CHAPTER TEN

After an hour sitting in his mother's rocking chair, his attention alternating between his father's labored breaths, ways to track down Langston and the Royals game on the muted television, Jake got up and wandered through the house. The kitchen hadn't changed in twenty years. The same dishes he ate off as a kid dried in the dish rack next to the sink. He opened the fridge. Pre-packaged lunch meat, some lettuce, a jar of pickles and a six-pack of Budweiser. He shut the door, and wandered past the living room and down the hall.

He ran his hand along the wall where he and Nicky first attempted dry walling. A fight over something stupid that spilled into the hallway. Jake got Nick into a headlock, swung him around and put his head into the wall, punching through the plaster below the framed school pictures of them from a couple years before.

Nicky's face and hair were covered with white powder and chunks of dry wall, looking like some sort of half-assed ghost. They alternated wary glances between each other and the hole, wondering how bad Stony would whip their asses.

Jake took the worst of the whipping. Not because he had to, but because he could take it more than Nicky. They both learned how to tape, mud, sand and paint the next day. Over and over again, day after day until they more or less got it right, or until Stony got too drunk to really care. Mom came in when Stony went on a beer run and switched out the bright light bulb for a dimmer one to help hide the tape seams.

He stood by the closed door. Mom and Dad's room. Jake remembered running in there and climbing in bed with Mom during thunderstorms when Stony was gone. If Stony was home, Jake just trembled beneath the blanket in his own bed. He once tried to crawl in with his parents, but Stony shoved him to the floor and called him a pussy. Jake passed his parents' door without opening it. He hadn't been in the room since Stony made him go in there with Nicky to pick out the dress Mom would be buried in.

There were two doors on the right. One for Janey's room, one for the room he and Nicky shared. He peeked into Janey's. No remnants of her childhood, just a pitted, black-iron bed frame and a twin mattress next to a tiny lamp with a timeworn cone shade and a copy of the Bible perched atop a scarred nightstand. Her old dresser retired to the corner of the room under the only window, a thin gray layer of dust gathered on its barren surface.

Jake stood at the closed door to his old room, one he'd opened and shut thousands of times. He placed his hand on the knob and jerked it away on contact as if the knob was red hot. Too early to tackle that one. Instead, he returned to the living room.

Stony slept, drawing in hitched, raspy breaths. Jake went to the refrigerator, drew out one of the cans of beer, and went out the side door, past the carport to the back deck. The deck looked down the hill toward the pond a hundred yards away. The algae-covered water partially hidden by a row of untrimmed evergreens, lit up by the bright moon. He cracked open the beer, took a deep pull and dropped into a yard sale, plastic-strapped chair at a damaged wood table that saw its best days twenty years ago. Stony never believed in throwing anything away.

He pulled out his cell phone and scrolled through his contact list. He made three calls—one to a dirty cop he knew in Kansas City, one to a dope head in Independence and one to a mid-level gorilla named Matthews who worked for one of Keats' competitors in St. Louis.

The cop and the dope head never heard of Langston, and Matthews didn't answer. Jake left a message, but doubted he'd get a call back. The last time he saw him, Jake broke both his legs with a sledgehammer after trashing two of his cronies. He tossed the phone on the table and stared at the black water of the pond.

He and Nicky used to fish at the pond every chance they got. Stony kept it well stocked, one of the few nice things he did for them. He and Nicky would dig up fat earthworms as thick as your pinky in the muddy banks. On the constant lookout for snakes hiding in the overgrown weeds. Skipping rocks to see whose could make it all the way across on the days the fish weren't biting. Pulling out long catfish and feisty crappie, and flinging the guts at each other while cleaning them under the carport.

The pond where Janey found Nicky three years ago. Sprawled out on the sun bleached dock with its cracked boards and rusty nails, fishing pole dangling in the murky water, an empty heroin syringe next to him. Track marks up and down his arm, a ghost of a smile on his acne scarred face, and glassy eyes staring to the heavens, forever lost in the gray skies above.

Janey eventually got hold of Jake. He'd spent the day staking out the place of a derelict who owed Keats a grand. After six hours sweating in his truck, Jake picked the lock on the back door of the grungy two story the guy lived in, searched the place and found over thirty-six thousand dollars hidden under a floor board in a bedroom. Jake gave Keats the grand the guy owed him and kept the other thirty five for himself. He'd been on cloud nine with his newly-acquired wealth until his cell rang ten minutes later. From top of the world to hell in the span of sixty seconds. He still regretted staying in his truck throughout the funeral. Coward.

Jake finished the beer and crushed the can, contemplating having another. Sounds of his father's pain carried from the living room, like an old door creaking open. The setting sun sparkling like diamonds off the surface of the pond drew him back to his tenth birthday, sitting on the bank with Nicky by his side, tracking the blood red sun as it dropped below the horizon. Nicky's arm draped over his shoulders. Feeling the sheer intensity of his love for his older brother, the idol. Crickets chirping, an occasional car droning by on Old Highway 83, bullfrogs croaking. Peaceful. Happy.

Stony emitted a long and soulful groan dripping with agony. Jake pictured him bent at the waist, clasping at his cancer-ridden abdomen underneath the howling timberwolf afghan. The tears that rolled from Jake's eyes earlier were gone, nothing but salty remnants on his cheeks. Whatever emotion passed through him earlier disappeared in that handful of tears he shed on his knees in front of his father. He rubbed his kneecap and the lump of scar tissue. Could still hear the sound. The sound that changed his fate. He thought of Nicky, dead on the dock and his mother laying cold in the ground. He felt that white leather belt cracking across his back and the gold ring breaking his skin.

The clock of his diminishing forty-eight hour deadline ticked away.

The moaning from the living room devolved to a pitiful wail, driving Jake to his feet. Half-moon craters indented in the skin on his palms from clenched fists, crimson lines forming. He took in the murky waters of the pond and waited for some sense of compassion or pity to wash over him. Something to drive him to the living room, to relieve the pain and suffering of the man who brought him into the world. When no such feeling came, he grabbed his phone off the table and searched until he got the number he wanted.

"Yeah," he said when a woman from Hospice House answered. "I need to talk to someone about getting my father in there."

CHAPTER ELEVEN

While his father slept in his chair, Jake grabbed his laptop out of the truck and booted it up at the kitchen table. He turned on the hotspot on his cell phone and pulled up the Internet. The signal was weak and his search for anything related to Shane Langston was painstaking slow. He found a few references to a Shane Langston and a car dealership, a fuzzy picture of Langston at a charity event in Sedalia, but nothing of any real help. Frustration grew. He scrolled through names in the Warsaw directory, trying to come up with someone he knew that he could hit up for information, but came up snake eyes. At midnight, he gave up, drugged Stoney according to Janey's list and carried him to bed.

Jake spent a restless night in Janey's old room. The moonlight through the window lit up the gold leaf on the Bible cover. Why the hell did Stony have the Bible in the first place? He'd declared on multiple occasions there was no God. Maybe the Bible belonged to his mother. She took them to church on occasion when Stony didn't bother to come home on Saturday nights. Otherwise, it wasn't worth listening to his diatribes about the money grubbers of organized religion.

Perhaps it was the same Bible Stony hit Mom with when Jake was seven. Lying on his bed with the pillow over his head until his mother screamed and something broke. Enraged, he jumped out of bed and stormed into the living room, just in time to see Stony

50

towering over her with her Bible in his hand, like an overzealous preacher to an unrepentant sinner. When Stony struck her across the face with it, Jake threw his skinny frame at his father, tiny fists swinging and swearing. Stony held a palm out on Jake's head, holding him at bay, laughing. When he tired of his offspring flinging obscenities and punches, the laughing stopped. Without a word, he punched his middle child in the face with the ragged ring. Jake told people he earned the scar on his cheek from a pickup football game.

The moonlight faded to sunlight. With no more sleep in his near future, he padded to the kitchen and fixed a pot of coffee. He needed to track Langston down, but couldn't very well do it while playing caregiver to his father. He couldn't ask Bear about him, and had no idea who still hung about Warsaw to make inquiries. Maybe Janey would know something.

Jake popped a couple of pieces of bread in the toaster, the morning mist rising over the pond out the window above the sink. He'd finished buttering the toast when Janey's car crunched in the driveway. He poured an extra cup of coffee and went to meet her in the living room.

"Everything go okay last night?" she asked.

Jake shrugged. "Fine, I guess. He was pretty quiet."

"You sleep okay?"

"Not really. Strange being back in this house again. Lots of ghosts."

"There were some good times too, weren't there?"

Jake sat quiet for a moment. "Not many, but a few."

Janey sipped her coffee and Jake leaned back on the couch. Keats popped into his head. He'd want an update and Jake had no idea where to begin. How was he going to find a local drug dealer in a town he hadn't been to in sixteen years? Since his sister worked in the sheriff's office, maybe she had a clue.

"Janey, you ever hear of a guy named Shane Langston?"

Janey's brow furrowed and she looked at him sideways. "Why?"

"Someone in Kansas City asked about him."

"Who?"

"Does it matter?"

"Yeah, it does. What do you need him for?"

"What do you know?"

"He's a mean, drug dealing scumbag. Every sheriff in four counties would love to get their hands on him. Tell me why you're asking. You mixed up in something, big brother?"

"No," Jake said with a wave of his hand. "My boss asked me to poke around since I was heading this way. You don't know where I can find him?"

"He's got a car dealership in Sedalia. That's about all I know except he's extremely bad news."

"What kind?"

"The worst kind. No telling how many bodies he's buried from what I hear."

"No," Jake said, "what kind of dealership?"

"I don't know. Lincoln, I think. Maybe Ford."

"So he's not some local little drug head?"

"Far from it. He's as bad as they come. But, it doesn't matter either way because you're not going anywhere near him."

"All right, forget I mentioned it." Crap. A half-assed lead, but not the bounty of information he hoped for. He'd assumed Langston was going to be some little white trash bottom feeder he'd have no trouble finding and taking care of. This was going to be harder than he thought.

Janey held the coffee cup in both hands, her elbows resting on her knees, eyes fixated on the floor like it would tell her how to start the next uncomfortable conversation.

"About Dad…" she said.

"I made an appointment for later this morning to see if we can get him into Hospice House in Sedalia. You want to go with me?"

Janey shook her head. She lit a cigarette and inhaled deeply.

"You sure that's best?" she asked, apparently forgetting she brought up the idea the night before. His temper rose a little.

"Don't you? He's on his last legs, Janey. You can't care for him the way he needs to be and I sure as hell don't want to."

"I can't pay for it. I ain't got two dimes to rub together."

"Don't worry," Jake said. "I got it covered."

"Where'd you get that kind of money?" Her eyes narrowed.

"I've been working steady and have some squirreled away. He have any life insurance?"

She took another drag and crushed out the cigarette in the ash tray on the coffee table. She pulled a few pieces of paper from her purse and passed them over.

"A few thousand dollar whole life policies Mom took out on him. Might not be enough to cover all the burial, but should take care of most of it. Just doesn't seem right sticking him in some hospital. Wouldn't be what he wanted."

Jake got to his feet, on the verge of shattering the coffee mug in his hands, sick of her utopian memories of Stony.

"Who gives a shit what he wants? He never gave a damn what we wanted. He's lucky we don't leave him here to rot alone."

"Jake," Janey said, wide eyed, shocked.

"No." He cut her off with a hard wave of his hand. "No more of this poor old Stony crap. You brought me here to do what you can't and that's what I'm going to do. I'm getting him in that place so they can at least make him relatively comfortable for the last hours of his miserable life. You don't like it, I can hop in the truck and head back to Kansas City."

"No, don't do that. I just meant…" She trailed off, her lip quivering.

"I know what you meant," Jake sighed. He sat next to her on the couch and placed his arm across her bony shoulders. No sense in being a dick to her. "It's the right thing to do."

Tears brimmed in her eyes. She wiped them with the palms of her hands. "You going now?"

He nodded. Though the appointment wasn't for another two hours and the drive north to Sedalia took forty minutes, he wanted to get the hell out of the house. Maybe go sniff around Langston's dealership.

"I'm gonna check on him," she said. "Call me when you find out something."

She shuffled to the master bedroom. Jake slipped on his shoes, grabbed his wallet and keys from the coffee table, and darted from the house before she opened the bedroom door and let the smell of death touch him again.

*****

Jake drove to Warsaw in silence, snapping off the radio when he started the truck. The thick morning air produced a light fog that rose off the highway and swirled behind the truck. He noticed he'd put the ring back on some time in the night. He removed it, setting it in the spare change cup under the dash and spent the ten minute drive over the winding and dipping roads thinking about the last of his stash and how big of a chunk this would likely take out of it. Would Keats really give him a fade into the sunset bounty if he took this Shane character down?

He pulled off Highway 65 and headed toward downtown Warsaw, wanting to grab a cup of coffee at Casey's before continuing to Sedalia. Traffic was scarce, only a handful of locals in pickups and jalopies passed by on the two lane road, until the unmistakable whoop of a siren and flashing blues and reds in his rearview mirror. Jake cursed under his breath and moved to the side of the almost non-existent shoulder.

The cop waited in his car for a minute, likely running his plates, leaving Jake to sweat out whatever caused him to get pulled over. The cop grabbed the roof, yanking his massive frame out of the car, and sauntered to Jake's truck, his hand resting on the butt of his service pistol. Jake kept his hands on the wheel in plain view.

"You rolled that stop sign, boy," the cop said as he swaggered to the window. Hanging jowls obscured by a neatly trimmed black beard, his brawny frame stretching the seams of his uniform. Jake's image reflected in the cop's mirrored sunglasses.

"The hell I did," Jake replied, matter-of-factly. "You need to get a prescription for those cheap-ass sunglasses. You steal those from the Dollar Store?"

The cop dragged his top lip over his teeth and sucked in a deep breath.

"You got a bad attitude, boy. That kinda talk is gonna get you in a heap of trouble around these parts."

"Heap of trouble around these parts? What is this? Fucking Hee Haw? Better having a wrong attitude than being a fat-ass cop in some piss-ant Ozark town."

The cop glanced up and down the road, probably checking for potential witnesses, grabbed the door handle, opened the truck door, and stepped back.

"You better get your ass out of the truck. Somebody needs to teach you some manners."

Jake swung his legs out, stretching his muscular frame as tall as he could. He rested his big hands on his hips and puffed his chest.

"You gonna teach me manners, fat boy?"

The cop feigned a punch to the head that Jake ducked. He dropped his hands and scooped his thick arms through Jake's arm pits and squeezed him in a bear hug. He started laughing. Jake clapped the man on his back and joined in as the cop twirled him around.

James "Bear" Parley held his old friend tight for a moment then set Jake back on the ground. His brown eyes twinkled as he removed his sunglasses. He gripped Jake by the shoulders at arms' length.

"Son of a bitch," Bear said. "It's been a long, damn time. You look good, buddy."

"So do you." Jake didn't realize how much he'd missed Bear until the mountain stood in front of him.

"Bullshit, I look like the goddamn Michelin tire man poured into a cop uniform."

"Can't believe James Parley is the sheriff."

"Yup, elected three times in a row."

"Must be doing something right then. Must be tough to stay popular around here."

Bear snickered. "As long as those who vote like me, I'm good. The shitheads who I bust aren't going to vote anyway, so fuck 'em. Janey said you were in town for your dad. Poor, miserable bastard."

The mention of his dad wiped Jake's face clean. He had flashes of late nights in the woods behind his house with Bear when they were kids. Sitting in the dark, smoking cigarettes and drinking beer lifted from Stony's stash—Jake talking, Bear listening. Bear letting Jake hide out at his house. Bear watching TV at Jake's and running with him to the woods when Stony rumbled into the driveway. You could tell the level of Stony's inebriation by how he pulled in. When the gravel flew, so did Jake. Only Bear knew the full story.

"Yeah, heading over to Hospice in Sedalia to see if they can get him in there."

"Seems like the best option to me."

"Don't have any other choice," Jake said. "I can't and don't want to take care of him. Figure my job is to make sure somebody does."

"You should check out the nurses while you're there."

"What do you mean?"

Bear grinned. "There's one in particular you might find interesting."

"I'm not going to pick up chicks in a hospice where I'm taking my dying father, man."

"Just trust me, okay? Check them out while you're there."

While Jake cyphered through Bear's cryptic clue, the two stood in uncomfortable silence as the sunlight gleamed against the faded scar on Bear's forehead.

Jake pointed. "I see you still got that scar from the Valley Bar."

Bear rubbed at the spot. "Yeah, that was a hell of a night. How many beers and whiskey shots did Stony feed us?"

"Enough. You remember which Crane brother started the shit with Stony?"

"Matt started it then his brother joined in. Hell, Stony fell off that bar stool and only spilled half a beer on Matt. The way those two assholes carried on, you woulda thought your old man took a piss on both of them."

Jake laughed. "We whipped their asses in the parking lot though."

"Yeah, you only got a busted lip and a black eye. I got a beer bottle in the head and twelve stitches."

They stood in silence for another moment as if in honor of the memory.

"So," Bear continued, "how long you gonna be in town?"

"Till it's over, I guess. Kinda in between jobs and I don't have a hell of a lot of pressing concerns back home."

Bear's cell phone rang and he answered it with a gruff greeting. How could Jake subtly ask about Langston? Bear had to have some bead on his whereabouts, but it would raise too many questions. Bear grunted into the phone and hung up.

"I gotta run," he said. "Tell you what. You get Stony situated and give me a call. We'll grab some brews and head out on the lake, catch some catfish and get caught up."

Jake held out his hand and Bear grabbed it, giving it a couple of shakes and flashing his pearly whites like he'd just won a million dollars.

"Goddamn," Bear whispered. "It's good to see you, man. Don't forget the nurses."

He pumped Jake's hand one more time with a wink, donned his sunglasses and headed back to his patrol car. Jake leaned against the body of the truck and waved as Bear drove off. Forgetting about his coffee run, he climbed in the cab of the truck, cranked the engine over and drove toward Sedalia to find a place for his father to die.

CHAPTER TWELVE

Willie drank his mid-morning coffee on the porch as the cook arrived in a beat up, black paneled van. The cook eyed the house through the windshield and climbed out, all bones in tattered, denim shirt sleeves. The van door screeched with rust as he opened and shut it. He took off a ragged John Deere ball cap, ran his hands through stringy, russet hair and replaced the cap as he approached the porch.

He stopped short of the steps, regarded Willie for a moment and pulled out a pack of Marlboro's. He lit one, inhaled deeply, and walked the perimeter of the house as he smoked. Willie stayed on the porch and waited for the cook to come around the other side. It didn't take long.

"Place looks like a shithole," the cook said.

"It is. Got it cleaned up inside, though. We should be good to go."

The cook took one last deep drag and crushed the butt into the dirt.

"I'm Dexter."

"Willie."

Neither man made a move for the customary handshake.

"How many you have here now?"

"Me and three others. They're inside waiting."

"Call them out and help me get the stuff out of the van. Then, send 'em home," Dexter said. "Shane says you're pretty good in the

59

kitchen, so we won't need 'em yet and they'll be in the way. You good with that?"

"Yup." Whatever got the money rolling in. As Dexter walked back to the van, Willie went in the house to rouse Bub, Howie and Bennett.

*****

With time to burn before his appointment with the Hospice House manager, Jake used it to cruise to Langston's dealership, which sat on a busy corner a few miles from Hospice. Jake circled the block a few times, checking the place out, and finally parked up in front of the showroom. Polished Navigators with sparkling windshields guarded the front door.

He got out and perused the lot, milling around trying to formulate a plan. A beanpole in a cheap suit spotted Jake and slinked over with a flash of teeth. His name tag read "Brad."

"Mornin', sir. Anything you're looking for in particular?"

Yeah, your dickhead owner in a body bag. Can I get the bag in black or is that extra?

"Just browsing," Jake said, running his hand along the window of an overpriced sedan.

"We have some great specials. Trying to clear out last year's models." Brad invaded Jake's personal space and lowered his voice to a conspiratorial tone. "I can make you one hell of a deal."

"That a fact?"

"As sure as I'm standin' here. Our owner's got to make room for a new shipment. Practically giving these things away."

The opening Jake needed. "Your owner?" Jake asked. "Shane Langston, right?"

Brad nodded. "That's him. Great guy. He's willing to…"

"He here today?"

"Mr. Langston? Not at the moment, but he's authorized me to

make each of our customers…"

"Any idea when he's coming in?"

Brad stopped his sales pitch and took a half step back, his eyes narrowing. "Do you know Mr. Langston, sir?"

"Just met him a coupla times around town. Told me to stop in and look him up if I was interested in a car."

Brad managed to revive his salesman's smile. He didn't buy it. "Live around here, do you?"

"Warsaw."

"And where'd you meet Mr. Langston?"

"You ask a lot of questions, Brad."

"It's my job, sir," Brad said, the smile faltering. "You know, get to know my customers. Find out what they're really after." Jake wanted to punch him in the nose and knock the smile the rest of the way from his face. He hated sales people.

"Appreciate the attention, but I think I'm going to just browse around for a while. If I need anything, I'll flag you down."

"Take your time…Mr.?"

"Maxwell. James Maxwell."

Brad extended his hand and Jake took it, the grip weak and sweaty. "Let me know if there's anything else I can do for you."

Jake wandered toward the south end of the lot. When he glanced over his shoulder, Brad regarded him for a moment before turning away. Jake walked the line of cars leading to the building and waved off a couple other salesmen before they got too close. When Brad trekked to the far corner of the lot to help an elderly couple, Jake made a beeline for the showroom and the offices behind it.

Three new cars with jaw-dropping window stickers covered the showroom floor. Two employees sat at desks talking on the phone, oblivious to his entry. Across the polished tile, a service bay bustled with mechanics while bored customers watched *The Price is Right* from a muted television mounted in the corner. He turned left down a short hallway past the restrooms and around a corner to the office area. The first one had Brad's name stuck to the door on an engraved metal plate. Jake resisted the urge to shove the clutter of paperwork covering the desk to the floor. He passed three empty cookie cutter offices to one in the back with Langston's name plate; a closed door with no window. An alarmed emergency exit dead-ended the hall beyond Langston's office.

Jake checked around and tried the knob. Locked. This was a stupid idea. What would he do if Langston sat in the office with his feet up? Shoot him in the head in a crowded car dealership? He should leave the detective work to the cops and stick to being the muscle. But Keats' clock ran and he had nothing else to go on. A quick glance at the lock revealed it was old and cheap. He could pick it in seconds and maybe find something useful inside.

He double checked the coast was clear and took out his wallet. He thumbed past the credit cards, generally too rigid for this kind of deal. You could bend them to the point where they couldn't be used or snap them in half. Instead, he selected a thick, laminated and expired gym membership card.

Jake pushed in the door to get a look at the locking mechanism. No trim to get in his way, so he slid the card into the vertical crack between the door and the doorjamb. Once he felt the bolt, he bent the card the opposite way to force the bolt back into the door. After a few seconds of wiggling the card, the door popped open. He checked over his shoulder one last time and darted inside, shutting the door behind him.

Light filtered in the office from partially opened blinds on the south wall. Jake turned the angle of the blinds down so nobody could see him from the lot. Get in and get out. He set the timer in his head for sixty seconds and began his search.

He walked behind the large, tan veneer desk and opened desk drawers, finding nothing but invoices and bank envelopes addressed to the dealership. A batch at the back of the drawer, rubber-banded together, was addressed to Marion Holdings c/o Shane Langston.

Forty-five seconds left. Nothing much on the desktop except a phone, a monitor with an empty docking station for a laptop, and a half-used, five-inch memo pad with Langston Motors printed on them.

Jake moved to side-by-side file cabinets on the far wall, four feet high with three drawers each. The first set was locked. The ones closest to a window overlooking the lot opened. Nothing but office supplies and a few dust covered trophies from a softball team Langston Motors sponsored. Twenty seconds left. What was he looking for? He scanned the room one last time, his gaze ending at the window where Brad approached with the elderly couple in tow. Jake pressed against the wall as Brad looked toward the window. Get the hell out of there.

As he stepped toward the door, sunlight from the window filtered on the desk. From that angle, indentations showed up on the writing pad. He ripped off the top few pages and stuffed them in his jeans. Opening the door, he peeked down the empty hallway. He engaged the lock and quietly closed the door, hearing the bolt thunk.

He inhaled and hurried to the bend in the hall—almost knocking over Brad.

"Can I help you, Mr. Maxwell?" Brad asked, his smile gone. Brad may have just been a smarmy salesman, but he smelled something fishy. Had he seen Jake through the blinds?

"Just looking for the bathroom," Jake replied.

"Back toward the front. You passed them on the way in."

"Thanks," Jake said, skirting around him. He popped in the bathroom and waited, washing his hands for effect. He counted to twenty and left the building. He started his truck and stared out the windshield, the air through the vents drying the sweat on his brow. If nothing else, he could stake out the dealership and wait for Langston to show. Then what? Could he kill him in cold blood? If it came down to Keats' goons killing Jake or Jake taking out a scumbag drug dealer, he could probably do it. There had to be another way.

He lifted the middle console and rooted around until he found a pencil. He took out the notepad pages from Langston's office and lightly rubbed the graphite back and forth against the indentations. White letters appeared through the gray. 5145 Southbend Avenue. Pulling out his cell phone, he plugged the address into his navigation app. 3.2 miles away. The clock on the truck dash said he had another twenty minutes before his appointment at Hospice. As he drove through the lot, he glanced in the rearview mirror. Brad stood in the safety of the showroom, his cell phone pressed to his ear. Jake should've punched the guy.

*****

5145 Southbend Avenue was a non-descript, rectangular, steel building, the kind you'd see farmers build to store their equipment. Forty feet high, and a hundred and fifty feet long, the corrugated steel building sat on the east end of town with a large bay door in the front and a man door at the corner. A dirty, white cinderblock small engine repair shop sat idle to its left and a pasture with a handful of cows grazing by the fence on its right. Jake parked up in front of the steel building. A small plaque next to the door read "Global Distribution Center" above the address. No trucks, no cars. It felt empty.

Jake drove along a narrow dirt road around the side of the building to a back lot adorned with a couple of forsaken cars abandoned in a tall collection of weeds. A door with a reinforced window stood below a single bulb in cobwebbed housing. He kept the truck running and walked to the back door. Locked. A look through the window revealed nothing but a small, cluttered maintenance shop and a darkened door leading to the rest of the building. He didn't have time to mess around inside. He had to get to Hospice.

*****

Jake sat in the manager's office, who explained, in excruciating and unnecessary detail, the dying process and what his father could expect over the next several days or weeks. But Jake's thoughts were about the Global Distribution Center building and its link to Langston. All Jake cared about was that Hospice had a room and he'd have enough money to cover it if Stony didn't hold out too long. If he did hold on, Jake would be calling Keats for some additional work in the near future.

Jake signed his name to a number of lines on the extensive paperwork below legalese clauses he didn't bother to read. Sign here, initial there. Page after page. The woman said he could bring Stony in that afternoon as they had a vacancy.

"We'll take good care of him, Mr. Caldwell," she continued. "Don't you worry."

"I'm not worried." Jake pushed up from the chair. The woman reached across the desk and extended a bony hand with impossibly long fingers. They wrapped around Jake's hand and a shiver went up his spine; it was like shaking hands with Stony's skeleton.

He ventured to the hall. The exit to the left and a long hallway with a number of doors leading to the rooms on the right. A fat woman in a muumuu the size of a circus tent talked in hushed tones on a cell phone, a box of Kleenex in her free hand. A young couple scurried past, the woman crying into the shoulder of a suited yuppie. Jake started to follow them out, then remembered Bear's advice to check out the nurses so he took several tentative steps along the hall.

The first few doors were closed. In the next, a withered old man hooked to beeping and purring machines by tubes running from his arms focused on a soundless television playing from a wall mount on the opposite side of the room.

A nurses' station sat at the end of the hall. A nurse in light blue scrubs wrote on some charts with her back to him as he approached.

She had long, wavy champagne hair and strong, sinewy arms protruding from a short-sleeved top. She shifted her weight from foot to foot as she wrote, and Jake couldn't help but admire a very nice backside. She glanced over her shoulder as his boots clomped on the thin carpet. The corners of her mouth turned up to reveal a perfect row of gleaming, white teeth. Now he knew why Bear wanted him to check the nurses. He'd have to thank him later.

She set the pen on the chart, turned, and stepped forward. The woman working at a computer stopped pecking and alternated her glance between her and Jake like they were two fighters squaring off.

"Oh my God." The blonde nurse clasped a hand to her sensuous lips. "Jake? Is that really you?"

"Hi, Maggie," he said, heart thundering at the mention of her name. She threw herself into his arms and held him in his second hug of the day. Jake had to admit he liked Maggie's much more than Bear's.

CHAPTER THIRTEEN

Dexter may have been short on personality, but he made up for it in precision. Willie gazed around the living room and kitchen area at their setup. It was going to be a long cook, but in the end they'd rake in enough cash for Willie to get away from the life. He and Dexter prepped until noon, then stepped out the front door to have a smoke in the clearing by the van.

"You worked for Shane long?" Dexter asked.

"Few years," Willie said.

"He speaks highly of you. Well, as highly as Shane speaks of anybody."

"That's good to know." Yeah, that was definitely good info to have.

"He trusts you, but not your fat buddy." Dexter took a last drag and crushed the butt on the heel of his boot as he exhaled, then put what was left in his shirt pocket.

"Bub's a necessary evil. Can do stuff to people I can't do."

"Like what?"

"Like break their face," Willie said. "We went to high school together. He dropped out to work for one of Shane's dealers. I came on board after I dropped out the next year."

"How'd you get above him in the food chain?"

"I have a brain. Bub ain't the sharpest crayon in the box, but he'll do what you tell him to do and that's all I need."

They went back inside and worked in silence, moving chemicals here and there, adjusting valves and beakers. If only Willie paid better attention during his high school chemistry class, maybe he'd know how this exactly worked. He may be a redneck hillbilly, but he'd done some research on meth.

Methamphetamine had been around for a long time. Speed, crystal, glass, crank, tweak, rock, tina, ice, shards. The main ingredient ephedrine or pseudoephedrine was found in many legal drugs like decongestants, Nyquil Nighttime Cold Medications, Sudafed and diet pills. The national crackdown on scoring ephedrine had led people like Willie to find some creative sources of the drug.

The familiar tense knot formed in his belly. Guilt because of what they were making and who they'd be selling it to. Picturing his mother hunched over in the shack she called a house, smoking what he cooked from a dirty glass pipe made his skin crawl. But it wasn't like he invented the shit. He forced his thoughts to turn to dollar signs.

"You know they used meth during World War II?" Willie asked. "My great grandfather flew bombers over Germany and told me they used to call meth 'Pilot's Chocolate.' You know, to help fight fatigue." Dexter said nothing, just kept setting up tubes and beakers. Willie gave up trying to make conversation.

Since they were in the Midwest around farming country, Dexter's basic cook method used the readily available anhydrous ammonia. Mix it with the right quantities of pseudoephedrine, and sodium or lithium, and boom, you get meth. The hard part was getting enough pseudoephedrine, but this guy seemed to have ample supply. Willie didn't ask where Shane scored it and Dexter didn't offer.

Willie never touched the product because it scared the shit out of him. His customers snorted or smoked it, flooding their pea brains with dopamine, wide eyed and tweaking for days at a time, continuing to chase the first high until they ran out of product, or crashed and burned. The tragic downside wasn't worth feeling like Superman for a short time. He had dreams of breaking free from this life, maybe having a family with kids. Getting strung out on this poison wasn't going to help make that dream a reality.

"You ready?' Dexter asked.

Willie zipped up his protective yellow suit and stretched the straps of the full-face respirator wide, slipping it over his head. He drew in a deep breath, soaking in the musty air of the old house, and pulled the respirator over his face. Pressing his hands against the filters, he inhaled deeply, the rubber sucking against his face ensuring he had a good seal. Dexter waited, tapping his foot impatiently.

"Let's do it," Willie said. Hopefully, for the last time.

Chapter Fourteen

It took the thirty minute drive from Sedalia to Warsaw for the smile to dissipate from Jake's face. But not even the joy of seeing the only woman he ever loved again could stop the prospect of dealing with Stony and Keats' looming deadline from pulling down the corners of his mouth. Stony was straight forward, but how to track down Langston? A trip to the car dealership, some worthless phone calls and a locked up warehouse wasn't going to get him very far.

He might not survive the next forty-eight hours, but if he did last that long, supplies were needed. He took the exit ramp for Walmart, weaving through abandoned carts in the parking lot to an open space on west side. He walked toward the store, giving a wide berth to a sloppy woman with a booger-picking kid lazily clad in pajamas at two in the afternoon, and then helped an old woman finish loading her car, offering to take her cart back to the store. She looked like Hap Anderson's mother. Hell, it could've been. He hadn't seen either of them in sixteen years.

Pushing the cart toward the Walmart entrance, a flash of denim caught his eye between two cars. A tall, heavy set man in overalls stood next to a rust bitten El Camino, Iron Maiden cranking from backseat speakers that probably cost more than the entire car. The fat man retrieved something from his pockets and palmed it to the driver. An obvious exchange of money for drugs. If Langston ran the drug trade in Warsaw, one of his dealers could lead Jake in the right direction. But which one was the dealer and which the customer?

The choice was made for him when the El Camino's glass packs rumbled and faded away. Jake parked the cart with a pile near the entrance, swinging the cart around so he could check out the fat man without being too obvious. He headed his way, so Jake went inside. No better place to track someone than inside a busy Walmart.

An ancient greeter offered a pleasant hello. Jake nodded to him then approached the discount shelves near the entrance. He grabbed the closest item, an "As Seen on TV" miracle garden hose, and pretended to read the back of the box. The fat man moved past in a wave of body odor. Jake waited a moment and followed. If he lost sight of the guy, all he would have to do was follow his nose.

The fat man picked up some high calorie snacks and a case of cheap beer, and made his way back to the front. Along the way, one of the boxes slipped off the pile toward the floor. With surprisingly fast reflexes, the fat man snagged it before the box hit the floor. Big and quick. Good to know. The lines at the registers were six deep so Jake headed to his truck.

Ten minutes later, the man hefted himself into a beat up truck and rumbled out of the parking lot. Jake followed, keeping some distance between them. Did this guy work for Langston? Maybe Langston's local supplier?

The truck rolled toward downtown, bouncing up and down with each curve of the road. Apparently new shocks were not high on the owner's list of priorities. A Benton County Sheriff's car passed and the fat man's head turned toward the side mirror to ensure it kept going. Jake followed the right guy.

A few minutes later, they cruised down Main Street and the truck turned toward the Community Center. Jake passed and angle parked in front of an antique store. With the courthouse and jail to his back, he walked down an inclined sidewalk, pausing at the corner of the building, the Community Center in front of him. He snuck a peek around the brick. The fat man stood twenty feet away in an empty back alley talking to two other guys with matching hair styles—too long and too dirty. Jake overheard something about some guy named Willie, a shipment and a warehouse.

Jake considered tailing the guy in the hopes that he could lead him to Langston, but that could take time he didn't have. Besides, being stealthy was not in his wheelhouse of skills. The fat man could tell him what he needed to know or Jake could beat it out of him. Jake stepped around the corner and the trio in front of him stopped talking and watched his approach.

"Afternoon, fellas," Jake said. The three of them stepped back into a neat line covering the breadth of the alley. The fat man in the middle, the other two on either side like matching white-trash bookends.

"Help you?" the fat man asked.

"Maybe. For your sake, I hope so." Jake stopped within arm's reach, his hands relaxed at his sides.

"What the fuck is that supposed to mean?"

"I need some information and you're going to give it to me."

"Or what?"

"Let's not let it get to that," Jake said. "I saw you dealing at the Walmart."

The fat man moved with surprising quickness and grabbed Jake by the shirt, slamming Jake against the brick wall of the building while the two long-haired guys pressed in on either side. They were identical twins. Not big, but ugly and wiry.

"Who the fuck are you?" the fat man asked.

Jake grinned. "You're gonna find out in about two seconds if you don't take your hands off me."

"Kick his ass, Bub." At least Jake had a name to work with.

"I ain't gonna ask again, dickhead," Bub said.

"I'm not here to start any shit. I just need some information."

"You a cop?"

"Do I look like a cop?"

"You look like an asshole," Bub said.

"I'm gonna be if you don't take your hands off me and take two steps back. Last warning."

Bub's face remained inches from Jake's, his breath a horrible concoction of cigarettes, garlic and teeth that hadn't been brushed in a week. He released Jake and stepped back. Not a big one. The twins remained on either side, clenching their fists. The one on his left held something behind his leg. Arm down at his side, angling his body away.

"Okay," Bub said, "what do you want?"

"A guy who owes me some money. Shane Langston."

The twins shot a look to Bub who, to his credit, remained stone-faced. But his eyes gave him away. The same look in the eyes of a guy at the poker table who didn't like the last card the dealer laid down. The reason some guys wear sunglasses at the table—eyes never lie.

"Never heard of him," Bub said.

"That so? Looks to me like you do."

"What's he owe you money for?"

"That's between me and him. Look, I'll make it worth your while if you point me in the right direction."

Bub clearly considered the proposition for a moment, then glanced to one of the twins. "Hank, point this asshole in the right direction."

Hank swung his arm high and wide, aiming at Jake's head. Too slow and telegraphed. The two foot metal pipe whistled overhead as Jake ducked, twisted and unleashed a vicious jab into Hank's solar plexus. His fist sunk in and the air whoofed out. Hank was done.

Jake kept low and shot his good leg out at the other twin, not catching him flush with the back kick, but a solid enough to provide some distance. Bub swung a haymaker at Jake's head that he easily side-slipped. Bub's over-swing carried him toward the brick wall of the building and Jake helped him along that path with a palm strike to the back of his head. His face cracked into the stone with a satisfying smack. He threw a jab and a left hook to the glass jaw of the advancing twin who was unconscious before he hit the ground. Jake turned back to Bub.

Bub breathed heavy, eyes dazed and blood running down his chin. Hank wheezed on his hands and knees, trying to suck in air. Bub raised his fists in a fighter's stance and edged forward. Jake danced to the side, keeping Hank between them. Bub tried to move forward and circle around, but Jake mirrored him, waiting for him to do something stupid.

"Stand still, you chicken shit," Bub grunted.

Jake grinned, continually circling. "Tell me where I can find Shane Langston and I'll let you walk out of here with your ugly teeth intact."

"You talk big for running away."

"So catch me, fat boy."

"Go fuck yourself." Bub lunged. Jake shot out a straight jab and caught the taller man squarely in the eye. Bub stopped cold, and Jake followed with a jab to the gut and a swinging elbow to the chin. Bub dropped to the ground on top of Hank. That had to hurt worse than Jake's punch.

Jake started forward when the wail of a siren closed in fast down the hill from Main Street. He had no desire to tell Bear his reason for rousting the local drug dealers and he'd never make it down the other side of the back street before the cops got there. A door marked "Deliveries" beckoned from the brickwork a few feet away. Jake darted to the door, which opened into a cluttered storeroom, dimly lit by interspaced overhead fluorescents casting shadows on dusty furniture and shelves lined with knick knacks. He made his way to a set of stairs and climbed to the main floor, to the front door and back out to Main Street.

A small crowd of onlookers stared down the hill toward the Community Center, the flashing lights of the police car bouncing off the adjacent buildings. He jumped in his truck and smacked the steering wheel. Though he had no doubts Bub worked for Langston, he was no closer to finding his target than when he started. Wait, Bub had said something about a warehouse. Maybe it was the Global Distribution Center.

Jake turned into a gas station and parked in the back corner. He grabbed his cell phone and scrolled through his contacts list. Dwight owed him a favor. He answered on the second ring.

"Dwight, Jake Caldwell," Jake said.

Silence filled the line followed by a heavy sigh. "What do you need?"

"To collect on the favor you owe me."

"What favor?"

"The favor where I spotted you the five hundred bucks you owed Keats and didn't break your face. Or do I need to come over and remind you?"

"Oh, yeah. That favor. What is it?"

"You still a computer pirate?"

"Among other things."

"Need you to see what you can find on a Global Distribution Center in Sedalia." Jake read him the address. "Looking for ownership records, tax filings, anything interesting you can dig up."

"What's this for?"

"Don't worry your shitty comb-over head about it. Just call me when you get something." Jake's brain flashed to the bundle of envelopes in the back of Langston's drawer. "Oh, and find out what you can about Marion Holdings and its ties to a guy named Shane Langston."

"Who's that?"

"Just a guy I'm digging into. And keep it quiet. Call me as soon as you can later today?"

"Today?"

"Yeah, unless you want that visit. I'll even forgive the last two hundred you still owe me."

Dwight grunted. "I'll call you in a couple hours."

Jake hung up, pleased the wheels were turning. Slowly, but they were turning. Time to head home and deal with Stony.

CHAPTER FIFTEEN

By three o'clock, the sun blazed overhead in a cloudless sea of blue and the temperatures climbed to the upper eighties. A light breeze blew in from the west, a tornado of fallen leaves swirling in the drive. Jake and Janey worked in unison to deposit Stony's gaunt frame into the front seat of the truck. As Jake leaned over him to fasten his seatbelt and tuck in the afghan around his legs, he caught a sour whiff of body odor mixed with the smell of old, wet leaves. Stony cried out and grasped at his belly. Jake muttered sorry and quickly pulled away as the seatbelt clicked.

He shut the door to the pickup and faced Janey's tear-filled eyes. Jake had the conflicting urges to yell at her for being emotional over their rotten bastard of a father, and to comfort her with a warm hug. Instead, he settled for the middle of the road and shoved his hands deep into the pockets of his blue jeans and alternated glances between Janey and the fascinating chunks of gravel at his feet.

"You sure this place is gonna work?" she asked.

Jake covered the details with her earlier in the living room. No matter who their clientele, Hospice House did miracles comforting the dying and their families. More than a man like Stony deserved, but he decided not to antagonize her with that point. She dabbed the corners of her eyes with a tissue from her pocket.

"It's a nice place, Janey. He'll be fine there and they'll make him comfortable for the homestretch."

"And the nurses? They seem okay?"

"Better than okay." Jake grinned.

"What?" she asked. "What are you smiling about?"

"One of the nurses on his wing," he said. "Maggie."

"Maggie? Your Maggie?"

Their reunion flashed across his brain. The way his shirt smelled like her all the way back to the house, the lilac drifting into his nose. The feel of her body perfectly against his, taking him back to a sleeping bag under the stars in the woods. Her naked, eighteen-year-old body entwined in his, firm breasts molded against his chest, still warmly inside her, her delicious sweaty brow. He could still feel her soft lips grazing his ear as she whispered she loved him.

"Yeah, my Maggie. How did you not know she worked there?"

"I don't pay attention where every resident of Benton County works."

"She still live over there?" he asked, pointing over a clump of trees and a rise of land.

"As far as I know. I don't pay attention to where every resident of Benton County lives, either. I've got too much other stuff going on to track your old girlfriend. She left town a few months after you did. Came back a couple years later."

"She looked good. Real good," he said.

"Well? What did she say?"

"Nothing much." Jake shifted from foot to foot, anxious to get going. He wasn't sure if the anxiety came from the prospect of getting rid of Stony or possibly seeing Maggie again. "She gave me a big hug, we talked for a few minutes and I headed here."

"Bull," Janey said, playfully pushing Jake back into the body of his truck. "You haven't seen her since forever ago and that's it?"

Forever ago. A wave of guilt slapped away the happy vision of Maggie. He kicked a rock with the scuffed toe of his boot and sent it into the brush.

"I left her," he said at last, pissed for letting the happy thoughts rip south so quickly. He glanced to Janey, the joy fading from her face like the air sputtering out of a pierced balloon. "I left you. I left Nicky. I left everyone behind like the selfish prick I am."

"But you're back now." Janey put a cool hand on his arm. "You're back now."

"Yeah, but just to fix things. That's all I know how to do," he said, shuffling around the back of the truck and climbing in.

Janey stepped on the running board, crossing her arms on the open window. She reached forward and picked up a corner of the afghan, wiping a tiny trail of spittle from their father's chin.

"Maybe Stony isn't the only thing you came back to fix." She dropped her eyes then herself back to the ground and walked to the house.

Stony slumped against the seat, head lolling on his shoulder, the exact pose he modeled after Jake and Nicky would find him passed out in a bar and haul him home. This time, instead of passed out against the door, bloodthirsty cancer cells chewed him up from the inside.

Jake fired up the truck and rolled down the hill to Poor Boy Road. As he did, he looked up to a grassy clearing overlooking the picturesque valley, the clearing where many years ago he last held Maggie Holden. The night he fled Warsaw for good.

CHAPTER SIXTEEN

Jake hit the outskirts of Sedalia heading toward Hospice House. Would he end up this way? Being driven by someone else to die alone. It was possible. Life was full of wicked twists and ragged turns. He'd never have guessed he'd be a leg breaker for the mafia when he was a dumb, hormonal teenager. They skipped that option on career day.

At seventeen, Jake had the world by the tail. He owned the starting running back and linebacker positions for the high school team, all but promised a full ride scholarship from Kansas State University to go play for the legendary Bill Snyder, and he was madly in love with the head cheerleader. Every muscle on his tall physique popped and he could run down the sun, lean and solid as a rock. He ran his own summer training routine getting ready for his senior year, chopping logs in the woods behind the house and hoisting them up the hill, building endurance and stamina. This would be his time to shine, to get away from Stony.

He talked about escaping Warsaw incessantly. Anyone who listened heard his grand scheme of playing Division 1 football for a top twenty program. Jake would make something of himself, something beyond scrapping for jobs like Stony, or schlepping away for minimum wage at the lumber yard like Nicky. Something more than getting stoned on cheap beer at a smoky, local bar, throwing punches, and fishing on the lake with a bad hangover.

Every time he talked about getting out, he directed it at Stony. Each whip of the belt, each bruise that showed up on his brother's face, and each promise Stony broke provided the fuel that burned his excellence on the field. His disdain for his father grew with every weight he pressed, every bone-crushing tackle he made, and every mile he ran. The anger would have eaten him whole, if it hadn't been for Maggie.

Strikingly beautiful with cascading hair and a taut, athletic figure, Maggie could stop conversation in a room with a smile. She and Jake fit together like perfect puzzle pieces, both burning with the desire to get away and do something meaningful with their lives.

As he broke the city limits of Sedalia, a dark row of heavy clouds rolled in from the northeast, still a way off but likely to dump on the area within the next couple hours. His knee ached in familiar places as the atmospheric pressure changed and he rubbed the scar to make it go away. Stony groaned as the truck bounced over a pothole and Jake was cast to the worst night of his life.

Jake and Bear skipped rocks by the creek and drank beer lifted from Stony's stash in the fridge, Jake's sweat-soaked T-shirt thrown over his brawny, tanned shoulders. Bear left his shirt on, not wanting to endure Jake's jokes about his weight. They talked about football and the upcoming two-a-day practices on the Warsaw High field. Their senior year and they'd be the Dynamic Duo. Bear held them up on the line and Jake knocked them down. Ten games, graduation and they'd both be gone to Kansas State.

Jake reached into the stream and tossed one of the last two beer cans to Bear. They drank and continued the rock skipping contest. Stony hadn't shown his face for three days. He and Bear would cruise the watering holes in town daily until they found Stony's beat up Ford. The truck moved so at least they were certain Stony wasn't dead in a ditch somewhere. Jake could give two shits if Stony came home, life moved easier without him. Nicky had a job and brought home the occasional groceries, but he showed up almost as rarely as Stony. Jake and Janey cooked a decent meal together, and nobody kept him from rolling up the hill late at night to be with Maggie.

"I'd better get going." Bear crushed his empty beer can and belched loud enough to shake the bark from the nearby trees. "My mom's making meatloaf tonight and will beat my ass if I'm late."

"You'd better watch the weight or you're not going to be able to move on the d-line," Jake said, draining the rest of his beer.

"Suck it, Caldwell. I'm an all-powerful, monstrous beast of destruction."

"Teams will tremble at your feet."

"They will beg for mercy," Bear shouted. "I set 'em up…"

"I knock 'em down," Jake responded, bumping knuckles with his best friend.

They trudged up the hill, Jake with the axe over his shoulder, Bear carrying an armful of logs. The sun burned overhead, just beginning its descent to the west. Janey read a book at the picnic table snuggled under a grove of trees in front of the house. Stony chained the table to a nearby tree for some reason. Nobody could figure out why. One wrong move would turn the thing into a pile of kindling. Janey waved as the two approached.

"Your sister's looking good, Caldwell," Bear said, waggling his eyebrows.

"Keep your dick away from her. She's too young."

"Sweet sixteen, baby. Old enough."

"Fifteen, perv. Not sixteen until next month and still too young and thin for your ass. You need one of those mama's in the muumuus."

"You can come for dinner, you know," Bear said, stopping at his car. "My mom loves you. I think she'd adopt you if Stony would let her."

"Stony wouldn't give a shit. I'd tell her to start the paperwork if it wasn't for Janey."

"All right, later dude. Tell Maggie hey."

They bumped fists again as Bear jumped into his Chevelle, cranked the key, and waited for the engine to catch, the endeavor always a bit of a gamble. Would it or wouldn't it? Today it did and Bear tore out of their driveway and on to Poor Boy Road in a cloud of dust.

Jake went inside the house and smelled something cooking in the kitchen. Janey made her green bean casserole and Jake's stomach growled. The leaping deer clock on the wall read five o'clock, five hours until he could hook up with Maggie *at their spot after she snuck out.*

Jake and Janey ate in the living room in front of the television that night. Burt Reynolds jumped his Trans Am over the bridge to elude Sheriff Buford T. Justice in Smokey and the Bandit, when the familiar muffler of the old man's truck roared up Poor Boy Road. An engine revved to redline followed by the clunks of gravel flying in the driveway. Jake's head swung to Janey, her eyes growing wide.

"That doesn't sound good," she said.

"It's not," Jake said, jumping up. "Go to your room and shut the door."

He didn't have to ask her twice. She padded down the hall and disappeared into her room. Moments later, the truck door squealed open, glass bottles clinked together and broke on the driveway. The door shut and Jake clenched the armrest of the chair, staring ahead at the TV, the muscles in his jaw already aching with tension. He could bail to his room, or out the back door, but he represented the buffer between Stony and Janey. The old man hadn't hurt her, but the possibility of a first time couldn't be discounted. It wouldn't happen on Jake's watch.

The front door banged open, and an unshaven, dirty mess lurched against the frame. Three days worth of booze, smoke and body odor rolled across the living room and made Jake wince. The old man swayed and scanned the room from side to side as if trying to figure out if he went to the right house. His eyes locked in on Jake on the third sweep.

"Where's everyone at?" Stony asked, slurring, leaning against the doorway like it would collapse if he moved.

"Janey's in her room. Nicky came home from work, but went back into town to hook up with some friends."

"So what the hell are you doing?" Stony said, the corner of his mouth drawn up in a sneer. "Not out finger bangin' your little blondie?"

Jake remained stone faced as his father laughed and staggered past to the kitchen. He grabbed a cold beer and plopped in his recliner. He chuckled at his joke, but stopped when the vein in Jake's forehead pulsated with anger.

"Whatsamatter?" He took a long pull from the can, foam on his upper lip and amber liquid dripping down his chin. "Can't take a joke, you candy ass?"

"I can take a joke," Jake said. "I'll wait until you say something funny."

Stony took another slug. He wiped his mouth on a dirty shirt sleeve and pointed at Jake with a long, bony finger.

"Listen, smart ass," he said. "I'll whip your ass if you don't keep your mouth shut. You think you're a big man. Big football man fucking the hottie prom queen. You think you're better than me?"

Jake was well-conditioned to not engage his dad on any level of confrontation. Stony was on a three-day bender and though he could barely stand, Jake couldn't bring himself to fight him, a line he wouldn't cross, no matter what Stony did to him.

"I don't think I'm better than you."

Stony's finger wavered in the air, and it took a good ten seconds for Jake's statement to seep in.

"Good, you miserable little son of a bitch." Stony sank back in his chair. "Cuz you ain't better than me. Big football star. Mister college bound douche bag. Ain't nobody better than me. Especially you. Now go fix me something to eat."

Jake stood without a word, went to the kitchen and heated some of Janey's casserole on a plate. He waited a minute for the microwave to finish and took the warm food to the living room. Stony slumped in the recliner, out cold, the empty beer can tilted toward the floor. Jake took the can, turned off the light and left Stony there. He knocked gently on Janey's door. She opened it enough for her red, curly head to show.

"Go to Darla's house for the night," he said. "He's passed out now, but he'll wake up eventually and I don't like his mood."

"What about you?" Lines creased her forehead.

"Don't worry about me. I'm going to hook up with Maggie. I might just take a sleeping bag and crash up on the hill. It's warm out. I'll be fine."

Janey grabbed a bag, stuffed a few clothes in it and peeked in the hall. The two tiptoed to the front door, though a parade of trumpeting elephants could trample through the place and Stony wouldn't twitch a muscle.

Jake escorted Janey a quarter mile up the road to her friend Darla's house, as small as their own, but better maintained. Darla's folks didn't make a lot of money, but they were kind, hardworking people who knew what the Caldwell kids faced at home and would take any of them in without a word when needed.

Janey safely deposited, Jake walked back toward home, past the front yard and up the hill into the woods, following the moonlight touching the dirt path that climbed to the Spot. He waited, taking in the moon-kissed tree tops with his knees drawn up, hugging himself with his brawny arms. He thought of his dad passed out and how they had to escape him. It was fucking ridiculous.

Maggie arrived with her spirit-lifting aura twenty minutes later. They embraced and kissed, said a few words and kissed some more. She couldn't stay. Her parents were still up and working on something for church. She snuck out her window, but needed to get back. They promised to get together tomorrow and parted ways.

He trudged back down the hill, his work boots crunching leaves and twigs. A rabbit darted across the path, diving into the opposite brush. He wished he'd brought his sleeping bag. But the day's work and the beer left him wiped out; he didn't have the energy to walk back to the hill. Stony would be out until morning anyway.

The chainsaw sounds of his dad snoring in the chair shattered the silence of the house. His father hadn't moved an inch in the hour Jake was gone. In the bedroom he shared with Nicky, he peeled off his clothes and dropped on to his bed in his boxers, staring at the ceiling and thinking about Maggie. His leg dangled off the side of the bed, sweeping back and forth. Jake counted the pendulum sweeps of his big toe brushing the bare wood. He counted to sixty before falling asleep.

He dreamed of a monstrous shadow chasing him through the darkened Warsaw streets. The normally wide Main Street squeezed together to nothing more than an alley, and he darted from door to door trying to escape. The stores were all locked and the windows dark. Long, pale faces with black eyes stared out from inside the shops as he screamed for help. Every time he approached a door, the faces drew back and disappeared into the blackness. The thump of the shadow's heavy footsteps drew closer and the impact ring of metal meeting metal. The narrow Main Street triangulated to a point, trapping him. As the shadow approached, Jake pressed his back into the unyielding wood and screamed aloud.

He woke in a sheen of sweat, heart racing from the nightmare. The light from the hallway backlit the figure hovering over him with something in hand. Jake smelled beer, dirt and sweat.

"You want to leave, boy? Let me tell you somethin'. You ain't goin' nowhere."

85

His father raised the dull silver pipe, eighteen inches long, an inch in diameter. The pitted pipe descended and crashed into Jake's knee as it dangled off the side of the bed. Pain erupted like a volcano, sending piercing, fiery waves of agony through his body. A second swing of the pipe crashed between Jake's hands grasping at his shattered knee and sent him reeling into darkness.

CHAPTER SEVENTEEN

Willie smoked and sweated outside the house, the four o'clock sun peeking through the trees to the west. He hated wearing the hazmat suit, but better to sweat it out than let the chemicals seep into his skin. Dexter kept an eye on the process inside the ramshackle house, making sure nothing boiled over. Thank God they neared the end of the run. Dexter creeped him out.

Bennett crashed in the back of the pickup truck, where he'd pretty much been since his noon arrival, snoring loud enough to wake a hibernating bear. Even from this distance, Willie could smell the alcohol and weed seeping out of his pores. He, Bub and Howie tied one on last night at the Turn It Loose bar. Bennett said poor Howie lay wrecked in their trailer back home puking his guts out. Willie gave him until six o'clock to sleep it off before getting his ass back to work, or he'd let Shane know Howie wasn't pulling his weight.

Bub rumbled up in Willie's truck. He slowly poured himself out of the cab, wincing with each step as he made his way to the house.

"What's wrong with you?" Willie asked.

Bub coughed and drew in a deep breath, pressing his hand to his side. "Think I broke a goddamn rib."

"From what?"

"Some big fucker jumped me and the Sterretts down by the Community Center."

Willie stepped off the porch. "One guy took all three of you? Who was he?"

"Don't know. Big. Solid. Short brown hair. Was asking about Shane. If we knew where to find him."

Sirens wailed in Willie's head. "Cop?"

"Don't think so. Didn't look like it anyway."

"Maybe a fed?"

Bub lit a cigarette with painful movements that made Willie ache. He'd had his ass kicked before and recognized the telltale movements. "Never seen him before. Said Shane owed him some money and he wanted to know where he could collect."

"What'd you tell him?"

"Told him to fuck off. Like I'm gonna give him Shane's address. Then Hank took a swing with a pipe at his head and it was on. Man, that guy could fight. Like one of those ninjas in the movies. Don't think we hit him once."

"What then?"

"In about five seconds, both Sterretts were out cold on the ground, and he had me by the throat. Police sirens went off and the guy just disappeared like a fart in the wind. Cops didn't even see him and didn't want to jack with us. Just told me to get the hell outta there."

Bub ground the cigarette in the dirt. What should Willie do? Tell Shane? Probably not. Shane would send him on some witch hunt for the guy and he had enough to do. Besides, Willie didn't want to mess with any man that could take down Bub and both the Sterrett twins at the same time.

"Go take a rest next to Bennett," Willie said. "We're finishing up here."

Bub nodded and limped to the truck bed. He slid back and passed out before Willie got to the front door of the house.

Back inside, Willie learned from Dexter the Meth Master for the next couple of hours. His final product had a crimson hue, chunks of rock like faded rubies. Dexter called it "Devil Ice." He offered to let Willie try some before pounding a crystal to powder and snorting it. His eyes bugged and he howled a primal scream.

"That's some good shit," he said. "You don't know what you're missing, kid."

Willie knew exactly what he was missing. He took a long pull of bottled water and his mind drifted to the girl. Little Halle who wasn't little anymore, almost legal in the eyes of the law, though still too young for Willie to even think about. But think about her he did.

Willie wandered back outside and lit a cigarette, leaning against the rickety front porch railing. It wasn't her centerfold body, perfectly tan and smooth which was all Bub ever saw. It wasn't her cascading hair or her soul-penetrating icy blues. For Willie, it was her smile, full of promise and a lust for life, that got his motor racing, even if she never cast it in his direction. He fantasized of chance meetings around Warsaw, long strolls around the lake, making out under the moonlight in the back of a sweet truck he'd probably never own. In the darkness of his trailer when his hand would reach below, she'd peel off her shirt, always the orange tank top, reach behind and unclasp her bra. Willie would reach forward and caress those perfectly round, soft breasts and lick the sweat from her cleavage.

"What the hell are you thinking about?" Bub asked, lying on his side in the truck bed, propped up on a meaty arm.

Willie jerked from the fantasy as if he'd been shocked in the ass by a cattle prod.

"Nothing."

"Bullshit. You had that stupid, faraway grin on your ugly mug and judging from your banana wood there, I'm guessing you were thinking about Halle."

"Shut the fuck up."

"Man, I'm telling you, we should pick her up sometime. She's always wandering around town. Take her down to the lake...take her down everywhere."

An image flashed of Halle at the hands of a fat animal like Bub and his stomach rolled. He flicked the cigarette toward the truck. Right now, Bub ogled over Halle and joked around. But eventually he'd quit joking and his pea brain would try to turn fantasy to reality.

"Don't even think about it, Bub."

"Or what?" Bub must've been feeling better and clambered forward, dropping his boat-feet to the ground. He demonstrated the unwavering loyalty of a dog, but even a dog could turn and kill the man holding his leash. To set things to order, the master pulls on the leash and the dog obeys. Willie needed to yank on Bub's leash.

Willie reached on to the porch rail and picked up his butterfly knife. With practiced dexterity and a glimmer of sunlight on silver, he exposed the blade, locked the handles together and threw the knife at Bub's feet. The blade buried itself inches from his toes. Bub's fleshy jaw hung open. Willie puffed as wide as his skinny chest could expand.

"Touch Halle and I'll cut your balls off. Got it?"

Bub closed his mouth. He kicked the knife over and winced back on to the truck bed, scooching back like a crab while holding his side. "You're a crazy sumbitch, you know it?"

Willie played the part of the powerless pawn working under Shane, and it felt good to throw his weight around. He nodded and went back to the house. Dollar signs rolled as he shattered the sheets of Devil Ice and bagged the results. With those dollar signs translating to bills in his pockets, he floated back to Halle and picked up with the imagined scenario in the pickup truck. This time, instead of sex, the two of them left Warsaw together for the bright lights of Kansas City.

CHAPTER EIGHTEEN

Howie Skaggs teetered on the side of his bed, holding his throbbing head in his hands. With his eyes clamped shut against the piercing daylight blasting through the smoke-yellowed windows of the trailer, he grabbed his cigarettes off the end table. Without opening his eyes, he lit the cigarette and inhaled deeply, holding the smoke in as the nausea stirred in his belly. He glanced at the clock and groaned. He'd been in bed all day and now had only an hour to get to the cook house by six o'clock or Willie would have his ass.

Hank Williams, Jr. nailed it; the hangovers hurt more than they used to. A few years ago, he could've pounded the same amount of beers at the bar as he did last night and been right as rain today. But the mileage on his body since then had taken a toll. He had a vague recollection of dancing with Marcie Wallows to the music blaring from the blown juke box speakers at the Turn It Loose. He opened his eyes and touched the top of his head, wincing at the bump and the memory of Daryl, Marcie's husband, busting a pool cue across his noggin for groping his old lady while they grinded to some techno-pop garbage. Bub threw the man into the parking lot. Howie glanced to his swollen knuckles. He and Bub took turns pummeling the guy's face raw. When Daryl slid down the side of a rusted out pickup with half an ounce of consciousness, Howie walked back in the bar and picked up where he left off with Marcie. Either she didn't know her husband just got his ass kicked like a narc at a biker rally, or she didn't care.

Someone hammered on the door to the trailer. Probably Willie there to get him back to the cook house. Howie slid to the edge of the bed, trying to find the will to stand. The door thundered again.

"All right, all right," Howie shouted, recoiling at the reverberations in his beer-soaked brain. "What the hell is so important?"

He flung open the trailer door and froze. Not Willie, but Bear with his paw on a holstered pistol. Randy Daniels, one of the local deputies who everyone called Sad Dog, leaned against the squad car, his sturdy arms cradling a shotgun. A pale hulk with a thickset face, and cropped, red hair, Randy wore his patented "don't fuck with me" look. Howie was one of the few people in town who knew why people called Randy "Sad Dog," but it wasn't worth the ass beating Randy would lay on him if he told anyone.

"We need to talk, Howie," Bear said. "Mind if I come in?"

"As a matter of fact, I do." Howie stepped outside and closed the door behind him. "What's up, Bear?"

"You're up," Bear said. "You and that shit heap Bub beat the hell out of Daryl Wallows last night. He's up in Clinton in a hospital bed with his jaw wired shut and three broken ribs."

Howie cursed internally. Bear's sights had locked on him and wasn't about to let it go. His mind did a quick inventory of the trailer. His unlawful pistol and a couple of stones of Devil Ice he'd pilfered from the cook house sat on his dresser. Shane's angry face floated across his mind's eye. He was in deep, deep shit.

"Don't know what you're talking about," Howie said.

"Yeah, you do. You okay? You look nervous all of a sudden. Something inside I need to be worried about?"

"Nah," Howie said, anxious to get Bear away from the trailer. He tried passing Bear, appearing casual. "Let's go to the station and talk about it."

Bear stopped Howie in his tracks with an arm to his shoulder. "Hey, you ain't getting in my car in your goddamn boxer shorts. Go cover up that little dick with some clothes."

Howie turned and glanced over his bony shoulder. Bear breathed down his neck. He should've known they wouldn't let him go in by himself. He tried to dart inside and pull the door shut, but Bear grabbed it, stepping inside and pushing Howie back.

"Hey," Howie yelled out as Bear passed. "You ever hear of unlawful entry?"

"You a fucking lawyer now? You invited me in. Besides, it's pretty rude to try and slam a door in a cop's face, Howie." He crushed Howie against the wall with his substantial bulk. "What have you got to hide in here?"

"Nothing," he muttered, eyes cast down, praying Bear wouldn't look to the bedroom. The freaking gun and baggie sat in the open. No such luck. Bear saw them and smiled.

"Well, well, what have we here?" Bear said, clamping on Howie's neck. Daniels caught him as Bear shoved Howie out the door. "Cuff him, Sad Dog."

Daniels face-planted Howie on the uncomfortably warm hood of the Crown Vic and Howie grunted as the handcuffs bit into his wrists. Wearing only boxers, there was nothing to frisk so Daniels pulled him upright and leaned him against the car. Things crashed and banged inside his trailer for a few minutes before Bear came out with the butt of the pistol in one hand and the bag of Devil Ice in his other. A pair of jeans and a shirt draped over his arm. He tossed the clothes on the ground when he got to the car.

"Jesus God," Daniels said. "This guy smells like ass."

"He's getting ready to smell a hell of a lot worse," Bear said, examining the pistol. He handed it to Daniels who checked it to ensure it wasn't loaded and placed it on the hood of the cruiser. Bear held up the baggie, the afternoon sun lighting up the red rocks like a half-ass prism. "What's this?"

"It ain't mine," Howie said, ashamed the lamest and most tired excuse crossed his lips.

"Yeah, I'm sure it isn't. Where did you get it?"

"How should I know if it ain't mine?"

Bear grabbed Howie's face, digging his powerful fingers into his cheeks.

"Don't dick with me, Howie. Where did you get it?"

A million comebacks flooded Howie's brain. Should he continue to plead ignorance, or maybe try feeding Bear enough information that he might cut Howie loose? It took a few seconds to conclude silence was the only response to guarantee Shane wouldn't slice his balls off and feed them to his mountain of a bodyguard. He clamped his lips together.

"Nothing?" Bear said. "Fine, we'll take you in and have a little discussion. You're on probation, right?"

Howie had six months remaining from a previous illegal weapon and meth possession charge. He'd served fourteen months in the county jail with no desire to go back. But he didn't answer Bear.

"Well," Bear continued, releasing Howie's face. He put a thick finger under Howie's chin and raised his head so their gazes locked. He dangled the Devil Ice in front of him. "You better start figuring a way to help yourself out, Howie. I don't know what this red shit is yet, but I'm guessin' it ain't Jolly Ranchers."

Bear motioned to Daniels who wrestled Howie to the back of the squad car and shoved him inside. They climbed into the front and talked as if Howie wasn't even there.

"Well, what do you think?" Daniels asked.

"I think some heads are gonna roll over this, Sad Dog." Bear held up the baggie and flicked the rocks inside. "Some heads are gonna roll starting with this shithead in the back."

CHAPTER NINETEEN

About the time Bear pulled Howie out of his trailer, Jake pulled up to the Hospice House entrance. The single-story, cream-brick building rested at the back of a long, macadam driveway that set it apart from the traffic of Highway 50. Jake crept up the drive, the thick pine trees on either side thinning out until the building spilled in front of him. He stopped at the entrance, shut off the engine and stared across his old man to the front door. He'd phoned ahead to the director to let her know he was on his way. Stony's gaunt face rolled from the window. Bloodshot eyes squinted at him.

"Where are we?" Stony rasped, his bony hands tightening over his stomach. Though it had been a decade since Jake heard the man's voice, the mere sound of it raised his blood pressure. The last conversation involved him saying "Hold on" when Jake made a rare call to talk to Janey.

"Hospice in Sedalia," Jake said.

Stony's thin lips curled upward into his patented shit-eating grin before a coughing spasm racked his body. It took a good minute for the fit to pass.

"Aw, man." He wiped his mouth with the back of his hand. "Fucking Hospice? Am I that bad off?"

"Yeah, you are," Jake said. He focused on a crushed bug on the windshield, hands alternating between his lap and the steering wheel. Another coughing spasm lurched Stony forward. He covered his mouth with the sleeve of his gray shirt and Jake noted specks of red as he pulled his arm away.

"How long you been home?"

"Couple of days."

"Staying long?" Stony asked.

Jake ground his teeth. When the hell would someone come out and get him? "Just long enough. Not a day more."

Stony reached a shaky hand to the door and pushed himself up in the seat. He squinted across the cab.

"You doing okay? You look good," Stony said, his demeanor catching Jake off guard.

"Doing fine, Stony," Jake managed, his white knuckled hands squeezing the steering wheel.

"You got your mother's eyes. I ever tell you that?"

"I don't recall too many lucid father and son exchanges in our past."

Stony chuckled a couple of breaths before erupting into a cough that rocked his body. Jake waited for this spasm to pass and handed him a bottle of water. Stony managed a couple of sips, wiping a bit from his chin with the back of his hand.

"You ain't gonna get many lucid conversations with me past this one either. I'm so doped up I'm lucky if I remember my goddamn name half the time."

This civil exchange with his father put Jake in an emotional upheaval. Your mother's eyes…his self-deprecation. It did nothing but raise Jake's hackles. Why did it take the decrepit old bastard crawling into his death bed to become civil? Jake sure as hell wasn't going to give him the satisfaction.

"I'll make sure they spell it right on your tombstone," Jake said. Pain on Stony's face from the shot flashed, followed by a knowing huff of resignation. His old man knew it. Too little, too late.

"You know what I keep dreaming about? Playing catch in the front yard with that scuffed up, old football you got for Christmas when you were six or seven years old."

"Ten."

"Took you a year to be able to catch two in a row. Taught you good, didn't I?"

"It was either catch the ball or get your boot up my ass. Guess either I was a slow learner or your foot got sore."

Stony's gaze moved from Jake's face to the gold ring sitting in the cup holder next to him. He picked it up, a smile breaking across his face.

"Damn," he said. "Haven't seen this in a long time. Figured you took it when you skipped town. And you kept it all these years to remember me by?"

"No. Just wasn't going to let you do any more damage to anyone else with it," Jake said, turning his gaze from the windshield to see his father's smile disappear. Jake needed to get him out of his truck before he screamed.

As if on cue, a couple of nurses in bright, flowery scrubs emerged through the front door with an empty wheelchair. Jake waited for Stony to pop the ring on his finger. Instead, he caressed the rough surface and dropped it back in the cup holder.

Jake got out of the truck and opened the passenger door. The two nurses worked together to load Stony's bony frame into the wheelchair. They pointed across the lot to an empty space in front of a line of evergreens where Jake could park and disappeared with Stony into the building.

As Jake pulled forward, he resisted the urge to gun the motor and careen out to the highway and disappear. Just hearing Stony's raspy, three-pack-a day-for-forty-years voice box grate syllables in his direction cracked the door of past shadows. Jake had worked hard over the last decade to push them into a room of their own, to contain them and not let them wash him away. Now, with a few spoken words, the waste of welfare opened the door.

Jake drove into the parking spot, absently rubbing his knee. He had to see this through. If he bailed now, Janey would hunt him down. Stony would continue to haunt his dreams. The sound of the pipe shattering his kneecap would echo in his ears. He'd keep seeing Nicky in every junkie he met in Kansas City.

He hopped out of the truck and slammed the door too hard. As his boot heels beat relentlessly on the parking lot, his resolve built. With each step toward the entrance, his certainty solidified this was meant to be. It might be hours, it might be days, but Jake would be there when he drew his last phlegm-filled breath. When Stony died, Jake wouldn't need that room of past shadows any longer. He would be free.

CHAPTER TWENTY

Halle Holden dropped her backpack on the couch, the old sofa groaning in protest under the weight of textbooks. She'd skipped cross country practice, telling Mr. Monroe she suffered from "female issues"—her excuse when a rare bout of laziness rolled through her. Today, she couldn't handle the track coach's running regimen he probably pulled off the Internet. Mr. Monroe may be a decent Biology teacher, but he was a lousy track coach.

She checked out each room, thankful her mom wasn't home from Hospice. Lately, they'd butted heads anytime Halle explained her teenage rationale for doing whatever she did. You'd think being a straight-A student and on the Varsity track and cross country teams as a sophomore would buy her a little leeway from an occasional beer, joint or slightly missed curfew. Her mom cut her zero slack.

She donned her favorite pair of running shorts and a tank top, and admired herself in front of the floor-length mirror in her tiny bedroom. She twisted to and fro, admiring her muscled legs and how her ass looked in the aqua shorts. The summer of running those Ozark hills paid dividends. The boys at school already noticed how she'd grown over the summer. Even her big crush, Senior Mason Dell, did a double take yesterday when she passed by. At least that's what her best friend Alicia said.

On her iPod, Sara Bareilles asked how big her brave was as Halle trotted out the front door, down the driveway and on to the chipped pavement of Poor Boy Road. She figured she could work in a quick three or four miles before meeting Alicia at their spot. Hang there for a couple hours and be home before her mom got back from her shift. Perfect.

The late school bus rumbled by as she hugged the side of the road. A lone face peeked from the back of the bus, little hands pressed against the dusty glass. Tyler Garrett gave her a wave with his little elementary school hands. Halle gave him a big smile and waved back. She babysat for Tyler on occasion, his house not far from the place she and Alicia discovered a few months ago.

It looked abandoned when they first approached, knee high weeds growing around a sunken, wooden porch. A thick layer of dirt and grime covered the windows and a screen door hung on for dear life by one hinge, rapping gently against the flaking front door. There were no cars, no lights, no sign of life anywhere. She and Alicia squirreled around the outside, wiping away the dust into makeshift peepholes in the windows. The place was furnished, but no doubt abandoned.

They didn't venture inside that day, but over the ensuing weeks became brave and wormed their way in through an unlocked back window. The dusty pictures on shelves and old bills scattered on the floor clued them in there wouldn't be an angry owner barging in.

Halle jogged at a brisk pace along Poor Boy Road, thinking of the bonding memories she and Alicia forged at the old house over the last five months. She giggled recalling their first marijuana smoking experience. Stoned to the bejesus and talking about boys. She reached the hidden path to the drive and ducked below arching tree branches, not thinking twice that the normally closed green gate lay open. She ran through dark shadows that mixed on the dirt path with spatters of light piercing the thick tree cover.

Rounding the last curve leading to her secret house, she expected to spot her Alicia sitting on the lawn chair waiting for her arrival. Instead, a white panel van and a familiar rusted out pickup truck were parked in front of the house. She slowed to a walk, panting hard, each step slower than the one before as her brain worked the scene in front of her.

Flickers of yellow moved through the front windows but she kept moving forward. What was she doing? It reminded her of those crappy slasher movies she sometimes watched with Mom. They made fun of the bimbos who just had to find the source of the commotion. Blood dripping through the ceiling? Hmmm, let's go upstairs and look. Home alone in the dark, a loud thump comes from the basement. Better go investigate. Yet here she stood, being that bimbo.

Her mother's voice saying "curiosity killed the cat" rang in her head, yet Halle crept along the tree line of the clearing, approaching the house from a blind spot on the side. As she reached the front porch, she glanced to the pickup. Two pairs of feet stuck out of the truck bed. Her heart stuck in her throat and her hand shot to her mouth. *Oh my God! There are dead people in that truck.* Then one of them raised a leg and spat a rattling fart.

Every fiber screamed at her to get the hell out of there. Instead, she slid to the sagging porch, carefully setting her weight toward the edges where the rotting wood was best supported and less likely to groan and give her away. She inched to the window.

Inside, two figures worked elbow to elbow amongst tables of pots, tubes and beakers, dressed in yellow plastic suits she recognized from the movies whenever someone waded through hazardous waste. They wore gas masks under the hoods and one swung a hammer, smashing something on the table. The other one grabbed handfuls or red crystals and weighed them in quart-sized Ziploc bags. With her attention fixed on the crystals, she failed to notice the figure doing the hammering had stopped and now stared straight at her.

Halle's heart thundered, and her face grew hot and flushed. The man with the hammer pulled back the hood and removed the gas mask, his face crunched in disbelief, as if he needed an unimpeded vision to believe what he saw before him. She recognized him and had a pretty good idea the content of those baggies wasn't rock candy.

"Oh, fuck me," Willie Banks mouthed. He moved toward the front door and Halle ran like a bat out of hell past the back of the house and into the woods.

CHAPTER TWENTY-ONE

The manager told Jake it would take them a little while to get Stony situated in his room. She suggested he hang out in the waiting room or go get something to eat. Outside, he soaked in the sun when his cell rang. Dwight.

"What do you have?" Jake asked.

"Did you know some of this shit is flagged by the FBI? The FBI, Caldwell."

Interesting. "So did you get it?"

"Yeah, but this wipes our slate clean. In fact, you should be paying me with whatever proceeds you're gettin' from whatever the hell it is you're doing."

"Come on, Dwight. Just give me the info and we're even."

"Okay, Marion Holdings is the one the Feds flagged. It's an ownership group with a shitload of properties including a chain of restaurants, bars, car washes, convenience stores, warehouses and a car dealership."

"What dealership?" Jake asked.

He heard a shuffle of papers. "Langston Motors in Sedalia. This holding company also owns title on the Global Distribution Center you mentioned."

"Why was it flagged by the Feds?"

"I had to hack into the FBI database to do it and you can't hang around there too long. You can only bounce your signal around so many times. Best I could see it was for concerns with drugs and money laundering. The thing is, the FBI files are all about Marion Holdings. Nothing about this Global Distribution Center."

"That doesn't make much sense," Jake said.

"I see it all the time. The spectrum of competency in the FBI is broad. Everything was flagged except for the Global Distribution Center. It's a new site in the last six months. Doesn't look like they've either put two and two together, or done another search since the new site came into the picture. Gotta love the efficiency of our government."

"What about Shane Langston? He's the owner of Langston Motors."

"Langston Motors? Hell, he's the principal of the holding company. He owns all of it. Guy's a freaking millionaire."

"You found it that easy?"

"Easy? Hell no. I had to look through six different databases to connect the dots. You're lucky I have OCD. Doubt anyone else could've found it. We even now?"

"Yeah, you did good, Dwight. Stay away from the casinos."

He checked his watch. He had about an hour to kill so decided to head over to the warehouse. His time was running out with Keats. If he couldn't get to Langston or chickened out of killing him, maybe he could come up with something to hang Langston out to dry.

*****

Minutes later, he turned into the empty lot of Global Distribution Center. Jake followed the side road around the corner of the warehouse, heading toward the back.

He got out of the truck and checked the back door. Still locked. He checked the door frame but couldn't see any alarm contacts, and, given the age of the building, decided to take a chance it wasn't wired. He shoved his Glock into his waistband and pulled a sledgehammer from the back of the truck. With a grunt and a swing, he cracked off the doorknob, ready to bolt if sirens sounded. He pushed open the door and examined the frame. No wires, no alarm.

The door opened into a small maintenance shop. A few workbenches were covered with tools and an overhead hoist hung above a grease spot on the floor. With nothing of interest there, Jake headed through the door on the opposite wall. It opened to a single, vast expanse, dark save for light filtering through cobwebbed windows set along the roofline. The lone occupant of the warehouse, a large John Deere tractor, rested along the west wall with an office area toward the front.

He rummaged through the office and found nothing of interest except a thick layer of dust on the desks and chairs. He turned to leave when a muffler rumbled outside and the large bay door began rolling up. His slid behind the open office door, peering out to the warehouse floor through the crack. Seconds later, a black panel van drove inside and blocked his view of the tractor. The garage door screeched down, taking out the flood of sunlight. Jake slid the Glock from his waistband and held it by his leg, adrenaline surging.

A bulky Hispanic man dressed in jeans and a beige jacket climbed out of the passenger side and walked around the front. He spoke in Spanish to the driver then climbed into the cab of the John Deere. The tractor fired up, its engine echoing in the empty warehouse. Over the top of the van, Jake watched the tractor roll forward a few feet and stop. The driver's door squealed open and the man in the tractor climbed down. More doors creaked, probably the back of the van, followed by the scrape of dragging metal. Jake closed his dry mouth and he prayed they wouldn't come this way.

A few minutes later, the scraping metal sounded again followed by van doors slamming shut. Back in the tractor, the Hispanic man reversed it to its original spot. He got back in the truck, the bay door opened and they were gone. Jake waited until the door closed and the sound of the van faded into the distance.

He emerged from behind the door, pointed the Glock and eased into the warehouse. Empty. Nothing but him and the tractor. What the hell were they moving it for? He crossed the warehouse and stood by the huge tractor tires. He pulled out his cell phone and turned on the flashlight feature. The bright LED lit up the dirty floor and revealed the source of the scraping sound. A large, orange grate which rested underneath the tractor tires. Jake shined the light through the gaps to an empty trough. Probably a drain for washing down equipment.

He climbed into the tractor and fired it up. He'd never driven one and it took him a minute to figure out the controls. Those guys didn't move this beast for the hell of it. Something must lay underneath. He managed to roll the tractor forward a few feet then killed the engine. Climbing down, he wrested the bulky grate from the floor without throwing out his back.

Inside the empty trough, a rectangle shape outlined the metal with a small, circular ring at the top and a hinge on the opposite side. He knelt on the floor and yanked the ring. The metal raised on the hinge revealing a compartment, about three feet long and a foot wide. Jake whistled at the contents.

Inside, clear plastic bags of white powder glistened. Probably not baby powder. A cheap, black-leather duffel bag sat in the space. Jake leaned down and unzipped the top. Strapped bricks of dollar bills. He thumbed through the pile. Maybe fifty thousand. Now what the hell should he do?

Langston owned the warehouse and this had to be one of his stashes. Jake should take the drugs and the money and get the hell out of there, but what would he do if he got stopped by the cops, several kilos of what he assumed to be cocaine in his truck? He left the drugs in the trench and grabbed the duffel bag. Heck, he needed the money more than Langston and considered the find the spoils of war.

Jake set the duffel bag to the side, closed the lid and wrestled the grate back in place. He clambered up the ladder to the cab to back the tractor up, but figured he had just as good a chance of driving the thing through the warehouse wall. Leave well enough alone. Instead, he grabbed a rag, wiped down everywhere he touched and ran out the back door with the duffel bag, picking up his sledgehammer along the way. A minute later, he rolled out of the parking lot with the fifty grand locked in the tool box on his truck.

Now what? He had Langston's money, but what about the drugs? He headed back toward Hospice, searching the shops on the way. Finding Bigfoot would have been easier than finding a pay phone. Spotting one at the edge of a dilapidated strip mall, he called in an anonymous tip to the police, giving them the location of the warehouse and where to look. He wiped the phone down with a rag and drove away with a grin on his face. A rare win for the good guys.

*****

By the time Jake got back to Hospice, Stony slept. The room was homey, with brown, threadbare carpet and wallpaper with flowers and vines. Sepia maybe, who knew. He never claimed to be an interior decorator. A basic dresser sat along the wall at the foot of the bed with a mid-sized, flat-panel television on one end of the wood. A ceiling fan rotated lazily overhead. Jake plopped in a recliner, running a visual circle between the window with a view of the sun-drenched parking lot, the spinning blades of the fan and his father who lay on his side, his face crunched in agony.

A heavy-set nurse in pale blue scrubs floated silently into the room, checking the IV hooked into his father's hand. After writing some things on a chart, she slid over to the chair where Jake sprawled, interrupting his attempts to come up with a way he might reveal to the cops Langston's ties with the warehouse.

"Hi," she said in a soft, practiced manner. "I'm Judy and I'll be looking after your father at night. If you need anything, let us know."

She patted Stony's leg and slipped out of the room. Overall, Jake had to admit, an impressive display by the staff. Regular hospitals either acted like they didn't care with a calculated indifference or they over-schmoozed to make you think they did. The rhythmic rocking of the chair and the cool breeze from the ceiling fan hypnotized him and he dozed off.

He held an absurdly large fishing pole in his hand at the banks of the pond behind their house. The rod as thick as a small sapling and the reel as big as his head. A blood-red line dove into the murky water.

Across the dock, Nicky sat on the edge fishing, his feet dangling in the water. His thick mane of black hair hung on his shoulders and he bobbed his head back and forth like he jammed to a tune. A needle gleamed in the sunlight next to him.

"Nicky," Jake yelled, but all that came out was a tiny squeak. A chill ran down Jake's back as he realized what day this was even though he wasn't here when it happened. The dock, the needle, the smile on Nicky's face.

Nicky's head continued to bob to the music in his head. He picked up the syringe, examining the icy contents. Jake tried to move his feet, but they were buried to his ankles in the mud. The rod sang and burned in his hands; the buzzing of the cicadas grew in volume, every sense amplified a hundred fold. A sweaty sheen covered Nicky's brow. Even across the lake, Jake could smell the heroin in the syringe, his panic rising.

Nicky's head stopped bobbing and the smile disappeared from his face. The song in his head had ended. He set the syringe on the dock and dropped his fishing pole in the water, peeling off his T-shirt and undoing the belt holding up his ratty, stained jeans. As he wrapped it around his skinny bicep and cinched it tight, Stony sauntered down the hill from the house toward the pond, a square bottle of Jack Daniels swinging by his side.

"Dad," Jake yelled, this time finding his voice. "Dad, help!"

Simultaneously, his father and brother put their index fingers to their lips, shushing Jake. Nicky picked up the needle. Jake screamed and twisted, pulled and tugged. Nicky put the needle to his arm and pierced the bulging blue vein.

Nicky's thumb hovered over the plunger and he looked over to Jake. Sadness and gut-wrenching anguish draped his face. "Got no choice, little bro. You left me here to die."

Nicky pushed down. His brown eyes rolled back in his head, which lolled back and forth. His mouth gaped in a knowing grin as he lay gently back on to the weathered pine boards.

At the same moment, the line on Jake's rod and reel jerked, the top of the rod bending impossibly. Jake used all his strength to crank the handle, bringing in the line a few inches at a time. Across the way, Nicky coughed and twitched. The more his older brother sputtered and gagged, the faster Jake cranked the reel.

A figure rode below the surface of the pond, following the tiny wake from the thick fishing line as it sucked through the water. Jake spun the reel, drawing in the line as if Nicky's life hung in the balance.

With his catch mere feet from the bank, Nicky twitched one last time and the light disappeared from his eyes as if someone flipped a switch. Light to dark. Life to death. Fade to black. At the same moment, the figure launched itself out of the water and landed face to face with Jake. His father, waterlogged and motley skinned, the green lake water filling his eyes, a mouth full of jagged teeth and black ooze.

"It should've been you, Jake," Stony said.

Jake yelled and jumped out of the recliner, frantically swiping away at imaginary threads of the dream. Nurse Judy rushed in.

"Everything okay, Mr. Caldwell?"

"Yeah," Jake replied, sweaty and shaky. "Everything's fine."

The dream rushed back and his mind's eye saw Nicky dead on the dock. His mother's grave with her fine blue dress draped over the headstone. The Dad-thing from the lake camped in Stony's chair in the house, swinging a thick lead pipe in a scaly, muscular arm.

"You sure?" she asked.

"No." He grabbed his keys off the dresser and left without a glance back.

CHAPTER TWENTY-TWO

Halle ran for her life down a rutted dirt path leading from the house and through the thick Ozark woods. Overgrown branches tore at her clothes and scratched her sun-kissed skin. The path narrowed, then serpentined, ever covered in a thick canopy of green. Sunlight penetrated the growth in splotches, lighting her escape route. Limbs cracked and snapped as they crashed through the brush behind her.

Though her heart thundered with panic and frightened tears blurred her vision, she widened the gap from her pursuers. Hours of blasting around the track at school finally paid off. Another half mile to reach Highway 83 where there might be some traffic. Rounding a hook in the path leading to the final straightway stretch, she kicked in the afterburners and her hope snapped away with an agonizing pop in the hamstring of her right leg. She stumbled and fell, biting into dirt and leaves. As she tumbled to a stop, the shouts grew closer.

Eyes darting to either side looking for cover, she scrambled to her feet and hobbled into the brush. She crawled in a few yards, found a protective oak and pulled herself to the other side away from the path. Her back bit into the sharp edges of the bark as she slid low and slumped against the base. One hand grabbed her injured leg, the other clamped against her mouth to stifle her frantic panting. She reached for her cell phone, then remembered it wasn't there. She'd give anything to call Mom. Would she ever see her again?

"Where'd she go?" the approaching voice said, gulping air between words, heavy feet pounding the ground. Sounded like Willie Banks.

"She's going for the highway," another said in a heavy twanged accent. "Keep going. We gotta get her or it's gonna be our asses."

The footsteps thumped on the path and she huddled in the brush. God, what could she do? She couldn't stay here because they'd come back. She couldn't go back to the abandoned house because the others might be there. The Cleary house up the hill on Poor Boy Road lay a good half mile away and would be tough going in the heavy woods on an injured leg. But what options did she have other than to dive deeper into the Ozark woods? With a whimper, she pushed to her feet, using the old tree for support, her hamstring screaming.

She slid to the side and eyed the steep hill she needed to climb when a hand grabbed her by the throat. Steely fingers bit into her flesh and shoved her up against the tree. The dark eyes of her attacker bore into hers, the plastic suit crinkling. A wet, red tongue flicked over ragged teeth. The man pulled his face close to hers, his eyes wild and crazy.

"Gotcha bitch."

*****

Thirty-five miles away in Sedalia, Jake burst out the front door of Hospice House and gulped the fresh air greeting him. He clasped the back of his neck with both hands, heart thundering like he'd run a marathon. He'd heard about people having panic attacks. If this wasn't one, it did a pretty damn good imitation. He would have been on the road back to Kansas City in the next sixty seconds had Maggie not strolled across the sparsely-filled parking lot toward him.

Her strong, bronzed arms swung by her sides, hair bound in a French braid draped over her shoulder. Just her presence brought

Jake back into focus. Her face scrunched with worry as she drew closer.

She reached out and touched his arm. "You okay?"

Her electric touch sparked a torrent of feelings. Love and regret, happiness and longing, joy and pain. He wanted to go back in time to their spot on the hill where the world still didn't make a hell of a lot of sense, but they at least had each other.

"Yeah, I'm okay," he lied. She squinted her eyes and pursed her lips. Even after sixteen years, she could tell when he was full of it.

"Uh huh. That's what I thought. You just check in?"

"Couple hours ago," Jake said. "Stony's sleeping. I dozed off and had a helluva nightmare."

"About your dad?"

"And Nicky. Jumping back here…"

"Brings back a lot of memories." She dropped her arm back to her side. Their hilltop off Poor Boy Road reflected in her eyes. She'd aged, but man did she age well, more beautiful now than at eighteen.

"Maggie," he said. "I don't know what the hell to do."

Jake waited for her response. He'd done some pretty unspeakable things over the last decade, things he wasn't proud of, things that would land him a good stretch in prison if he'd been caught. Those he worked for counted on him because he proved to be an unflappable, unshakable rock. Yet, standing by the entrance to the building where his father lay dying inside, and touched by a woman he'd never stopped loving, Jake was weak and vulnerable.

"I know what to do." She wrapped her arms around him and pulled him close, burying her pretty head into his chest. "Let's get the hell out of here."

He inhaled the flowery scent wafting off her hair. "Don't you have to work?"

"Nope. I'm done now."

She slid her arm around his elbow and grabbed his bicep, pulling him toward his truck.

"Where we going?" Jake asked.

"Stony's in good hands. You got any beer up at your house? I could sure use a cold one and I'd like to know what you've been up to for the last sixteen years."

"Guess I could do that."

The setting sun loomed large in the clear autumn sky as they left Hospice House and headed south. He stole glances at Maggie as they drove. Maybe not all past shadows were dark.

CHAPTER TWENTY-THREE

The Wild Man ate Halle up with his crazy eyes, reminding her of the gnashing, roaring monsters in her childhood book *Where the Wild Things Are*. Bennett Skaggs huffed back up the trail when Wild Man gave an ear-piercing whistle.

"Yeah, my pretty," Wild Man said. The vise grip on her neck burned and his free hand traced her neck to her shoulder. Halle shivered and groaned as his fingers touched the top of her breast. Visions formed of her naked, crumpled figure lying on the forest floor while these animals had their way with her.

"Let her go, Dexter," the voice behind Wild Man said. Dexter's hungry expression crashed to tight lips and an eye roll of disappointment.

"Fuck that," Dexter said. "She's coming with us."

Willie Banks came down the trail over Dexter's shoulders, the hood of the suit bouncing behind him. Bennett lagged behind, red-faced and breathing heavy. Willie had a gas mask in one hand and a large, black pistol in the other. Willie creeped her out. Always staring with lustful hunger on his pockmarked face. However, he also appeared to be her only chance out of this situation.

"Willie, help me," she said, the breathless speech of the panicked. He twitched at the mention of his name coming from her lips.

"Jesus Christ," Dexter said. "The bitch knows your name?"

"Of course she does, you moron." Willie drew up beside Dexter and pulled his hand away from Halle's throat. "How big a town you think we live in?"

"This is a problem," Dexter said, drawing his gaze down Halle's body. Goosebumps erupted on her skin. "A problem I can take care of...eventually."

"You ain't takin' care of nothing but bagging up what's left in the house," Willie said. "This is *my* town and she's now *my* problem."

He gripped Halle's arm and dragged her sideways away from Dexter. She went willingly, glad to be out from under the vulture's gaze, even if it was Willie Banks doing the tugging. Dexter grabbed her other arm and her hamstring groaned in protest. Willie set off toward the house but Dexter held his ground, turning her into an absurd wishbone contest.

"You know, the boss won't put up with no witnesses to the operation," Dexter said. "It ain't gonna happen."

"Let's get her back to the house," Willie said. "We'll secure her, finish bagging the stuff, and get Bub and Bennett on the move."

"You should quit using our names," Bennett said.

"You went to fucking school with her, Bennett. She cheered you playing football last year. Get up to the house."

Bennett trudged up the trail like a little kid being sent to his room without any supper. Dexter gave Willie a squinty "this shit ain't over" look before following Bennett.

"You okay?" Willie asked softly when the others were out of ear shot.

"Think I blew my hamstring running." A glimmer of optimism burned like a fire through Halle's body. Maybe she could charm her way out. "Can you help me get home?"

Willie drew his head back, eyes wide with disbelief. He dropped his gaze to the gun in his hand.

"Home?" he said, pushing her gently up the slope after the others. "You ain't going anywhere. What the hell are you doing back here, anyway?"

Halle winced with each step, like someone stabbed her with a knife in the back of her leg. The urge to drop to the ground and vow to go no further tempted her, but Dexter kept a close watch over his shoulder; he probably wanted her on the ground.

"Was going to hang with my friend at the house, but she didn't show," Halle said, stopping. She couldn't run, but she didn't want to go in the house. Bad things would happen. "I haven't seen anybody at that house for months until you guys showed up," she continued. "Come on, Willie, let me go. I won't tell anyone about you being here. Hell, I don't even know what you were doing."

Willie waved the pistol forward, motioning her to move again.

"I don't know what to tell you," he said. "I'll try to keep you safe, but in the end...it ain't gonna be my call."

As they crested the small hill and the ramshackle ranch lay ominously before them, Halle had the sick feeling Willie having a thing for her wasn't going to be enough to keep her alive.

CHAPTER TWENTY-FOUR

As Willie prodded Halle up the hill in the descending darkness, Sheriff Bear plopped the baggie of red rocks on a scarred wooden table in the dimly lit holding room at the Benton County Jail. Howie slumped in a creaky chair, his skinny arms hugging his torso, the death sentence in a bag in front of him.

He was screwed. If he said nothing, Bear would beat the shit out of him and he'd spend the last of his teen years in prison for meth distribution. Given his moderate but significant juvenile rap sheet, Judge Cronin would have no qualms sending him away. Willie and Shane might make some minor attempts to keep him happy and quiet, but in the end, Shane would count him as too big a liability and Howie would end up with a steel shank shoved through his ear in the exercise yard.

If he told Bear any tidbit of information, Bear would beat the shit out of him to get more, get pissed when he didn't get any, and send Howie in front of Judge Cronin who'd send him up the river. Shane wouldn't worry about keeping Howie happy. Howie would end up ass raped in the shower for his loose lips with the same steel shank shoved through the same ear.

The third option? Tell Bear whatever he wanted to hear in exchange for immunity from prosecution and a relocation package for himself and his brother. If worse came to worse, he could leave

Bennett behind, though Shane would kill him. Their chances of staying alive with a pissed off Shane roaming the lands weren't great, but they were better than prison, and would probably save him a beating from Bear. But, turning into a rat? That made his stomach harden.

"Howie?" Bear asked, leaning forward on the table, his paws interlocked in front of him. Howie was so lost in thought he hadn't noticed Bear sit at the table.

"What? You're seriously going to break my balls over a few little rock chips?"

"Yeah, I am." Bear's dark eyes bore into Howie's, forcing Howie's gaze back to the Devil Ice. "You know how long I worked to get this crap out of my county? You know how many skulls of shitheads like you I've cracked? How many of my kids' games I missed? How many lives you've destroyed spewing this poison around? Do you have any idea, Howie?"

Howie shook his head, almost imperceptibly like a nervous tick. His brain thumped from the horrific hangover and the slap delivered by Deputy Sad Dog when he put Howie in the room. Sad Dog Daniels never liked Howie, and now hung back in the corner behind Bear, arms crossed and a sadistic smirk pasted on his red-faced mug.

"So, what is this?" Bear asked, picking up the bag of Devil Ice and waving it in front of Howie. "What's it called and where'd you get it? You cooking in my town again, Howie?"

"No, sir," Howie said. "That bag ain't mine."

"Oh, well hell." Bear dropped the bag on the table and kicked his chair back. "We might as well cut him loose, Daniels. The bag ain't his."

Sad Dog laughed. "Must belong to his scumbag brother."

"Ain't his either," Howie said.

Bear stretched his arms to the heavens and adopted the voice of the local Baptist minister. "Lord, it's a miracle. This bag of red rock just magically appeared on your bedside table next to an unregistered pistol, neither of which your dumb ass is supposed to have because you still have six months of probation, am I right?"

Bear moved around the table and directly behind him, the thundering pulse in Howie's neck visible. Howie closed his eyes and readied his mind for Bear's fist to crash into his skull. Instead, Bear leaned forward, his thick fingers digging painfully into the meaty space under Howie's collarbone. His face close enough that his beard tickled Howie's cheek.

"I can help you, Howie," Bear said, his scratchy voice low, almost an intimate whisper. "I'm the only one in this entire county who can actually help you. I can help you because I don't want you. I want the sumbitch who is bringing this shit back into my town. You're going to tell me or I am going to throw you in a cell with Big Dick Sanders who hasn't had a warm body to snuggle up to in a couple of weeks and would love to make his acquaintance with your tight, white ass. When Big Dick is done, I'm going to beat you so bloody your momma is going to need to fetch your dental records so Doc Thompson can identify your remains."

Howie winced as Bear's claw dug harder into the muscle of his neck. His mind raced. Bear hurt him and itched to do more. Sad Dog waited across the room with a hungry look, like a Doberman anticipating the attack command from his master. Howie pictured Shane and Willie safely at the house sipping drinks and counting money. That fat tub of lard Bub Sievers would go on being a waste of oxygen while some tattooed lifer in prison took out his frustrations on Howie's ass. Mostly, he worried about his brother. If Howie gave Bear anything useful, Bennett would die a horrible death at the hands of Shane.

"What's the street name for this?" Bear growled, clamping harder on Howie's collarbone. Howie howled, stamping his foot to dissipate the pain, worried his collarbone would snap like a toothpick if Bear applied anymore pressure.

"It ain't got a street name," Howie cried. When the words escaped his lips, Bear released his death grip, but kept his hand on Howie's throbbing shoulder.

"What's it called?"

Howie desperately tried to figure out how much he could say. "Devil Ice, I guess."

"Where'd you get it?" Bear asked.

"I don't know," Howie said, howling again as Bear clamped on to the collarbone again.

Bear gritted his teeth. "Don't say I don't know to me again. Where did you get it?"

"Hank Troy," Howie said, expelling the name of a small-time local dealer who he hated.

"When did Hank Troy sell it to you?"

"Last night at the Turn It Loose," Howie said. In truth, he hadn't seen Hank in a couple of weeks but hoped his lie would help the pain in his shoulder go away. Instead, it intensified.

"Hank Troy has been in County for the last ten days, you dumb son of a bitch. Nothing pisses me off more than some dickless tweaker jerking my chain. Did Hank sell this to you?"

"No," Howie whimpered, tears forming in his eyes. Panic rose through his skinny frame and the truth bubbled to the surface. One more ounce of pressure from Bear and he would spill everything and that would be the end of him.

"Give me something and I'll make the pain go away." Bear clamped down further.

"Shane," Howie said, the pitch of his voice near a howl.

Bear's eyebrows shot up. "Shane Langston?"

Before Howie could even nod, a knock sounded on the door. Bear jerked his head to Daniels to answer the door. Daniels got up and moved to the door of the interrogation room. Howie crimped his shimmering eyes shut.

"Sheriff Parley," a deep voice said. "I suggest you take your hands off Mr. Skaggs."

"Who the hell are you?" Bear asked, releasing the pressure from Howie's collarbone.

"I'm Mr. Skaggs' attorney and I'd like a moment alone with my client. Now."

Howie's eyes opened wide, as surprised as Bear and Deputy Daniels at the dark-suited figure in the doorway. How in the hell did he get an attorney?

Bear edged away from the table, rubbing his fingers with his opposite hand, no doubt trying to get circulation flowing through them again. He studied the card the lawyer offered then crumpled it in his hand. "We're not done here, Howie. Not by a long shot."

*****

Halle drew her knees together and rocked back and forth on the edge of a bare mattress in the back room of the abandoned house, dreading the opening of the door. Muffled voices emanated from the other side as Willie and Dexter argued. She caught brief snippets of the conversation which centered around her.

Someone had painted the window shut and it wouldn't budge. She came close to tossing a chair through the glass, but realized she wouldn't clear the window sill before those animals pounced on her. She'd hobbled around the room on her bad leg searching drawers in a nightstand and a dresser for some kind of weapon, but got nothing for her efforts but filthy hands.

Her mind raced at potential strategies to get out of this mess, but saw little chance. Dexter wouldn't let her go. Bub Sievers would love to come into the room and have his way with her, maybe the Skaggs brother would join him. Mom was strong, what would she do? She'd always taught Halle that nothing was given to you. No matter the situation, you had to work for what you wanted and not rely on anyone else but yourself. Especially, a man. But her mom also said you draw more flies with honey than vinegar. Willie liked her, despite her young age. If she could charm him, he might keep her alive long enough to get out of this. As if on cue, Willie's voice drew closer to the door, which cracked open seconds later.

"You go play with your girlfriend," Dexter said. "We'll see what the Man has to say about it."

Willie entered, red-faced and tight jawed. He shut the door behind him and ran his hands through his long, frazzled hair. He'd replaced the plastic suit with ratty, stained jeans, holes in the knees, and a well-worn blue denim shirt, the cuffs rolled up.

"What's going on, Willie?" Halle asked.

Willie focused on the dusty floorboards for a moment before dropping on the edge of the bed. "I ain't gonna lie to you, Halle. You're in deep trouble."

"What for? I didn't see anything."

"Yeah, you did," Willie said. "You know it and I know it. The question is what are we going to do about it?"

Tears welled up as her mind raced to the dark, macabre places this situation could lead. There wasn't any way she would get out of this unhurt. She'd never wanted to hold her mother more in her life.

"Just let me go home," she said, eyes wide and pleading. "Please, Willie. Let me go home. I won't say anything. Hell, I don't even know what I saw."

"Ain't up to me. I'm gonna do my best to keep you safe. I can control these animals out here, but when…the boss gets wind of this, I can't say what he's gonna want to do. He's not big on loose ends."

"But I don't know anything," Halle said, a tear falling on her cheek.

"Yeah, you do." Willie wiped the tear from Halle's cheek then walked out leaving Halle to imagine her fate.

CHAPTER TWENTY-FIVE

Jake pulled up the drive to the old homestead, Maggie sitting quietly in the passenger seat. Jake was thankful she left her car at Hospice House. Halfway between Sedalia and Warsaw, Maggie had rested her hand on top of his. Jake was surprised sparks didn't fly from the electricity coursing through his veins. They spoke little as they rolled up and down the highway hills. Jake wanted to talk but had trouble coming up with anything to say.

He parked in front of the house and listened to the engine tick. A few loose leaves drifted on the truck's black hood before dashing away in the evening breeze. Jake rotated his broad shoulders toward her.

"Maggie…" he said, before trailing off. Once he looked into her eyes, his train of thought completely derailed. He worked his mouth open and closed as if the mechanical motion would fire the synapses of his brain.

"How 'bout that beer? I've got a few minutes before I need to get home." Maggie flashed her deep dimples, saving him.

They got out and walked into the house. Even with Stony gone, it still smelled musty and decayed, and he reminded himself to open the windows once he and Maggie were done. He grabbed a couple of cold beers and headed back to the front door. He scanned to the left where Maggie now wandered fifty yards away through the uncut grass, toward their spot on the hill. She glanced over her shoulder and gave him a nod to follow. He double-checked the locked toolbox on his truck and waded through the grass after her.

Once past the yard, Jake picked his way along the narrow path he must've trodden a thousand times in his youth. Tree branches and weeds had taken their toll on the well-worn trail, but he could climb the hill with his eyes closed. The day's falling sun cast his shadow out front as he emerged into the clearing. Maggie faced the expansive valley below, her back to him.

"I never get tired of this view," she said. Jake walked beside her, admiring the explosion of fall colors from the sun-kissed tree tops. He handed her a beer. She popped the top and took a long pull, licking the tiniest bit of foam from her upper lip.

"It was one of the few things I missed about this town." Jake took a swig of his own beer. He sat on the ground, his knees drawn up in front of him. Maggie followed suit.

"Was I one of those things?" she asked, turning her gaze from the scenery to him. Jake resisted the overwhelming urge to kiss her.

"Yeah, you were," he said at last. "This spot brings back a lot of memories. We had a lot of good times here."

"And some bad times, too," she reminded him. "I came up here every night for a month after you disappeared, staring out at this same valley, crying in anguish and anger. Just waiting for the crunch of your boots coming up the path, but you never came."

The multicolored foliage swayed in front of them, almost hypnotic. "I can't explain why I bailed the way I did."

"You don't have to explain. I know why."

"It doesn't make it right, though," he said.

"No, it doesn't," she replied. The pain resonated in her voice. Pain he caused. "I tried to find you, you know. Nobody knew where you went or even heard a whisper about you for a couple of years."

Yet again, intense guilt settled on his shoulders, his back aching from the weight of it. He'd run away from Stony, but left one

"Oh, no," Maggie said, raising her hand to her mouth.

"Yeah. She's about six years old, dirty face in hand-me-down clothes that didn't match. Like her dad rolled her in a pile of clothes that Goodwill rejected and accepted what came out. But, underneath that dirt, I saw her innocence, her beauty. She's pleading at me to stop hitting her daddy with these big, brown, tear-filled puppy dog eyes. I just stopped, fist raised, blood dripping from my knuckles and it came to me that I wasn't hitting a slab of meat like I was Rocky. I was hitting a real person, a father. He may have been a scumbag, but a sinking feeling of despair grabbed hold and jerked me out of this robotic state I put myself in. I saw then that I was no different from my father and if I didn't stop, I'd permanently turn to stone."

Jake swallowed, looking sideways at Maggie who sat in silence, absorbing the story.

"What did you do then?" she asked after a moment.

"I flushed the heroin down the toilet and took the bottle of Jack. Left him there bleeding on the floor. Paid the five hundred he owed my boss out of my own pocket and began to think about how to get myself out from the rock I'd crawled under. I've been paying people's debts out of my own stash to keep from beating them, which I can't keep up forever. But I can't stop because I still hear the bone of that finger cracking. I can still see that little girl when I close my eyes at night. They're the ghosts of reality that haunt me, but I think they're still there to remind me I gotta get out of that kinda life."

The burnt-orange sun rested just above the horizon, blasting a golden hue over the valley. The temperature dropped as the westerly breeze picked up, slapping the chill against their faces. Jake took off his jacket and draped it over Maggie's hunched shoulders.

"Do you think people can change?" he asked, wincing as he waited for her response, afraid of what it might be.

She regarded him, her eyes searching his face. "Yes. Yes, I do. I think you already started down that path. You just need the inspiration to keep going."

He breathed out. The worry about her running off when he told her the truth carried off in the Ozark evening breeze.

"I was worried you'd go busting down the hill away from me."

"I can't say it's not a little scary, but I'm not running away," she said, an uptick flashing at the corner of her mouth.

"What about you?" he asked.

"I've been here mostly. A couple months after you left, I needed a change of scenery and went to live with my grandparents up north. Then, Dad died in a car wreck a couple of years later. Mom used the insurance money to send me to school in Columbia and get my nursing degree. She got sick after I graduated and I came home to be with her."

"Is that how you got hooked up with Hospice?"

She swallowed the last drops of her beer and set the empty can on the ground. Jake remembered her mom well—tiny in frame, fiery in spirit. Maggie was their only child, her pride and joy.

"She fought like hell, Jake," Maggie said. "It was six months from diagnosis until I buried her. The Hospice staff was so great I couldn't see myself working anywhere but there."

"So, now you're by your lonesome in the house on the hill?"

"Not exactly." Her hair danced across her face from the wind and she hooked the locks over her ear to hold it back.

"Married?" he probed.

She glanced up beneath long eyelashes. "No, just me and my baby girl."

Jake drew back. What the…? Baby girl? He closed his dangling jaw before any leaves or bugs flew in.

"You have a baby?" he choked out. Maggie registered the shock on his face and laughed.

"Well, she's not exactly a baby anymore. Teenager. She's growing up so fast I can hardly keep track."

"What happened to the father?"

She eyed the darkening ground. For a moment he thought she

wouldn't tell him.

"He's gone," she said. "Didn't quite work out."

"Sorry," he said, still stunned that Maggie was a mother.

"Yeah, me too." She stood. "But speaking of which, I'd better get home. She's probably wondering where I am. And I still have to make some food for one of my patient's family."

"I thought volunteers did that," Jake said.

"I'm a volunteer."

"I thought you worked there."

She tilted her head and smiled. "Not all the time."

She climbed to her feet. Jake pushed his large frame off the ground and faced her.

"I'd love to meet your girl sometime," he said.

"We'll do that. You going back to Hospice tomorrow?"

"Yeah, I'm going to check in with Bear and Janey, but I'll be there in the morning sometime."

"I don't suppose I could hitch a ride with you," she said, bumping him playfully with her shoulder. "I kind of abandoned my car so I could spend some time learning what my ex-boyfriend has been doing all these years."

"No problem." He reached out and took her hand in his. "He didn't scare you off?"

She rose to the tips of her toes and leaned in, kissing Jake on the cheek. It was soft and delicate, a whisper that sent shivers along his spine.

"Not yet, anyway," she said, handing him his jacket. She walked the backside of the hill toward her house and disappeared into the darkened trees. A myriad of stars popped one by one in the sky as the darkness took control of the daylight, leaving Jake to wonder why the hell he ever left her in the first place.

CHAPTER TWENTY-SIX

The pole lights of Main Street flickered to life, but all was already quiet. They pretty much rolled up the Warsaw sidewalks after five o'clock. Bear sat with his back to his desk, eyeing the oak tree in the middle of the Benton County Courthouse square, recalling the time he and Jake climbed to its highest heights with their pockets full of acorns and spent hours throwing them at passersby. Every once and awhile, some unfortunate soul would settle against the base of the tree, and they'd keep score on direct hits to the head. Bear usually won and held it over Jake; he rarely beat him in anything.

The pleasant image faded and the stark reality of the present trumped the simpler times of the past. The shithead Howie Skaggs had been in the interrogation room with his lawyer for the better part of two hours and Bear teetered on the edge of tossing the lawyer out and violating Howie's civil rights. He'd never actually do something like that to jeopardize his case, but he hated sitting around with his thumb up his ass. Howie had stood on the edge of the waterfall, about to jump off and give them Shane Langston on a silver platter when the lawyer showed up.

A knock sounded on the door behind him. Deputy Daniels leaned against the frame with a cup of coffee.

"He still in there with the lawyer?" Bear asked.

"Yeah. You seen the guy before?" Daniels crossed the room and sat in the chair opposite the desk. Bear spun around.

"No, but Langston has more than a few bloodsuckers at his beck and call. Damn it…we almost had him. Another sixty seconds and he would've spilled his guts."

"We ain't getting nothing out of him now," Daniels said.

Bear reached out and held up the bag of red rocks. "I'm not so sure. I've seen this variety before. There's a cook who works out of Kansas City who makes this red stuff. Saw some files on it when I was on the task force. Thought he was in prison somewhere. I do have another question, though."

"What's that?"

"How in the hell did the lawyer get here that fast? This is Warsaw, not New York City with a lawyer on every street corner. Somebody's giving ole Shane a heads up."

"Maybe somebody saw us driving him in and unloading him," Daniels said.

"Can't be that," Bear said. "The bloodsucker had to drive in from somewhere unless he just happened to be fishing out on Truman Lake. No, he was already on his way before we even pulled into town. I think it's a hell of a lot more likely we got someone in our house batting on both sides." But who could it be? There might be a couple guys who'd look the other way, but teaming up with Langston? "Book him for possession of the gun and meth," Bear continued. "Stick him in a cell and wait for me. I gotta go meet an old buddy."

"You want me to give Howie some company? Big Dick Sanders is about to start humping the bars of his cell."

"Nah," Bear said. "Let's leave Howie alone with his thoughts. I haven't given up on rolling him yet. My ability to prevent the penetration of his delicate posterior by a dick the size of a tree trunk might be the trump card I need to get his trap flappin'. You hear about the bust in Sedalia?"

Daniels shook his head.

"Cops got an anonymous tip about a drug stash in a warehouse.

Rolled up and found six kilos of coke in a floor drain."

"Six keys? Who owned the warehouse?"

"Beats the shit outta me." Bear shrugged. "I've never heard of the place. Global something or other."

"Somebody's gonna be pissed."

"Somebody's always pissed about something, Sad Dog. It's one of life's few certainties."

Daniels left and Bear locked the Devil Ice in his desk drawer. He stepped into the cool night and headed out to meet Jake on Poor Boy Road.

*****

Despite the cool autumn breeze, Willie had to wipe the sweat from his brow with the tail of his shirt as he, Bub and Bennett finished loading half the Devil Ice into Dexter's van and half into Willie's truck, their path lit by the gas generator lights Dexter brought with him. With each trip into the house, Willie noticed Bub eyeballing the closed door to Halle's room. He could hear the thoughts rolling through his enforcer's head and considered the size of the problem he had on his hands. His cell vibrated in his pocket. Willie checked the number and winced. He walked back inside the house, away from his crew and answered it.

"I hear we have problems," Shane said.

"Depends on what you mean by a problem."

"I mean a local teenage girl who saw you and my product with her own little eyes. I call that a problem."

"I got it under control."

"How do you figure?"

"She looked through a grimy window. I doubt she saw anything."

"I'm not taking a chance. Off-load the stuff to your storage area and bring the girl to me. I'll be at the blue house."

Damn. Other than an order to put a bullet in Halle's head and dump the body, delivering her to Shane was the last thing Willie wanted to hear. In either case, nobody would ever hear from her again. The blue house hid deep in the Ozark countryside, one of three houses Shane maintained in the area that only a handful of people knew about. How the hell could he get her out of this?

"Second problem," Shane said. "Where's your boy Howie?"

"He never showed back tonight and won't answer his phone. He was hungover as hell after last night so I sent him back to his trailer to catch a few z's before we broke this place down."

"You call him from this phone?" Shane asked, a razor edge to his tone.

"No, the other burner phone," Willie said. "What's going on?"

"Howie isn't answering the phone because he got pinched by Bear this afternoon. He's currently sitting in the Benton County jail."

Willie's gut cramped. "Oh shit."

"Oh shit is exactly what you should be thinking," Shane said. "He and your douche bag bodyguard beat the bejesus out of some guy last night and Bear hauled him in for it. In the process, they found an unlicensed piece and a bag of my product you guys have been cooking."

Willie's insides melted to jelly and he crashed at the tiny kitchen table, head resting in shaky hands. This was a disaster.

"I'm pissed, Willie," Shane continued, the tension in his voice drawn as tight as a trip wire. "Thought you had better control of your crew than this."

"Howie won't say nothin'," Willie said, but without much conviction.

"You got a hell of a lot more confidence in the little prick than I do. Let's talk more when you bring the girl. And bring that tub of shit Bub with you when you come. We gotta tie up some loose ends. Be at the house in an hour."

The phone silenced, and Willie held it with trembling hands. He glanced at the closed door holding Halle, mind racing at what could potentially happen when he got her to the blue house. What could happen to her? What could happen to all of them? Shane didn't like loose ends and right now they were as loose as a cheap hooker on a Friday night. Bub lumbered along the hall toward him.

"Hey, we're done loading and I wiped the place down," Bub said, sweat rolling off his fat jowls. "You look like all the blood ran out of your body. Everything okay?"

"No," Willie said. "I'll explain on the way. We gotta meet Shane after we dump the stuff at the barn. Loose ends."

Bub's eyes crunched with concern. "Shane don't like loose ends."

"Exactly. That's why things aren't okay. Let's go."

CHAPTER TWENTY-SEVEN

"You're going to end up in jail, man." Bear cracked open his third beer. "Jail or dead. People who work for Keats don't tend to have long life spans."

They leaned back in matching stamped steel chairs on the deck of Stony's place, the cracked wood frame table in between them. The crickets and bullfrogs around the pond sang a symphony, far more enjoyable and relaxing in comparison to Jake's normal balcony experience in Kansas City of car horns and police sirens. Jake had spent the last thirty minutes sharing the past sixteen years of his life, except for the mission Keats sent him on. Bear could probably tell him everything he needed to know about Shane Langston, but Jake couldn't figure out how to delicately launch into his orders to track down and kill the guy.

"Off the record," Bear asked. "You ever have to whack anyone?"

"This isn't the 1930s, man. Nobody calls it whacking."

"Have you?"

"No," Jake said. "When it came to getting deadly, Keats never sent me on those jobs. Guess he saw that line in me he knew I wouldn't cross. Besides, he had gorillas who liked doing that kind of shit. I've got my anger issues under control."

"What do you do with it? The anger."

Jake shrugged. "Push it down. Compact it into a little ball that I shove into a corner."

"What if the ball gets out?"

"I won't let it. Not after last time."

"What happened last time?"

Jake hesitated telling the story to a member of law enforcement. Then again, it was Bear. "Found a guy I was sent to collect on in Oklahoma. Found him in the parking lot raping a woman in the back of his van. I started swinging and it came to me how much he looked like Stony. Once I started pounding and kicking, I didn't stop until the woman pushed me back. Last I heard he spent the remainder of his days drinking his meals through a straw from his wheelchair. Not saying the guy didn't deserve it, but the fact I lost control like that scared the living shit out of me."

"What would you do if Keats asked you to kill someone?"

"I don't know. Guess it would depend on the reason. Would have to be something better than the guy owed Keats money. That's for damn sure."

"Even then," Bear said. "Even for something the guy deserved to die for like that asshole in Oklahoma. Could you stand over a cowering man and pull the trigger?"

Jake took a long drink and drained the can, crushing the aluminum and tossing it on the table.

"Exactly," Bear continued. "He may not have asked you yet, but it's coming one of these days, man. And once you cross that line, there ain't no going back. That will haunt you for the rest of your life, but it won't matter because Keats will own your ass."

Jake popped the top on his second can. "It doesn't matter because I'm getting out. But this isn't working an assembly line in a factory. I can't just toss my tools on the floor and say 'Fuck this job' and head out the door. A person doesn't up and quit on Keats. You have to exit gracefully."

"And carefully," Bear added.

"Very carefully. You have much experience with him?"

"Just some files when I was on the meth task force," Bear said. "Keats dabbled in meth and other drugs, but the old standard of booze, cigarettes and loan sharking are more his MO. Lots of bodies dotted-lined to him, but no direct proof of anything. Seems like one of the old school types like you saw in *The Godfather*. There's some rumors of gun running and extortion here or there, but nothing sticks to him. I ain't got proof of it, but pretty sure he got a buddy of mine tossed off the KC police force on some trumped up charges he planted."

"He's got that kind of pull with the cops?"

"Got that kind of pull with a lot of people. That's why you gotta be careful. I'll be pissed off if I read some news article about your dumb ass getting dragged from the bottom of the Missouri River."

"Whatever it takes, I'm out."

"Doing what?"

"Who knows," Jake said. "Maybe I'll move back here and come to work for you."

"You don't want this shit." Bear took another deep slug off his beer and belched loudly. "There's some really good people down here, smart people, wealthy people, people who want to relax, maybe fish a little and enjoy the fruits of their hard-earned labor as they fade away into the sunset. Unfortunately, there's also a bunch of shitheads who live for nothing but getting drunk or high. Think they're already so screwed in life that it has nothing to offer. Why not do it stoned? I tell you, drugs are going to be the death of me and I've never touched 'em. Got one in custody at the jailhouse with some red rock that's completely new to this area."

"Who is it?"

"One of the Skaggs boys. He's a lackey for the local supplier. Some low rent lawyer showed up out of thin air and cut me off. Even when you get them, you never really get them, know what I mean?"

"Is that why the 'Striving to be Drug Free' sign is gone?"

Bear huffed, but his eyes were serious. He downed the rest of the beer in one motion and popped the tab on another.

"You'll never get a town like Warsaw to be drug free. Too much poverty and the aforementioned shitheads. When I started, it felt like I was trying to build a sandcastle in the middle of a tidal wave. But, after a time, I had the meth production and distribution in vapor lock, man. It cost me years and a lot of blood, sweat and tears, but I locked up so many producers the Benton County Jail was about overrun. I had eyes and ears everywhere. You couldn't whisper the word meth without me hearing about it. If you said it, it was your ass."

"So what happened?"

A sneer crossed Bear's lips. "Shane Langston. Thinks he's the reincarnation of Scarface."

Jake stiffened at the name. Did Bear notice?

"The problem," Bear continued, "is he's smart, he's ruthless and he's got connections. Nothing near what Keats has, but he's got more than one person who he can call on for favors. I couldn't get anyone to flip on him and those who even thought about flipping ended up dead. I worked with the Feds and we sat on him for over a year. Couldn't get anything on him. The fucker was always one step ahead of us. Things quieted a bit before the Mexicans started carting meth up through Kansas City. It's making a comeback along with coke. Hell, they just found a ton of it in a warehouse in Sedalia, but now I also gotta deal with prescription drugs. Oxycontin is huge down here."

The Sedalia warehouse bust was good news. At least Jake's call to the cops didn't go unheeded. But he didn't want to hear the news about Langston's slipperiness. In his head, Langston was some skinny tweaker running product out of a backwoods trailer. If Bear and the Feds couldn't get anything on the guy, how was Jake supposed to take him down? He couldn't very well tell Bear he more or less just robbed Langston's warehouse, so he decided to probe for more information.

"Where's this Langston operating out of?"

"Got places all over Benton County. Hell, he has two houses we know about within ten miles of here. Has some car washes in St. Louis, a car dealership in Sedalia and owns a bar in Kansas City that his brother runs." His brother wouldn't be running anything anymore unless he could do it without a head. Time to poke Bear and see if he jumped.

"What if this Langston met with an untimely accident?" Jake asked, slower than he intended and too deliberate to be an innocent question.

Bear picked up on it and his eyes narrowed. "What the hell are you talking about?"

Jake shrugged off the question. "Nothing, just brainstorming solutions to your problem. Look, if you can't take this Langston out or overrun Mexico to cut off the supply, why not cut the legs off his dealers? Make it unhealthy to work for him."

"Easier said than done, my friend," Bear said. "You know the Banks clan down the road a piece?"

Jake ran through his rusty mental rolodex. "Earl Banks was a few years older than us. Ran around with that dumbass Lanny Sikes."

"That's the one. Earl's oldest boy, Willie, is Shane's main distributor in the county. Drives around in a rusted-out-jalopy truck, but stays pretty low key. The kid is smart, stays out of my way. His muscle, though, is Bub Sievers and that asshole does not stay out of my way."

"Related to Charlie Sievers?"

"Yup. You remember the ass whupping we put on Charlie and his buddies at the Valley?"

Jake held up his hand, pointing to the scar on his middle knuckle. He'd sliced it to the bone in a rainy, muddy parking lot outside the Valley Bar and Grill on the teeth of Charlie Sievers. Jake and Bear were eighteen at the time and had no business being in the bar. Charlie, a petty but big drunk, didn't like the fact the barfly women paid more attention to Jake and Bear than him. After some alcohol enhanced jaw flapping inside the bar, the confrontation spilled outside. Jake and Bear managed to take down Charlie and four of his running buddies amidst a backdrop of honky-tonk music, lightning flashes and rain drops the size of quarters.

"Is Bub as big a dick as his old man?"

"He's actually Charlie's nephew on his sister's side and he's a bigger dick than his uncle ever thought of being."

"I see you're married," Jake said. "Any kids?"

"Two. Jacob is eight and Madi's five. Don't get to see them enough. Trying to keep my mother-in-law Buella from imprinting on them. She's living with us."

"Buella? Yuck."

"Exactly, I think her bad mood comes from the name. Her husband Gene died ten years ago. I think it's because it was the only way he could get away from the woman." Bear smirked. "Speaking of old men, how's yours?"

Jake swirled around the beer can's contents before setting it on the table. "Dying."

"How you feel about that?"

"You a psychologist, too?" Jake asked.

"No, sir. We got one in town and he's as bat-shit crazy as some of his patients. I was there, man. I know what he did to you."

"Yeah, you, Maggie and Nicky are about the only ones. He recognized me today. We had a sixty-second conversation in the truck as I dropped him off at Hospice."

"Anything meaningful?"

"Nope," Jake said, "and we better not have any more. He can just die, rot in hell and I can get on with my life."

They stared down the hill at the darkened mass of the pond. Could Bear picture Nicky on the dock? Janey said he'd cleaned up the mess.

Jake's mind raced with a jumble of memories and half-assed plans of getting Bear involved with helping him take out Shane Langston. Keats wanted Shane dead, but Jake wanted out of the violent life, not to cross yet another threshold he couldn't come back from. If he helped Bear take down Langston, Jake could get him out of Keats' line of fire without having to do anything he'd later regret. But he had no idea how to enlist his old friend to his cause.

Bear drained the last of his beer and stood, stretching his arms high with a growl. "These chairs suck, Jake. Even the crooked ones I make in my woodshop would be better than these rusted death traps."

"Yeah, I don't think entertaining and worrying about the comfort of his guests was high on Stony's list."

"I gotta get home. It's great to see you again. Seriously, man. Since you might actually be here for a few days, we should go catch some fish. Got a new boat this summer. Might as well break it in."

Jake stood, and the two clasped in a manly hug with pats on the back hard enough to knock the bark off a tree. Jake walked around the side of the house to Bear's truck, still trying to come up with a way to spill the idea of teaming up to take down Langston. Every idea sounded too nefarious and he'd be forced to tell him the truth. Bear was his friend, but still the county sheriff. Bear swung one leg into the cab of the truck when Maggie ran across the yard toward them, a sprinting ghost in the moonlight.

Bear squinted into the darkness. "Is that Maggie?"

"Yeah," Jake said, wondering why his ex ran in the dark toward him. "She left a couple of hours ago."

"You don't waste time stoking the old flame, do you?"

Jake opened his mouth to say something nasty, but the panic etched on Maggie's face as she drew closer closed it. She'd changed from her scrubs into jeans and a University of Missouri sweatshirt, tattered at the collar. A few strands of hair had broken loose from a haphazard ponytail and pasted against her sweaty forehead. She stopped in front of Jake and Bear; fear shimmered in her eyes.

"Help me," she said, voice trembling. "Halle's gone."

"Halle?" Jake asked.

"My daughter. She's gone and I know something's happened."

CHAPTER TWENTY-EIGHT

Willie's pickup rattled east along Poor Boy Road toward the small town of Hastain, the engine making an unhealthy clank. They smashed Halle between Willie at the wheel and Bub, who chain-smoked with the passenger window halfway down. Bennett lay in the bed of the truck under a blanket, guarding the stash of Devil Ice. Between the smoke, Bub's body odor and the burning oil smell emanating from the engine, nausea and terror pushed Halle to the edge. She couldn't hold back the tears much longer.

"This ain't good, Willie," Bub said, breaking a silence that lasted an entire two minutes since he last made the same statement. "Ain't no fucking good at all."

"You mentioned it…several times," Willie said. "I'm telling you not to worry about it."

"You're in a dreamland, dude. Shane hates loose ends, and right now that's exactly what we are. We need to take this load and get out of dodge. You and me hit the open road."

"Rip off Shane?"

"That's what I'm sayin'."

"You wanna know what it feels like to have your skin peeled from your bones while you watch it happen? That's what Shane'll do to you, man."

"Not if we get out of the country," Bub said. "We sell this load off and head to Mexico."

"What happened to Canada?"

"I thought about it. Too cold."

"Well, good luck with your plan. Count my ass out. I ain't crossin' Shane."

Halle listened quietly, keeping her eyes on the road ahead. Bub's talk about crossing Shane and Willie's loyalty might be information she could turn into some kind of bargaining chip to keep her alive.

After four miles of the two-lane blacktop, Willie turned north on State Highway M for another mile and back east down a dark, narrow road. The faint glow of the headlights revealed a patchwork of black asphalt with no shoulder.

"Where the hell are we going?" Bub asked.

"The barn."

"And you're going to let her see exactly where it is."

"We don't have much of a choice, Bub."

"I won't say anything," Halle said.

"Just wait till Shane starts in on your pretty little ass, honey," Bub said. "You'll sing whatever song he wants you to sing."

Halle shivered and leaned into Willie.

Willie reached behind Halle and smacked Bub across the back of his thick skull. "Quit trying to scare her, dipshit."

"Don't matter," Bub said. "She either ain't gonna live to see the sun rise or is gonna wish she didn't."

Halle had fought her fear throughout so far, tried to show a brave face. But, when Willie didn't counter Bub's pessimistic assessment, bloody images of her lifeless body flashed in her mind and the tears she'd been trying so hard to hold back began to flow.

*****

"Whoa, slow down," Bear said. "What makes you think something happened to her?"

"I just know." Maggie shifted from foot to foot, a compact ball of nervous energy. "I just know."

"Maggie, she's a teenager. She's probably out with her friends."

"No," she said. "It's a school night and she's always home before dark. Always. She knows it's her ass if she doesn't make it back or at least call." Her eyes grew wet and her voice hitched. "Her backpack's there, she was home."

"Any sign something happened at the house?" Jake asked. "Some sort of struggle?"

"No, everything looks normal."

"Have you called around to any of her friends?" Bear asked. "Driven around to any of the spots she hangs out?"

"I called everyone I could think of. I can't drive around because my car's in Sedalia." She pressed her palms to her head, pushing in as if to hold back the nightmare scenarios that must be running through her head. "Nobody has seen or heard from her since school got out. Something's happened. I can feel it."

Jake placed both his hands on her shoulders, trying to settle her.

"Hey, we'll find her," he said. "Try and calm down and think. Where could she go? This town isn't that big."

"Tell you what," Bear said. "It's almost eleven. You and Jake cruise through town, go by the boat docks and the Swinging Bridge, and see if you can find her. I'll head out to some of the local hangouts on some back roads and see if I can roust her. I'll call you the second I learn anything. If we don't find anything in the next hour, I'll call in the dogs, but I don't want to start raising hell if she's out sneaking a beer somewhere with some peckerhead."

Maggie typed her information into Bear's cell phone. Bear patted her on the shoulder and climbed into his truck.

"We'll find her, Mags. I'll get the night deputies on board to keep an eye out."

"Thanks." Maggie wiped her eyes. Bear took off down the driveway and headed east.

"Come on," Jake said, putting his arm around her shoulders and steering her toward his truck. Bear's scenario with a beer and peckerhead sounded more feasible that something bad happening. Still, he wanted to support her and he always heard about trusting a mother's intuition. "Let's go find her."

Thirty minutes later after combing through every side street, park and gathering place in Warsaw, they'd come up with nothing. Jake called Bear who reported the same news from the various backroad spots he hit.

"Busted Trey Tompkin's kid with a six pack and a joint trying to get in Tammy Harrison's pants in the back of his old man's Chevy," Bear said. "But that's the only thing of interest I've seen. You check everywhere in town?"

"Everywhere but the Swinging Bridge," Jake said. "After that, I don't know where else to look."

They promised to hook up at the police station in thirty minutes. Traveling back toward Main Street, they headed to the Swinging Bridge—an old iron structure crossing the sloughs. Maggie fervently scoured the streets as they drove, starting every time she saw something in the darkness—not a frequent occurrence considering it approached midnight.

They cruised through Main Street seeing nothing but a shadowed couple kissing on the hood of an old Impala outside a bar, before rolling down the hill and pulling into Casey's parking lot. Maggie jumped out of the truck and went inside, exchanging words with an elderly clerk. She trotted back and climbed inside.

"Marge said a group of kids came in a couple of hours ago," she said. "They loaded up on Red Bull and junk food. Halle wasn't with them, but her friend Alicia was."

"I take it you didn't talk to Alicia before?"

"I tried calling her house but nobody answered," she said, "and she and Halle are tight. If anyone knows where my girl is, it's Alicia. Hit the road under the bridge."

Jake gunned out of the lot to the highway. A quarter mile later, he turned toward the Truman Dam and took a sharp right on a road his old man called The Fill.

A group of six teens huddled in the shadows of the cloud covered moon in front of a silver, newer-model sport pickup and an old black Mustang. Curious faces squinted against the light from Jake's truck, riding too high to be mistaken for a cop car. But it represented an unknown presence and they cautiously set bottles on the ground out of sight and extinguished smoking materials underfoot.

Maggie flung open the door before Jake even rolled to a stop and stormed a hard-heeled path toward a pale, dark-haired girl hiding at the back of the group. He couldn't tell from her body language if Maggie was pissed off or anxious. Probably both. He climbed out after her. Maggie grasped the girl about the shoulders and the five other teens backed away. They weren't sure where this confrontation headed, but they sure didn't want to be involved.

"Please, Alicia," Maggie said. "Have you seen Halle?"

The girl's bloodshot eyes were downcast against the glare of Jake's headlights. Drunk or stoned.

"Please don't tell my mom I was here," Alicia said. "I said I was staying at your house and she'll kill me."

"You give me a clue where my daughter is and I won't say a word."

Alicia opened her mouth to say something and then looked over to the boy by Jake. With an almost imperceptible tick of his head, Alicia's mouth closed.

"Don't tell her shit, 'Lecia," said a scraggly haired teen with zits the size of boulders exploding on his face. He glanced toward Jake before grabbing his open beer from the ground by the Mustang.

"Shut your hole," Jake said.

"Or what, old man?" The shithead raised the can to take a drink.

Nothing lit Jake's fuse more than outright stupidity. He could crush the kid with one hand. The kid didn't seem to think Jake would do anything. Time to prove him wrong.

Jake's hand lashed out and sent the beer can flying in a whirling spray of amber liquid and foam. He used his large frame to crowd the kid against the side of the Mustang, pressing in tight. The kid's grin disappeared as he tried to stare Jake down.

"You don't scare me," the kid said, trying to appear tough but doing a piss poor job of it. Jake crushed in tighter. If the window of the Mustang was open, the kid would have tumbled through. Without breaking eye contact, Jake reached over and broke off the antenna and held the jagged edge in front of the teen's bulging eyes. Jake wanted to cut the little smartass, maybe a nice line across his cheekbone to give him a permanent reminder of what being a dumbass could get you. Out of the corner of his eye, Maggie's eyes widened. The snap of a finger bone and a little girl's screams echoed in his head. Goddamn it. This was the kind of shit he was trying to get away from. But he had the kid's attention and didn't want to lose the momentum.

"I'd better scare you or you're dumber than you look," Jake said. "Now shut up or I'll carve out those zits with this antenna and leave your face like the surface of a bloody moon. Got me, ass wipe?"

The teen gave a couple rapid head jerks of agreement, his eyes locked on the jagged edge of the antenna.

"Where is she?" Maggie asked Alicia again.

Alicia took one more glance at the shithead by Jake's side and groaned.

"Fine," she said. "After school she talked about going for a run and then we were supposed to hook up."

"Where?"

"At my house and then we were going to our spot."

"Where's your spot?" Jake asked, stepping away from the kid, but holding the sharp end of the antenna at his head as a warning.

"An old house off Poor Boy Road. We found it in the woods one day. We go there once in a while to hang out. It's not far from yours. A quarter mile past Skinny Hart's place. You know, the house with those silly deer statues and gazing balls in front of it."

"Who lives there?" Maggie asked.

"Nobody," Alicia said, squinting like it was the stupidest question she'd ever asked. "Looks like nobody's lived there in a long time. There's a picture of a skinny guy next to a fat woman in the dining room, but that's the only personal thing there."

"So what happened?"

"She never showed at my house," Alicia said. "I called her, but she didn't answer. I figured you and her were doing something." She finally caught the frantic look in Maggie's eyes and softened. "You really can't find her?"

"No, I can't. Who else knows about this place?"

"Nobody, Ms. Holden. I wanted to tell some people and Halle said no. It was our little hideout."

"If you hear anything about her, you call me. Now, go home." Maggie grabbed Jake by the elbow. They climbed into Jake's truck which he threw in reverse.

"You were going to cut him, weren't you?" she asked.

He shook her earlier with his tale of his violent past and was afraid to say any more. *No way* perched on his lips, but he couldn't lie to her. "Thought about it. A few months ago I'd have done it in a heartbeat. Seeing their own blood tends to be a big motivator to get people to talk."

"What changed your mind?"

He glanced at her. "You. I don't want to be that guy anymore." He let the confession sit. "You know the place the girl was talking about?"

"Yeah, I think so," she said. "Sounds like old Royce Weather's place. Hell, he's been dead for years. I kind of know where the turn off is, but I'll never find it in the dark."

"Call Bear," Jake said. "Have him meet us at your place. We'll swing past to make sure your girl hasn't gone back home. If she's not there, I bet Bear can find the house."

He spun the truck around and started back out The Fill Road; the Swinging Bridge crossing the Osage River couldn't support traffic any longer. He glanced in the rearview mirror. The teens resumed their drinking, and the shithead flipped him off with a full arm extension.

They rolled to Highway 7, stopped, and waited for a few cars to pass.

"Tell me she's okay, Jake."

"She's okay," he said. As she dialed, Jake hoped he wasn't telling her a lie.

CHAPTER TWENTY-NINE

A quarter before midnight, Willie pulled into the driveway of his uncle's farm a few miles northwest of Hastain. He killed the lights and rolled along the dusty road, guiding the truck by the moonlight which danced in and out of the patchy clouds overhead. Though his uncle slept like the dead, Willie wasn't taking any chances on waking him. He wheeled away from the house behind a decrepit barn, slouching like an ancient relic in the darkness.

Willie opened the door. "Stay here and keep an eye on her."

"With pleasure," Bub said, drawing his tongue across his chapped lips. Willie started toward the barn, paused, and leaned back inside.

"You touch her, Bub, and I'll cut your dick off. Got it?"

Bub's nostrils flared like a bull, his mouth working on a reply but came up empty.

"Give me two minutes." Willie grabbed his portion of meth from the back and hauled the hefty bags around to a coffin-shaped box his uncle used to store miscellaneous tools. Willie set the bags on the ground and opened the box. He moved some blankets and tools out of the way and yanked on a ring hidden in the base. A three-foot by three-foot trap door opened, leading to a hidden cellar beneath the barn. He could hide Halle down here and say she got away. But then he'd have to contend with Bub and Shane. He grabbed the meth and carefully descended the creaky stairs into darkness. When he reached the dirt floor, he dropped the bags on the ground and groped around for cord of the overhead light.

The dull light from the dirty single bulb swung, pushing back the shadows. Fifteen feet square, the room held racks of rifles, machine guns and other weapons his uncle swore the government didn't want him to have. Enough weaponry to shoot Shane's house to hell and back, but Willie couldn't shoot worth a damn and Bub embodied one of the biggest targets you could find in Benton County.

He moved past plastic-covered shelves of dry goods and water jugs lining the far wall. Willie would burn the roads to get here when the zombie apocalypse hit. He picked up the meth bags and placed them in an old army foot locker in the far corner.

Back at the entrance, Willie killed the light and hopped into his truck. Minutes later they rolled back down the road to the highway, toward the blue house and Shane. Willie's grip tightened on the wheel with each turn of the wheels. The window to get Halle out of this mess shrank with each passing second.

*****

Jake and Maggie waited in Maggie's living room for Bear. They'd swept through like a tornado looking for Halle. It killed Jake to see the fire in her eyes extinguish like a blown out match when they found the house empty. To make matters worse, he got a text from an unknown number. The simple message read "Tick tock." Jake had less than a day to put Langston in a body bag or Keats would find one for Jake.

Maggie fidgeted on the beige, corduroy couch, rubbing her hands together like they were worry stones, waiting for her baby girl to come bounding through the front door. Jake sat in a brown, leather recliner next to the couch twiddling his thumbs, feeling helpless and hating it.

"It's going to be okay, Mags." Did the words sound as hollow as they felt? Would she see through his reassurance knowing things might be far from okay?

"Hope for the best, plan for the worst," she whispered.

"Who says that?"

"You used to," she said, head tilting in surprise.

Jake scrunched his eyes. "When?"

"All the time. We'd sit on the hill talking about what you were going through with Stony and football and school and Nick and Janey. Your head went in a million different directions back then. You hoped for the best because that's what would get you out of here. You planned on the worst because you knew life is full of curveballs."

"I don't remember saying it. Sounds pretty optimistic considering that as long as Stony was around, things were guaranteed to turn to shit," he said.

"I always loved that about you."

"What?"

"You could always see the light at the end of the tunnel," she said, a sad smile crossing her lips.

"Well, I was an idiot teenager."

She shook her head. "I think you're selling yourself short."

He rose and stood by the fireplace, examining the pictures on the mantel. He lifted the first one; one of her parents with their arms draped around an eight-year-old Maggie.

"That's my favorite picture of my folks," she said. "We took it at Silver Dollar City. Daddy was so happy he could spring for a vacation. He did just about anything to make me happy."

"Don't think he liked me much."

"He liked you about as much as any father could for the man who deflowered his baby girl."

"You told him?" Jake set the picture back on the mantel as if the frame was on fire.

Maggie laughed. "No, but I think he had a pretty good idea. I think he had bigger worries that you were going to turn out like your father."

"Then he was a smart man."

He stared at another picture of a beautiful, blonde girl with the same button nose and high cheekbones as Maggie.

"This Halle? Bet you're beating the boys back with a stick." He stole a glance at Maggie. "She's gorgeous, just like her mother."

"She is beautiful, inside and out. She's stubborn as mule, like her father."

"Who is…" Jake asked when headlights flooded the living room and Bear's horn blared. Maggie jumped from the couch. Jake set Halle's picture back on the mantel and followed her outside, clasped Bear's hand, then laid out what they learned from Alicia.

"I know exactly where it is," Bear said. "Not far from here at all. Got some flashlights we can use to scout the place out. Come on."

The three of them climbed into Bear's truck and they rolled out of Maggie's driveway and on to Poor Boy Road. Instead of moving right toward town, Bear spun the wheel to the left. They rode in silence through the blackness, the clock on the dashboard reading twelve thirty. A mile later, he slowed, leaning his bulky frame forward, squinting his eyes as he probed the passing landscape lit up by the headlights.

"There you are," he said at last, cutting on to a dirt path Jake didn't even see. He hopped out and opened a long, green gate then returned. They bounced along deep, rain-carved ruts for a hundred yards before rolling into a clearing. The truck's bright beams blasted the side of the old house in front of them, shadows jumping away into the deep woods. The three of them got out and Bear scanned the area. He popped open the strap of his holster and rested his hand on the butt of his gun. Jake stood beside him, taking in the house and surrounding grounds.

"Abandoned, huh?" Jake said.

"That's the word."

"Awful lot of fresh tire tracks for an abandoned place."

"Any chance Halle would drive down here, Mags?" Bear asked.

"No chance," she said. "We just have the one car and it's in Sedalia."

"Jake, stay here with Maggie." Bear eased his gun from his holster. "I'm going to check the house out."

"I'm coming with you," Maggie said, starting forward. Bear held his hand out.

"No, you're going to stay here with Jake," he said. "Something doesn't smell right."

Jake took Maggie's hand and pulled her to him. He leaned against the truck, feeling naked without a weapon of his own. Bear crept with his pistol resting on the outstretched flashlight. At the front of the house, he shined it through the window, then walked around the side and out of sight.

Despite the warmth, Maggie trembled as a late summer wind gusted through the trees. Jake agreed with Bear, something didn't smell right. The normal rustic, woodsy smell of the Ozarks had been replaced with an acrid stench.

Bear's flashlight appeared on the opposite side of the house and danced along the ground as it approached them. As he drew closer, he holstered his pistol and examined something in a white handkerchief in his hand.

"What's that?" Jake asked.

Bear held out a red shard into the lights of his truck. "A link. Meth".

"Red meth?"

"Devil Ice. I got a shithead in custody who knows exactly what it is."

"You go inside the house?" Jake asked.

"Hell, no. You smell it?"

"Yeah, like weird sweet-smelling cat piss," Jake said. "If that

155

makes any sense."

"Makes perfect sense if you combine it with the trash I saw inside the house through the windows and this chunk of meth. That's why we're not going in there. This is a meth lab and somebody cooked here recently."

"But...but...Halle could be in there," Maggie said, jumping forward. Bear grabbed her by the arm.

"You can't go in there, Mags, the house is full of poison. But don't worry, I checked the rooms through the windows and it's empty. I'll get my team here with the proper gear and we'll sweep through it. Once light breaks, we'll sweep through the woods as well, but I'm guessing Halle was here recently."

"Why do you say that?" Maggie asked, a slight smile raising her cheekbones.

Bear held out the white handkerchief and rolled his palm over revealing a silver iPod. Its illuminated face showed two things, Pink's song "Try" playing and the ominous sliver of red from the battery bar. Bear turned the iPod case over, the light from the truck revealed the name "Halle" crudely etched in the silver casing. Maggie stifled a cry. Jake pulled her in tight, holding her until her stiffness gave in.

"Come on, Mags." He led her to the truck and helped her in. He shut the door and returned to Bear.

"What are you thinking?" Jake asked.

"I got a cook house, a rock of new meth they're calling Devil Ice, which I also found in the trailer of a guy I have in custody who happens to work for my local dealer who happens to work for Shane Langston. Combine that with Halle's iPod and I'd say we've got ourselves a good lead."

Shane Langston again. Should he bust out the reason for his return besides taking care of his dying father? How would Bear react? He couldn't do it in front of Maggie. Soon.

At least they now had something to go on. Jake had the same iPod. His got a good six to eight hours of playing time before the battery ran out which put Halle here not long ago. Where the hell was she now?

CHAPTER THIRTY

At midnight, moving south on Highway M, Willie turned down a roughly paved unmarked road heading toward the water. He flipped the headlights to bright and slammed the brakes hard when a couple of deer flew across the road, missing his front end by scant inches. Willie instinctively threw his arm across Halle's chest to keep her from flying into the windshield. Bub grunted as his sausage hands crushed into the dashboard. As if Willie's nerves weren't frayed enough, he had to worry about a family of deer flying through the windshield and skewering him.

Bub yelled and reached for the shotgun in the rack behind their heads. Halle screamed at Bub's lunge and pressed her palms into the dashboard.

"Bub, what the hell?" Willie said.

Bub kept his hand on the gun, breathing heavy. "Little bastards coulda killed us."

"It's just a bunch of goddamn deer."

"I gotta do something…shoot something. I'm about to lose my fucking mind. We shouldn't be doing this, Willie. We need to bail."

"Relax, man. Smoke a blunt."

"I would if I had one."

Bub sat back in the seat and they drove on for another mile. Willie leaned forward, squinting through the midnight fog wafting off the road, searching for the turn off. He slowed to a crawl by a blue ribbon tied on a fence post off the road. At a gate blocking the road, he flashed his brights three times.

A bearded behemoth with a shaved head and a neck as thick as Willie's waist emerged from the darkness with a rife slung across his back and a pistol in his hand. Was that Rick? Hard to tell. Shane liked to rotate through his crew and they all looked alike, big and mean. Rick eyed the truck for a moment, called in something on a radio and opened the gate. Willie gave him a quick wave, getting nothing but a cold stare in return.

A quarter of a mile later, Willie stopped in front of the blue house, a sprawling two story nestled in a grove of thick Ozark trees off the water. The house was dark except for a patch of lights on the far end and a single bulb burning over the front door. A pair of boots stuck out of the shadows at the far reaches of the porch light. A heaviness settled in his gut. His chances to save Halle were all but gone. He smoothed his hair back and took a deep breath.

"Stay here with the girl," he said to Bub. "Let me make sure everything's cool with Shane."

"What if you don't come back out?" Bub asked.

"Then I guess you're fucked."

He climbed out, the rusty door screeching through the night like a banshee. He slammed it shut and walked the few feet to the front door.

"Go on in," the voice said from the darkened porch. "He's waitin' for you in the den."

Willie opened the door and took a few tentative steps inside to the smell of fried bacon and cigarette smoke. A light shined from the kitchen to his left and a figure flashed by the doorway. A bearded face he didn't recognize. He went right down the dark hallway, his heart hammering.

He emerged into a brightly lit den. A large head of a ten-point buck hung above a stone fireplace, regarding Willie with glassy eyes.

Bookending the fireplace were two comfortable leather highbacks. Shane lounged in one of them in blue jeans and a tight, gray T-shirt talking on his cell phone, his polished, black cowboy boots resting on a wagon wheel coffee table. Shane raised his eyebrows at Willie and waved him forward to sit on the brown leather couch.

"Yeah, he just got here," Shane said. "Uh huh. It won't be a problem, sir. I'll take care of it."

Willie's skin prickled, his nerves firing on all cylinders. He didn't know why Shane wanted him here, didn't know what he planned on doing with Halle, and had certainly never heard Shane call anyone "sir." He pulled out his cigarettes, hoping the nicotine would ease the nervous tremble in his hands.

"Willie." Shane hung up the phone and settled back in the chair. "Glad you could make it. Any trouble finding the place again?"

"Little tougher in the dark, but we managed."

"Where's the girl?"

"In the truck with Bub."

"You didn't invite them in?" Shane asked. "Where's your manners?"

"Thought we should talk first." Willie took a deep pull on his smoke. "I never heard you call nobody sir before."

"It's called respect."

"I suppose."

Shane plopped his boots to the floor and leaned forward, resting his steely arms on his knees. His jaw tensed as he picked up a large Bowie knife off the table and cleaned his fingernails with it.

"You know what I hate, Willie?" he asked after a minute of silence, holding his nails out for examination like he just got a manicure at a salon.

"Loose ends," Willie said. Shane raised his eyebrows. He pointed the knife at Willie.

"You're a smart son of a bitch, Willie. Loose ends make my ass itch. Loose ends are what get people in trouble and at the moment I have more loose ends than a frayed rope."

"Like what?"

"Now you're playing dumb." Shane set the knife back on the table. He got up and crossed the room to a bar, his boots thumping against the hardwood. He poured a finger of Scotch from a crystal container. Willie was fine that Shane didn't offer him one. Scotch tasted like turpentine filtered through a sweat sock. Shane took a sip, walked to the couch and sat next to Willie.

"You hear about Sedalia?" Shane continued. He raised his eyebrows like Willie should know what the hell he was talking about. Willie shrugged. "Someone hit my warehouse today. Took fifty grand in cash, but left the drugs and called the cops."

"Oh, shit."

"Exactly. I wondered who would be dumb enough to hit me. My first thought was our Mexican friends, but they wouldn't leave six keys of coke and call the cops. I figured it was someone who knew about the stash but didn't have the balls or resources to move the coke."

Willie focused on the imperfections of the polished wood floor at his feet. How the stain coated the wood, but pooled in black lines in the cracks. Like blood. Like his blood if Shane drew conclusions that weren't there. Did his inability to meet Shane's gaze spell guilt or insecurity? It didn't matter one way or the other because he learned long ago from his father to never stare an angry alpha dog in the eye.

"Let's see how smart you are, Willie," he said. "What are my loose ends?"

Willie wished Shane would've offered him a Scotch, something to calm his nerves. His mind raced through all that happened that day. How truthful should he be? After running through the pros and cons, he decided he might as well lay it out.

"Howie," Willie said, looking up. The police had Howie in custody, an easy one. Shane held up a finger signifying he'd scored one point.

"Your cook, Dexter," Willie continued. A second finger went up. "Bennett, Bub and the girl".

"That's five." Shane splayed the fingers of one hand. He drained the rest of the Scotch and set the glass on the table hard enough to jump the ice cubes in the glass. "I'm afraid I'm going to need my other hand to count the rest."

"Well, you really only need one more finger."

"So who is the last loose end?"

"Me." Willie crushed the cigarette butt in the ashtray.

"Very good. And who knew about my warehouse?"

"Me and Bub. Think I took Howie there once."

"Were Bub and Howie with you all day?"

Willie pressed his lips together and shook his head. "No, sir."

"Loose ends, every one of you. And since I hate loose ends, exactly what am I going to do about them?"

A cold sweat broke across Willie's brow as Shane picked up his hunting knife, fingering the wickedly sharp blade. He'd witnessed firsthand what his boss could do with one.

CHAPTER THIRTY-ONE

Twenty minutes later, Willie stuck his head through the open front door of the blue house and signaled for Halle and Bub to get out of the truck. Perfect timing. Halle had spent that eternity pressed into the driver's door, as far as she could get from Bub's wretch-inducing stench. He licked his lips and stroked his hand up and down his thigh while staring at hers. Why didn't she wear baggy sweats on her run?

Inside the house, Willie directed Bub to the kitchen and Halle followed Willie down a hall into a room as big as the high school cafeteria. He stepped to the side revealing a muscle-bound man with black goatee and intense eyes. She wrapped her arms across her chest and shivered. Willie introduced him as Shane. Her skin crawled as she shook his cold and clammy hand. Willie and Bub said Shane was dangerous and now, unable to meet that penetrating stare, she agreed.

"You must be Halle," he said. "Pleasure to meet you."

She said nothing, a mixture of fear and anger burning inside her. Fear at what he would do to her and anger at her lack of power to stop it.

"I apologize for this cloak and dagger business," he continued. "I'm sure you understand after what you saw at the house."

"I didn't...honestly, I didn't see anything," she said, eyes glued to the floor. "Just these guys chasing me through the woods. When can I go home?"

"Soon, if all goes well." Shane acted calm, but tension coated the air, like he held on by a very thin thread. "We have to figure out what you did see and what we're going to do about it. Why don't you go into the back room and get cleaned up while Willie and I talk?"

"Then I can go home?"

"We'll see." A phrase translating as *No*. If Shane had his way, she wouldn't set foot in her home again.

"I didn't see anything," she said again, forcing herself to look into those black eyes. Her cheeks ached with the tears that threatened to burst forth again.

"Well, we'll find out for sure, won't we?"

He waved her away and Willie took her by the arm, pushing her to the hallway. They passed a staircase leading down and stopped at an opened door leading to a wood paneled room with nothing but a queen-size bed and an antique dresser with a small lamp and a plastic alarm clock. She passed through the doorway and stopped to face Willie. His hands pressed on either side of the doorframe as if he were trying to hold it open. He represented her only chance at salvation and she had to convince him to help her.

"Willie," she whispered, glancing over his shoulder. "I'm so scared."

"You got a right to be," he said. His breath smelled like cigarettes and sour milk. It took everything in her not to cringe away. Instead, she reached out and gently touched his hand with hers, drawing her body closer to his.

"You gotta help me, Willie. Don't let them hurt me."

With her touch, the pulse in his neck visibly pounded, the wanting fire in his eyes. He checked over his bony shoulder.

"I'll do what I can," he said. "Hell, I don't know if any of us are safe. No promises."

Halle held her close proximity to him with her hand on his for effect before he closed the door. Shuddering with repulsion, she wiped her hands on her shirt. She was screwed if she didn't get out of here.

Hours later, after a futile search for an escape, she stood at the window, alternating glances between the spot-lit patio below and the morning sun rising behind the tree line across the gloomy lake. Would she see another sunrise? There was no way out of the room. They locked the door and posted a scary behemoth on the porch outside her window. Widow's peak on top, cascading mullet in the back, and beady eyes. He looked like a rat with a wig.

The long-haired giant on the porch cranked his rodent face to the light and winked. Rather than let him see her skin crawl, she dropped back into the bedroom. She plopped on the bed and hugged her knees tight, wondering where her mother was at that moment. Would she ever see her again? She had to be freaking out by now; if only Halle could get word to her. Maybe Willie would deliver a message.

Just then the door opened and Shane walked in. A giant black man with a shaved head in a tight, blue T-shirt guarded the hallway. Halle bet he ate little children for breakfast.

"It's time we had an honest chat, Halle."

Halle pressed against the window and clutched the sill behind her as the black man in the hall grinned before turning his back. She stifled a scream as Shane shut the door and stepped towards her.

CHAPTER THIRTY-TWO

Jake welcomed Maggie's head on his chest while they waited for Bear. Light from the television bounced around the room like a strobe, its volume on low. Some late night infomercial offering double the crap if you placed your order in the next ten minutes.

In a weird way, it felt like high school again, hanging out and watching the tube on the couch with his girlfriend. He had a fleeting sensation her mom would pop out of the kitchen asking Jake if he wanted anything to eat, or, if the hour drew late, her dad strongly suggesting the time had come for Jake to hit the road.

He slid his hand up Maggie's back and gently ran his fingers through her hair. She melted deeper into him, as if that touch shattered any lingering doubts about him like a sledgehammer against a mirror.

"God, I miss you doing that," she said.

"Sorry, thought you were asleep." He dropped his hand.

"No, don't stop. It relaxes me. If that's even possible."

Had it really been sixteen years since he'd last sat on this couch? Leg wrapped up in a cocoon of bandages, a hinged brace stabilizing his knee, wondering what in the hell he would do with his life. When Stony shattered the knee, he shattered the dream and the man she loved.

The athletic scholarship offers were dropped, the college coaches quit sniffing around and the gravity of Warsaw became a massive, immovable force holding him. He knew her frustration as he spiraled down the spiritual drain knowing there was absolutely nothing she could do about it. Jake retreated into a shell, and no matter how hard she tried, he wouldn't come out.

Medicaid paid for the knee surgery by the cheapest surgeon available. Stony said he'd take him to Kansas City to get it done, but never came home. Maggie and Bear ended up driving him. Jake spent the trip silent as the countryside rolled by, so full of anger and despair that a constant film of tears clouded his vision.

After the surgery, he did a rotation with Maggie for the first couple of weeks before toughing it out at home. On the rare times the old man came home, Stony mocked him, calling him "the cripple." Jake tried to put on a brave facade, but Maggie's face sank when Stony said it; she could see in Jake's eyes that he believed it was true.

Maggie did everything she could to hold on to him. Why didn't he let her in? She drove him to rehab in Sedalia before Jake decided to do it on his own with her help. She was there for every agonizing exercise, pushing him, comforting him. He walked again in three months and jogged in six, but his football days were over. Then, one day he left, just disappeared like a wisp of smoke, convinced he was doing the right thing.

Days turned into weeks, weeks into months and months into years. Not a day passed where she didn't cross his mind, curious if she ever wondered where he was or what he did. He thought of calling her so many times over the years, but too much time had passed and he was too afraid of what she might say.

In the past couple of days, he saw her bond with Halle in every glance at her picture and every determined step she made to find her. She needed her baby girl to keep her going and now a life without her hovered in the unthinkable realm of possibility.

"I don't know what I'd do without her," Maggie said, breaking the silence. Tears choked her voice. "She's my everything, Jake."

"We're gonna find her, Mags. Sun is coming up and we'll find her."

Hot tears coursed down her cheeks. He swept them away and continued stroking her hair. She slipped her hand around his waist and hugged him tight.

"Is there anybody we need to call?" he asked. "Her dad? Where's he?"

Maggie sat up and yanked a tissue from a box on the coffee table, dabbing her eyes with it.

"He's been out of the picture," she said. "I think not having a father figure around is what's fueled her rebellious nature."

"Nobody steady around?" His brain tried to form a mental image of her with another man, but thankfully nothing came to be.

Maggie grinned at his prying. "No. In fact, rumor around town is I'm a lesbian."

Jake busted out laughing. Maggie joined him for a moment before it died out. She took a deep breath. A heaviness settled in the air, something she wanted to say.

"Jake... I have to tell you something, but I don't know how."

"Just say it. I ain't goin' anywhere."

She stared at the tissue in her hand, shredding it piece by piece. "That's what you say now."

"Maggie, say it."

She straightened herself on the couch, facing him. "What do you remember about our last night together?"

His features sagged and his eyes dropped to his lap, the guilt literally pulling him down.

"I remember a wonderful night on the hill. You made a little picnic and we shared a bottle of some horrible tasting, cheap wine. We made love and stared at the stars, talking for hours. You tried to get me to see the brightness of the future, but I couldn't get over the opportunities lost."

She stroked his thumbs as he held her hands. "You remember

more than I thought you would."

Jake's lips pressed together. "It's taken me a long time to figure things out. Too long. The world I've been living in is a dark place full of pain and miserable people. It's a place I helped create when I was young, and I've lived there because it's all I know. It's like ghosts are chasing me."

Maggie moved closer and rested her hand on his shoulder.

"A place you helped create? You act like you brought this on yourself," she said. "It's not your fault. You may have continued the cycle but it was taught to you...taught on you."

"I know," he said. Empty words.

She lifted his chin. "Look at me, Jake, because you're not hearing me. It's not your fault."

"I know," he repeated.

"No, you don't. Coming back home has stirred a lot of memories and you don't just remember them now, you're feeling them. You have the knowledge, the facts of what happened with Stony that night. But it doesn't mean you understand it."

He shrugged. "What the hell difference does that make?"

"Until you understand it," she said, "until you understand him, you'll never escape those ghosts you're talking about. Until you understand it, you won't be able to forgive."

Forgive? Stony? "What in the hell makes you think I want to do that?"

"I think that's exactly what you came home for." She climbed to her feet and extended a hand. "Come help me make some coffee. I don't want to collapse in exhaustion while we're looking for Halle."

Jake took her hand and followed her to the kitchen. She handed him the coffee pot and faced the refrigerator. On the door, pictures covered every open space. Maggie and Halle together, cheek to cheek. Halle bounding the track in her Warsaw uniform, hair flying behind her. Halle with a group of girlfriends, arms binding each other together with blazing smiles of untapped futures. Then, in the corner, a picture of Maggie, Bear and Jake in front of Warsaw High School in their graduation gowns, Bear and Maggie beaming for the brave new world. Jake also wore a weighted smile in the picture, like his bleak future pulled at the corners of his mouth.

He filled the coffee pot at the sink. Just being in this place with her took him back sixteen years as he savored the breathtaking burst of pink erupting from the Ozark tree tops out the back window.

"After our last night, why did you go?"

"I don't know, Mags," he said.

"I don't know doesn't work. Make something up if you have to, but I need to know. You have your ghosts, I have mine. Mine is the image of you walking down the hill to your house all those years ago. I've seen your face in countless strangers, stopped in my tracks when someone's voice sounded like yours. I need to know."

He set the coffee pot on the counter and turned to face her, but couldn't bring his eyes past her bare feet. He shoved his hands in the pockets of his jeans. An immense and crushing weariness settled in his bones, the guilty feelings squeezing him, shrinking him.

"I've waited sixteen years to be able to ask this question," she continued. "It's haunted me because I loved you more than life itself back then. With you standing here in front of me now, it all seems so obvious. I never found anyone new. I always found a reason, some flaw with my boyfriends. I convinced myself it was because of Halle, but it was something else. It was you, Jake. I never stopped loving you. I have to know."

"There was more going on than I knew what to do with," he said. "Love for you, feeling responsible for Janey and Nicky, anger at Stony and this…this utter hopelessness at my dreams of getting out on the magic football carpet ride going up in flames. If I didn't leave then and there, I never would. I'd end up like Stony. Things didn't end up the way I planned."

"So you had a plan?"

"As good a plan as a stupid eighteen year old who doesn't know shit about shit can have," he said. He moved his gaze from her feet to her hurt eyes. "I was a coward. A selfish coward who only thought of himself. I figured I'd run away, and all that Warsaw held over me would fade in the distance. Once I recognized it wasn't going away, I didn't think I could come back empty handed. Figured I'd settle in somewhere, earn some cash and come get you."

"But you never did."

"No. Once you start running, it's hard to stop. I'd settle in somewhere new and it would be fine for a while. Then, I'd think of you and Janey and Nicky and Bear and Stony and the guilt would push me off to some other place. I figured I could outrun the ghosts."

She grasped him by the arms. "But we're not ghosts. The only past you're running from is lying in a death bed in Sedalia. You don't have to run anymore because there's nothing left to run from."

She pulled him to the refrigerator and pointed to the pictures of Halle. "Look at the good in the world," she continued, her thumb tracking the outline of Halle's face. "Just look at it."

"You did good, Mags."

She steeled herself. "No, Jake. We did good."

Jake's eyebrows furrowed together. He took a half step back and examined the pictures again.

"*We* did good," she repeated.

"We? You mean…"

"Yeah. Halle is yours."

The bombshell dropped. His mind was blank, too stunned to conjure up a cohesive thought. He gazed at the picture and the longer he stared, the more he saw. His daughter. Their daughter. He could almost hear Maggie's pulse racing with anticipation for his response. After an open-mouthed minute of contemplation, he leaned in and kissed her on the forehead, letting his lips rest there, absorbing the moment. Maggie wrapped her arms around his waist and squeezed him tight. The rising sun cast cheerful rays across the kitchen floor, silhouetting their united shape on the linoleum. He pulled back, cupping her face in his hands.

"Let's go find our daughter," he said.

CHAPTER THIRTY-THREE

A little after seven, Jake went out to meet Bear on the drive. His friend lumbered out of the cab of his truck, his uniform wrinkled with a dried coffee stain on one thigh. His eyes were narrow and hollow, and he needed a shave. Maggie flew down the front steps.

"Damn, Bear," Jake said. "You look like shit."

"Bears like their sleep and I haven't gotten much since you rolled into town. I take it no word from Halle?" Maggie's mouth turned low. "I spread the word among my guys to keep their eyes peeled and I got a crew heading over to the cook house. They're gonna scour the place and the surrounding woods and see if we can turn up something useful. Maggie, I'm going to steal Jake. I've got an idea his particular skill sets could help with."

What skill sets might those be? Those he was trying to get away from? Whatever it took to get Halle back. Everything had changed with Maggie's revelation in the kitchen. It was no longer about just finding her daughter, but finding his daughter too. Should he tell Bear about it?

"What about me?" Maggie asked.

"I need you to stay here," Bear said. "In case Halle or anybody else gets in contact with you."

"But they'd call my cell." Her eyes cast wide and pleading. "I can't sit here and do nothing. I'll go crazy."

"Please, Maggie. Just stay here. Somebody could come by or call with information, or Halle herself may come strolling up the lane. You won't be doing nothing. When was the last time you were in her room?"

"Yesterday, dropping some clean clothes on her dresser."

"You toss the place?"

Maggie stepped back. "No, she's a good girl. I don't have to loot through her stuff to know what's going on with my daughter."

"I know she's a good girl, but right now we're runnin' in the dark. I need you to go through every nook and cranny. See if there's any letters, notes, receipts, pictures. Anything out of the ordinary or anything that trips your pretty brain to give us another direction to look at. Look between the mattress and box springs, under loose floorboards, underneath jewelry boxes, every square inch of that room. Can you do it?"

Maggie started to say something, but instead nodded.

"Good," Bear said. "I'll call you in an hour or sooner if we find something. Jake, come with me, big guy."

"Where we going?"

"To the jailhouse. I got a problem a man with your unique talents could help with."

Jake grabbed Maggie's car keys and promised to get the vehicle for her.

"What's going on?" Jake asked when they turned on to Poor Boy Road and headed west toward Old 65 Highway and town.

"Remember the shithead I told you I got sitting in jail?"

"The one with the red rock and the lawyer?"

"Yup," Bear said. He reached Highway 65 and let an orange Challenger whip by. "The lawyer left with strict instructions to Howie Skaggs not to say anything to any of us. I tried talking to Howie in between searches for Halle, but he's wedged in tight. That's my problem."

"And I'm the solution?"

"I want to dump you in a room with Howie. I wasn't too worried when I originally talked to him, but now with the red meth and Halle's iPod at the scene, I think he can lead us somewhere."

"New rock you've never seen before," Jake said. "Recent cooking activity at a drug house and a mysteriously appearing lawyer."

"See? You would've made a good cop."

"What can I do?"

"He won't talk to a cop, but he might talk to you. You can look pretty mean when you try."

"What about his constitutional rights?"

"He has the constitutional right that I don't beat his ass. Beyond that, I don't give a shit at this point."

"You think this guy's gonna spill his guts to me? Sounds pretty fucking thin, Bear."

"It is thin," Bear said. "But we don't have much to go on other than rousting every kid in town, which we're pretty much going to do anyway, but maybe Howie gives us a direction. You lean on his ass until he gives us something useful. I've been chasing Shane Langston for a long time now. This is the best chance I've had to nail his ass so I'm pulling out the stops."

"What if the lawyer barks about police brutality?"

"You ain't a cop. I have some measure of plausible deniability."

"Doesn't sound very plausible."

"You want to help me or not, asshole?" Bear said.

Jake said nothing, letting his grin speak for itself. Giving Bear flack like the old days brought some normalcy to the world.

They exited the highway and rolled across the bridge toward town, the corner gas station busy with locals filling up for the day and getting their morning coffee. He wanted to break the Halle news to Bear, but said nothing as they arrived downtown. The shop owners angle-parked in front of their stores and were rolling out the sidewalks, preparing for the day's business. Bear pulled in front of the sheriff's office and shut off the car.

"There any cameras in the room?" Jake asked.

"One, but it will mysteriously stop working when we get there. Damn technology."

"Sure the lawyer won't come after me?"

"His lawyer won't even know you were here. We'll deny anyone has seen Howie since the bloodsucker left the night before."

Though he had reservations, Howie might lead them to Shane Langston and solve the problem both he and Bear suffered from. What could possibly go wrong? Well, a million different things, but if it took care of Langston and they found Halle, Jake didn't care.

"Okay," Jake said, opening the car door. "Let's do it."

CHAPTER THIRTY-FOUR

Howie Skaggs lay awake on an impossibly thin mattress that did nothing to mask the cold, hard metal of the bunk it rested on. He'd managed to doze for a bit, drifting in and out in between bleak bouts of imagined scenarios, most of which ended with his horribly painful death at the hands of Shane.

The lawyer spent his brief time with Howie grilling him on what he'd told the cops during his interrogation. Luckily, Howie didn't have to lie since the lawyer arrived before he had a chance to spill his guts in exchange for immunity and relocation somewhere out of Shane Langston's clutches. The lawyer promised to work on getting bail for Howie in the morning, and the man's demeanor left the impression on Howie's dim brain that he might potentially get out of this jam alive. At the same time, the dim brain told him the lawyer could care less whether Howie got out or not, and to keep his guard up.

A tall, thin man slept in the cell next to him. They must've brought him in during the night. The man's gaunt, bearded jaw hung open in a silent snore and a thin line of drool rolled down his cheek. His body odor and stale beer cologne wafted across the cell, mixing unpleasantly with the harsh smell of disinfectant from the jail. Two cells over, Crazy Wayne Kirtley, the town loon clutched the bars to his cell door and mumbled something to nobody. Wonder what he did this time?

The door to the bay clanked open, followed by the rhythmic thunk of a rolling cart with a bad wheel. Howie swung his legs off the bunk and set his shoeless feet on the cold, stone floor.

A uniformed cop stopped in front of his neighbor's cell and yelled at the man inside, calling him "Williams." Williams stirred and cracked his eyes. He sat up and wiped the drool from his cheek. The cop held a paper plate covered with a napkin through the slot in the bars. The inmate took it and returned to the cot seemingly oblivious to Howie's existence. The cop pushed the cart a few feet more and stopped in front of Howie's cell.

"Breakfast," the cop said.

Howie climbed to his feet and shuffled over to the door. He hadn't eaten for a day. Even the hard biscuit and two paper-thin slices of precooked bacon looked like heaven.

"When am I getting out of here?" he asked the cop.

"Beats the hell out of me. Ask the day shift when they get here."

"I want to talk to my lawyer."

"Tell someone who gives a shit because it ain't me."

The cop shuffled back the way he came. Howie poked at the food. The bacon was cold, but the biscuit was hot and tasted decent. Williams gnawed at his breakfast in the next cell.

"Whatcha in for?" Howie asked.

"Why?"

"Just making conversation."

Williams eyed him for a moment, his jaw working slowly on the biscuit.

"Possession of a controlled substance," Williams said.

"Small world. You from around here? I don't recognize you."

The man stuffed the rest of his biscuit in his mouth. He chewed for a minute, face working like he tried to figure out a complex math problem in his head.

"Kansas City," Williams said at last. "Was supposed to pick something up and got busted speeding. You want my bacon? I can't eat this crap."

Williams walked over with his plate in hand and Howie moved to meet him. Williams stuck the two pieces through the cell and Howie took them, popping them into his mouth.

"Thanks," Howie mumbled.

The man reached through the bars. "Hey, I'm Gus Williams."

"Howie Skaggs." He shook the man's hand. Williams' grip clamped from friendly to vise, surprising Howie with its power. He pulled Howie violently forward, slamming his face into the cold metal bars. Williams dropped the plate and produced a long, metal shaft of steel, filed to a sharp point.

"Shane says to have a nice day." Williams jabbed his hand through the bars and rammed the steel through Howie's eye, wide with surprise and terror. Just a millisecond of searing pain before the steel bit into his brain and cancelled any worries about what Shane was going to do to him.

CHAPTER THIRTY-FIVE

"What in the holy hell!" Bear bellowed from in front of the cell. Jake rushed across the yellowed linoleum to Bear who white-knuckled the closed bars.

Holy shit. The man inside the cell lay on his back, a steel shaft protruding from a hole that used to house his left eye. Blood pooled around the man's cropped brown hair, jaw hanging open in a silent scream, and trickled to the drain in the center of the cell, a copper smell hanging in the air.

"Jake, meet Howie. Johnston!" Bear slammed his fist into the wall as a rail-thin cop with a crisp uniform darted through the door and across the cell row.

He staggered back at the sight on the floor. "Jesus."

"Open the door," Bear whispered. "And call an ambulance."

Johnston fumbled with the keys before finding the right one and opened the cell. Bear trod carefully around the puddle of blood and knelt next to Howie. He touched his neck, checking for a pulse before shaking his head.

"Who was the last one in here?" Bear demanded.

"Inside the cell? Beats me," Johnston said. "I just got here. Howell came out with the breakfast trolley a few minutes ago, but he don't have keys to the cells and sure as hell didn't say anything about this guy being dead."

"Go get him. Now." Bear followed Johnston out of the cell and walked past Jake to the next cell. The man inside lay on his bunk with his hands folded behind his head.

"What's your name?"

"Williams," the man said, sprawled out like he lounged at the beach.

"I suppose you didn't see a thing," Bear said.

"Oh, I saw everything, Sheriff," Williams said, flashing yellowed teeth and waving a bloody hand in their direction.

In the next cell, Wayne Kirtley backed up against the wall, as far away as he could get. His eyes wide and wary.

"Man," Bear said. "This is gonna be a long fucking day."

*****

Halle trembled on the bed in the locked room of the blue house, feeling cold and empty as Shane perched too close to her, like a vulture in waiting. He had yet to touch her, but the threat loomed, his knife twirling deftly in his hands as he spoke. He'd spent the last thirty minutes asking about her, making small talk with little probing questions about her knowledge of the drug trade in Warsaw and Willie's crew in particular.

"So, what did you see at the house in the woods?" he asked, as innocently as if he'd asked a little girl if she liked puppies.

"Nothing," Halle said. "Honestly."

"Now, Halle," he said, a creepy grin on his face that caused a cold sweat to break on her brow. He crept the hunting knife across her leg, the razor edge scraping her bare skin. "We both know that isn't the case or you wouldn't have run. What did you see? And don't lie to me because I don't like people who lie to me."

Oh, Christ. What should she say? She stared at the knife, the words stuck in her throat. Shane stopped the blade and pressed the edge into her skin, drawing a line of crimson. Halle stifled a scream.

"I saw your guys in yellow suits," she blurted out.

"What were they doing?"

"Bagging up a bunch of red rock."

"Who was doing it?"

She fought the panic, watching her blood trickle down her thigh and on to the bed. "I couldn't tell. They both had masks on. But after they chased me in the woods and brought me back to the house, I knew it was Willie and Bub and Bennett. I don't know who the guy with the bad teeth was."

"Very good." Shane released the pressure of the blade. "What did they do with the bags?"

"I don't know," she said. "They kept me in the back room until we came here in Willie's truck."

"You came straight here?" Shane asked, resting his hand on Halle's thigh, the blade angled toward her stomach. Her throat tightened as she imagined Shane shoving it forward and gutting her like a deer. A sharp pang of regret sliced through her thinking about the last heated encounter with Mom.

"No, we stopped somewhere and Willie got out for a bit. He left me in the smelly truck with Bub."

"Where?"

Hot tears ran down Halle's cheeks. "I don't know. It was dark. Looked like a barn. Willie was gone for a couple of minutes, then he came back and we drove here. It was a little ways. Took us a while to get here."

"Willie or Bub say anything along the way about a warehouse?"

Warehouse? She shook her head.

"You're doing great, honey," Shane said, his breath hot in her ear. She trembled, scared his hand would slide up her thigh. Oh God, what would she do if it crept any higher? "What did they say in the truck on the drive?"

Halle wanted to lean away, but was too afraid to move. She smelled her own fear in the sweat trickling down her brow.

"They talked about you," Halle said after a moment. Maybe she could deflect Shane's attention off her. She had to keep his interest away from Willie who represented her one chance of getting out of here alive.

"Really? What did they say?"

"Bub said something about taking the stuff and splitting town, running away to Mexico or someplace where you couldn't find them."

"Mexico, huh?" The knuckles on Shane's hand holding the knife whitened with tension.

"But Willie told him to stop talking like that. That you'd find him and kill him. Willie stuck by you and said you were the boss and they needed to do what you said. Bub said he would run as soon as he could."

"Did he now?" Shane took his hard hand from her thigh. He walked over to the window, twirling the knife with his fingers. "Did they...hurt you?"

"No," Halle said. "I think Bub wanted to, but Willie stopped him."

Shane stuck the knife in a sheath on his hip. The coldness faded from his eyes for an instant, like he really saw a scared girl sitting in front of him. He crouched in front of her, taking her hands in his. His fingers were cold as ice.

"Thank you for your honesty, Halle," he said. "I want you to know I'm not going to hurt you as long as you cooperate. Do you believe me?"

Halle nodded. Like she had a choice.

"Now," he continued, "I'm going to have a little chat with Bub and Willie. I've got to figure out where things sit before we make our next move. You hungry?"

Halle shook her head. Her stomach was tied in knots and the thought of food made her want to vomit.

"Well," Shane said, "I'll have something brought to you anyway. You cooperate and this will be over soon."

Shane opened the door and the black mountain stepped over. Shane said something to him and the man walked down the hall. Shane offered her one last look and closed the door behind him.

She pressed the comforter against her bleeding thigh, counting out sixty seconds before combing through the room again searching for anything she could use as a weapon. She froze by the closet when shouts erupted from below, followed by glass breaking and a minute later a blood curdling scream from a man. She huddled on the floor and pressed her hands to her ears wanting to scream herself so she didn't have to hear the never-ending, agonizing cries coming from downstairs. After a minute, a door slid open and slammed against the stops. The muffled screams moved from the floor below to the porch outside. Several thuds echoed and when the screams stopped, she crawled to the window and peeked over the ledge.

The shocked mouth of the creepy rat guard hung agape on the patio before he faced the woods and vomited over the brick wall. Halle leaned forward and pressed her forehead against the warm glass to peer below.

Shane modeled on the patio, bare-chested and covered in blood, holding a crimson-dripping axe. His once slicked back hair draped across the side of his face. His chiseled chest heaved as he took in the mess at his feet. The scream rocketing from Halle's brain caught in her chest at what lay on the ground at Shane's feet. A pair of legs stuck out of denim overalls with Bub's worn brown boots at the feet, sliced muscle and white bone shards sticking out the top. A foot of bloodied patio separated the rest of Bub from his legs. Shane's gaze crept up the house to her window, his eyes wild and wide, blood splatters dotting his face like freckles. His madness a stark contrast to his cool demeanor in the room with her minutes before.

"He ain't runnin' now, sweetheart," Shane yelled to her.

Halle dug her fingers into her crossed arms, everything a haze. What had she done? She just wanted to get Shane out of the room. Though Shane had swung the ax, she realized she'd killed Bub by throwing him to the wolf. As her role in his brutal death sunk in, the scream sticking in her chest unleashed itself.

CHAPTER THIRTY-SIX

Bear kicked him out of the police station to deal with the death of his inmate, promising to call Jake's cell when Bear got free. Jake emerged under the worn, white porch railings of the red-brick structure. He read the etched stone on the front of the building that said it was originally constructed in 1856 as Benton County's first bank called the Mechanic's Bank of St. Louis, the most expensive bank building in Western Missouri at the time. Can't have been much competition.

His cell rang. Keats. "Good morning."

"Is he dead yet?"

"No. Getting close."

Keats's heavy breath crackled the speaker. "Close doesn't count and your time is running out."

Jake ran his hands through his hair, resisting the urge to tear it out. "What about all that bullshit about years of loyal service."

Keats chuckled. "You're trying to leave with all that knowledge turning around in that handsome head of yours. Those years of loyal service are the only reason you're not tied to a fucking chain at the bottom of the Missouri River. I'm giving you a way out, Jake. You gonna to take it or make me do something I don't wanna do?"

"I'm taking it."

"Good. I'd better get a call by midnight."

The line went dead and Jake pocketed the phone. This trip to see his dying father had evolved into a convoluted, A-1 clusterfuck.

Caught dead in the middle of meth, kidnapping, murder. His mind still hadn't wrapped around the fact he had a daughter. Why hadn't he been able to put the timeline of Halle's age together with the length of his absence? It seemed so clear now. His life wasn't worth much, but he'd give it up to get Halle out of this mess. That much he could do. But he needed Bear to make it happen and ensure Jake didn't end up in a body bag of his own. That would take a bit of work. Maybe he could see if those dumbasses he beat by the Community Center were around town.

He walked across the street, under the large oak on the courthouse lawn and stopped at the sidewalk, scanning up and down Main Street. Shit. Too early for the drug dealers to be out and about. He looked toward the shops, thinking of grabbing a bite at one of two open diners since he didn't have a car. He wasn't terribly hungry, but he once had an adventure in Colorado with an ex-army MP who drank more coffee than any other human being he'd ever met. The guy lived by the motto of "Eat when you can." Jake found that to be sound advice, and headed to the diner.

He stopped in front of a store called Lyla's Homemade Fudge, admiring the tasty looking treats and stained glass hanging in the window of the darkened store. Maybe he should've come clean with Bear about the reason he returned home besides waiting for his old man to die. What held him back? They shared the same goal, taking down Shane Langston. The only difference, Bear wanted Langston in a six foot jail cell. Keats wanted him six-feet under.

The diner hid behind a green awning across the street, a dozen heads sitting at tables. If the place was half full, maybe it wasn't half bad. He waited for an old guy in a red Cobra kit car to rumble past and crossed the street. Already muggy at eight in the morning, his shirt clung to the middle of his back.

As he got to the door, he peered inside. Janey's husband, Luther, sat alone at a table, scowling as he stirred his coffee and stared at the chipped Formica in front of him. It might have been sixteen years, but Jake recognized that slack-jawed look of stupidity. Older, balder and fatter, but definitely Luther. A plate of eggs and bacon lay untouched next to his cup. Luther's black, thinning and rumpled hair looked like he'd either just got out of bed or finished with a long night. Jake had no desire whatsoever to talk to his brother-in-law. He spun back toward the courthouse before Luther could spot him.

The troubled appearance of Luther made him think of Janey. He needed to stay close in case Bear wanted to resume the search for Halle. But only two blocks separated her house from the jail, and Jake had his cell. He strolled north at the end of the block on Van Buren and down the hill, the courthouse on the right and the old Roxy Theater on his left, no movie posters or any other signs of life. When did it close? He followed the tree-lined, crumbling sidewalk past Jackson Avenue and veered on to Osage Street.

The cheap, tan vinyl siding covering Janey's house hung crooked. Hardly surprising considering Luther probably did it himself. Sparse grass cropped up among patches of dirt and weeds. A broken walkway led to a front porch with a rusted, metal rocking chair that probably hadn't seen any action since Reagan occupied the White House.

Jake cruised up the sidewalk, the wooden steps groaning under his weight. The front door stood open, a ripped screen door in place to keep out the flies. Did he really want to go in? He knocked, a faded "No Solicitors" sticker slapped to the chipped, white paint. The appearance of the house would eliminate anyone from trying to sell anything.

Inside, Janey's head popped around the corner. She crossed a living room crammed with an ugly, beige couch and a recliner with cushioning threatening to burst through popped seams. Carrying a broom, she swam in a gray Disneyworld sweatshirt. She reached the door and pushed it open. An angry red welt stretched across her cheekbone.

"Jesus," Jake said. "What the hell happened?"

"Nothing." Janey walked back across the living room and into the kitchen with Jake following close behind. She swept dirt from a broken, red clay pot holding a handful of shriveled, green leaves.

"Luther?" Jake asked. Janey didn't confirm or deny it, but the slump of her shoulders solidified the truth. Jake resisted his first instinct to storm to the diner and beat Luther's ass.

"Been awhile since we had a blowup like this," she said. Jake picked up the pieces of the broken pot and searched for a trash can to dump them in. Based on the piles of dishes and crap everywhere, they could easily blend in just lying on the floor where they were.

"What happened?"

She swept up the last of the dirt and dumped it in a cardboard box on a round breakfast table. "It's my fault. I haven't been keeping up the house like I should because I've been dealing with Dad. He came home after being out all night and I started in on him."

"That gives him the right to smack you around? Has it happened before?"

"Once or twice. Not a bad record considering how long we've been married."

Jake could only shake his head at the stupidity of the statement.

"You should leave the dumb son of a bitch."

Janey laughed; a sad laugh. "And go where? Live on what? I'm stashing some extra money away, but I don't have enough to start over."

He could give her some, but that could raise unwanted questions about the source of the funds. "Where are the boys?"

"School. At least they'd better be." She sat at the messy table and took a sip of coffee from a chipped mug, "World's Greatest Mom" on the side. "You want coffee?"

"I'll get it," Jake said. He grabbed a rag off the counter, got some ice from the freezer covered with pictures of his nephews who he hadn't seen since Janey's last Christmas card. They were getting big and, unfortunately, taking after Luther more than Janey. Poor little bastards. He handed the ice to Janey who winced as she laid it against her swollen cheek. He poured a cup of thick coffee into a relatively clean cup. It tasted as bad as it looked.

Janey lit a cigarette and blew out the smoke as she looked into the yard, lip curled in disdain as if she just noticed the clutter of rusted junk, like they tried to have a yard sale a decade ago and left everything that didn't sell there. Jake leaned against the counter, anger boiling at what Luther did to his baby sister, despair at what she let her life do to her, and the ever present guilt for having put her in such a position in the first place.

"You stay at Hospice last night with Daddy?" she asked.

"No. Got him settled in his room. Been dealing with some other stuff."

"Maggie's missing daughter, you mean?"

He almost forgot she worked in the sheriff's office. Hell, everyone in town probably knew about Halle at this point. Not much of a point in letting Janey know Halle was his daughter. She'd find out soon enough.

"What have you heard?"

She flicked the cigarette ashes into the box with the broken pot. "Nothing other than nobody can find her. It ain't good though."

"You don't think she's holed up with some hormonal teenager or a girlfriend?"

"Not Halle. She stirs up a little trouble here and there, but she's a good kid. Spirited like her mom, but she wouldn't do anything stupid like disappear on her own."

"So what's your guess?" Jake asked.

"Beats the hell outta me."

"Tell me about Shane Langston or Willie Banks."

She took a deep drag of her cigarette and dropped the butt into her coffee mug.

"Both drug dealing criminals," she said. "Willie spent a few days in jail with us for possession. Langston is the one you have to watch out for. Mean as a snake."

"You work yesterday? See the kid they brought in?"

"Howie Skaggs? Yeah, I saw him. Bear and Sad Dog talked to him for a while before some lawyer showed up. Bear took off when he went to see you. Howie was sitting alone in a cell when I went home around midnight."

Best not to say anything about Howie still sitting in a cell, but without a pulse. He poured the horrid coffee down the drain and set the cup on top of a pile of noodle-crusted dishes.

"Where can I find Shane?"

"Why?"

"Don't worry about it, Janey. I just need to find him. It's important."

"What the hell have you got yourself mixed up in?"

"Nothing I can't handle. Do you know or not?"

She shook her head. "I don't know. Not sure if I'd tell you even if I did. He's a bad man, big brother."

Goddamn it. He wouldn't get anything out of her. "You working today?"

"No," she said. "Thought I'd go spend some time with Dad. He can't have more than a day or two. Bear told me to stay with him until the end." She climbed to her feet. "You're different, calmer. Figured you'd be out the door looking for Luther."

Jake set his jaw. "Oh, I'll deal with Luther. He isn't getting away with smacking my little sister around."

Janey set the makeshift ice bag in the sink. She placed her tiny hands on Jake's chest with a wide-eyed gaze taking him back to when they were kids. "Leave Luther alone. You'll make things worse for me and the kids. Go with me to Sedalia?"

"I should stay around here, keep looking for Halle. Just waiting for Bear to finish some things at the office."

Janey's brown eyes pleaded, like one of those weathered kittens from an animal shelter poster. "Please, Jake? You can come back

191

quick, but I need you there when I see him. At least at the start."

He couldn't resist those eyes. "Can you drive? I rode in with Bear, and I gotta get Maggie's car anyway."

"Let me go change."

She disappeared up a narrow staircase. Jake leaned against the counter. If his little sister believed he'd let Luther get away with this unscathed, she didn't know him very well. But he had bigger issues to deal with like finding his daughter and Langston. Luther could wait.

CHAPTER THIRTY-SEVEN

Neither of them could think of much to say on the ride to Sedalia. The low volume radio filled the quiet, a local country station that faded to static past Lincoln. Jake called Maggie and let her know where they were going. Still no word from Halle. Maggie's voice trembled and Jake could picture her sitting on the couch in the living room, rocking back and forth, biting her nails and eying the door. He also called Bear but it went straight to voicemail.

"So, what's your plan after he...you know," Janey said.

"Dies? I don't know. Seeing Maggie has been good."

"So, you might stick around for a while?"

"I didn't say all the memories were good, Janey. Hell, I don't know. Maybe it's time for a change."

Janey lit another cigarette, coughed harshly and cracked the window. Her aged Accord already smelled like a bar-room ashtray.

"It'd be nice if you stayed. You're all I got, big brother." She blew out another plume of smoke, her voice dropping to a whisper. "You promised you'd come back."

The miles of open fields darted past, dotted periodically with spotted cows and old farm houses. It didn't seem long ago when his eighteen-year-old self took in a similar scene as he hitchhiked out of town. He carried nothing with him at the time but a bag of clothes and a meager wad of cash.

Janey had sobbed and begged him to stay. He couldn't leave her and Nicky alone with Stony. What about the house? What about Maggie? She listed off a million reasons for him to stay, but none were powerful enough to hold him there. Though the doctors fixed his knee, and he limped slightly, the big dreams were dead. Nothing remained but a burning ball of anger. If he stayed, the ball would erupt and he'd kill Stony. Maybe if he got the hell out of Warsaw, he could breathe. If he could breathe he could let go and start to live. Until he could do that, there'd be nothing for him at home. He'd be no good to anyone or anything. He promised to be back in a few days, too much of a coward to tell anyone the truth. Nothing could quench the anger at what Stony took from him.

Now, the anger for his old man may have dulled, but it still held heat, like the embers of a dying fire. He rested his head against the cool glass of the Accord's passenger window. He was tired of the hate. Exhausted from carrying the guilt of what he left behind. Weary of the loneliness. Stony stole the dream with a couple of drunken swings of a pipe. Maybe when he died, he'd take the anger and the guilt with him to the grave. Maybe then Jake could start to live. With Maggie and Halle in the picture, he had something to live for.

*****

Thirty minutes later they rolled into Sedalia and into the parking lot of Hospice House. Janey coasted to the red-brick building and shut off the car. She yanked her visor and tried to adjust her hair to cover the bruise darkening her cheek. She slammed up the visor at the useless endeavor and climbed out of the car. Jake forced himself to follow suit.

Inside, soft music played in the hallway, one of those elevator-music mix tapes supposed to soothe and comfort. Though Jake found it annoying, he supposed it sounded better than stark silence. Outside of a closed door, a woman in a blue dress cried into the arms of a stoic gray-suited man. Further down the hall, a family laughed quietly as they passed around scrapbooks and ate cookies in a comfortable waiting area by the nurse's station. The laughter a welcome sound in this place.

They walked silently past the waiting area and down a softly lit, brown-carpeted hallway, lined with doors. Some were open, revealing empty beds and others occupied by patients with empty stares. The patients at Hospice lasted mere hours, days or even weeks. The doctors wouldn't give you a timeline.

Stony's door was cracked open a few inches. Janey and Jake waited outside after spotting a nurse inside moving deftly around the cords and monitors attached to their sleeping father, sunken eyes closed and mouth open. After a minute, she emerged. Late forties, dark hair streaked with gray and cropped short. She offered a tight-lipped smile.

"You must be Mr. Caldwell's children," she said. "I can see the family resemblance."

"How is he?" Janey asked. Tears dripped from her eyes like a leaky faucet you could never fully shut off.

"Resting." The nurse reached into her pocket and handed Janey a tissue. "We had a bit of a rough night, but we gave him some medicine to make him comfortable."

"How much longer does he have?" Jake asked. The nurse narrowed her eyes a bit at the coldness in his voice but, to her credit, the hardened stare disappeared as quickly as it appeared.

"We really don't like to speculate. You should talk to his doctor."

"Hours? Days? A week?" Jake pressed.

"If I had to guess, I'd say a day. His breathing is slowing, shallowing out."

"Has he said anything?" Janey asked.

"Not really," the nurse said. "He's cried out a few times but at this stage, he's not likely to say much. I'll be at the station if you need anything."

She patted Janey on the arm and left them. They entered the

room, the smell of death and antiseptic cleaner overpowering. Janey sat in a chair positioned by the bed and broke down as soon as she touched Stony's hand. On the other side of the bed, Jake leaned against the window cutout, as far from his father as possible.

Stony looked a hundred times worse than when Jake brought him in yesterday. With all that happened with Maggie and Halle, dropping him off at Hospice seemed like a week ago. Stony's skin was jaundiced, the color of an old bruise. He lay on his back with his head tilted into a thin, blue pillow, mouth ajar. His breaths were rattled, labored and few. Almost as if his body forgot how to breathe, and Jake envisioned long hours waiting for the last one.

Jake's limbs tingled, anxious and jittery. Watching Janey holding their father's hand and talking about the good things she remembered made him want to hit something hard. He'd rather be out with Bear looking for Halle, rather be sitting with Maggie. Hell, chasing some scumbag who skipped out of paying Keats down a dark alley would be better than sitting in this death room.

Janey blathered about Christmas when she was five years old. She thanked Stony for getting her the Tiny Town dollhouse she'd wanted, even though they didn't have any at Walmart in town. She wondered where he'd gotten it, how hard he must have scoured the earth for it. Jake wouldn't tell her he and Nicky got her the dollhouse. He and Nicky lifted the keys to the truck when Stony passed out. He and Nicky drove to Sedalia when they weren't even old enough for a license. He and Nicky switched price tags on the dollhouse with something less expensive so it fell within the range of the meager dollars they'd scraped together. He and Nicky wrapped it and put it under the tree. Stony took credit for it and the two boys were smart enough to keep quiet.

He couldn't take the lovefest anymore and pushed off the window ledge to leave.

"Jake," she said. "You can talk to him, you know? He can hear you."

"He doesn't want to hear anything I have to say." Jake grasped the footboard rail like he was trying to crush it with his bare hands.

"Sure he does. If you just…"

A low croak emanated from Stony. Janey stopped mid-sentence and they both leaned in when the sound repeated. Stony struggled to say something. His emaciated jaw fished open and shut, his eyes clamped as the sound came out again. Janey reached over and grabbed a cloth, dropping the end in a glass of water on a rolling tray. She wrung out a little and wiped it across Stony's cracked lips. Their father brought his lips together and drank in the few drops Janey offered. His eyes opened to a slit and his wandering pupils settled on Janey.

"Janey," he said, whispering, struggling. "My little Janey girl."

Janey sobbed, dropping her head to his shoulder for a minute. Jake stayed at the foot of the bed while she pulled herself together. When she raised her head, she stroked his cheek.

"I'm here, Papa," she said. "We're both here."

Stony's eyes cracked opened, a sliver of a dull glaze. His head rotated slightly toward Jake. His eyes crimped shut again, and a single tear rolled out and slid down his yellowed cheek.

"I'm sorry," he said. "I'm so sorry."

"Sorry for what, Papa?" Janey asked.

"Sorry," Stony repeated. His eyes unclenched and his jaw hung open. Jake held his breath. Was this it? Seconds later, the labored breathing came back. He slept again, the wet trail of the single tear clinging to the side of his weathered face.

"What do you think he was sorry for?" Janey asked, stroking their father's cheek.

"Lots of things," Jake said. "Most things."

Janey's dark eyes flared. "It is never too late to apologize for wrongs done." A phrase their mother used to say all the time. How in the hell did Janey even know about it?

"Just because he said it, doesn't mean I have to accept it."

"He's dying, Jake. What's done is done. You don't have much longer to forgive him."

He resisted the urge to slide on the jagged gold ring and punch Stony with it for dredging up this shit Jake had buried years ago. Instead, he unclenched the bed frame and walked out the door before Janey could say anything else. As he clumped up the hallway toward the exit, it occurred to him that today was the first time he ever heard his father say "I'm sorry" and the first tear he ever saw from the man's eyes. Too little, too late. One of Stony's favorite aphorisms.

He reached Maggie's car. Inside, his large hands rubbed the steering wheel like a worry stone. He closed his eyes, Stony's gaunt face looming large, the words "I'm sorry" tumbling out of his mouth and the tear rolling down his cheek. Jake pounded the dashboard with a fist, started the car and darted out of the Hospice House parking lot. The old bastard actually made Jake feel sorry for him.

CHAPTER THIRTY-EIGHT

Halle's throat burned from screaming, the image of Bub's bloody stumps sitting at Shane's feet forever carved in her brain. Her fear from being chased through the woods, kidnapped and locked in some house in the middle of nowhere was nothing compared to the unparalleled terror of Shane's sadistic brutality. Bub may have been a piece of garbage, but even he didn't deserve the fate she delivered him. Dear God, forgive her.

She gripped a long, rusty nail in her shaking hand, lodged between her first and middle fingers, under a pillow. Her fingertips were raw and bloody from working the nail up from the floorboard under the bed. If Shane came in and wanted to do anything to her, he'd be in for one hell of a surprise. If she could get it through his eye and into his brain, he'd drop hard like a stone. She had to wait for the right moment, lay still and act like she'd been shocked into a catatonic state. Although acting wouldn't be too hard given the circumstances.

A knock at the door jolted her awake. Her brain swam as it clawed itself back from sleep. How long had she been out? Through her window, the eastern sun floated in the distance, maybe ten in the morning. She focused on the golden knob rotating slowly and ran her raw thumb over the base of the nail, pushing it against her fingers and locking it in place.

"Halle?" Willie asked, poking his head through the door opening, his tone quiet and innocent. Was he afraid to come in? He slinked through the door and crossed the room, squatting at the side of the bed. She focused on the wall as if he weren't there, looking through him.

"Halle?" he repeated. "You in there? Listen, I know that was crazy with Bub. I know it's a lot to take in and it don't look like you're doing it too well."

A lot to take in? Was he freaking serious? Bub...in half...her fault. She squeezed the image from her head, her fear turning to anger when the bloody mess wouldn't go away, tightening her grip on the nail. Willie dropped his forehead on the side of the bed. She could use the nail. He wasn't looking, but her hand trembled, wanting nothing more than to let the spike of metal go. If she used it, was she any better than Shane?

"Do you believe in God, Willie?"

Willie jerked his head up as if surprised she spoke. "Why?"

"Do you?"

Willie leaned forward on the bed, searching the quilted pattern for an answer. "I'd like to think there is a God. That he created the Earth and there's a hell for those who deserve it."

"Does Shane deserve it?"

He glanced sideways at her. "I'm not gonna answer that."

"Do you deserve it?"

"I don't know," he said after a beat. "I always worry that what I'm doing is gonna condemn me, but I don't know what the hell else to do. I'm trapped here, same as you."

Halle reached out and rested her hand on his. "I wonder if I deserve it. I don't want to die, Willie."

"I got an idea," Willie said, placing his other hand on hers. "I got an idea but I can't do it with you like this. I think I can get us both out of this alive, but I need your help."

Help her? It seemed impossible. To get past Shane and the monster of a bodyguard would be miracle enough. But then there would be the creepy guy from the patio and at least three other people carrying big guns. Who knew how many others there were. She could stab Willie through those stupid brown eyes and try to escape on her own but she wouldn't make it to the front door. Willie was her only possible ticket out of here. She had no choice but to trust him.

Halle pushed herself up on to one elbow. "What's your idea?"

CHAPTER THIRTY-NINE

It neared eleven in the morning when Jake turned into Maggie's driveway. He fought off Stony's skeletal image with a single hot tear leaking out of those clenched eyes. He pulled in behind Bear's truck and stepped out.

Bear and Maggie talked on her front porch. Bear held a glass of tea in one hand and Maggie's hand in the other. Her red, puffy eyes found Jake as he climbed the front steps.

"Any word?" Jake asked.

"No. You go see your dad?" she asked. Jake nodded and offered a tight-lipped smile. Only Maggie, with her daughter missing, would have the kindness of heart to ask.

Jake handed her the keys to her car. "I took Janey and we went together. Now you're not stranded."

She stood. "I'm going to make a few more calls to Halle's friends. See if they've heard anything."

Jake took her hand as she passed and kissed her on her cheek. She returned the kiss and disappeared into the house.

"She's holding together better than I would," Bear said.

"She's strong. Stronger than me. Maybe her daughter has the same steel in her."

"She does. Everything okay with Stony?"

"Stony's dying. The sooner the better." Jake climbed on the porch and dropped into a rocker. "Get anything from the guy at the jail?"

"You mean the guy who slammed a shiv into Howie's skull? Nah. He ain't sayin' anything."

Bear set his glass on the wicker table between them and leaned forward.

"Who is he?" Jake asked.

"Don't know. Nobody in my office recognizes him. Can't run fingerprints on him because the scumbag burned them off somewhere in his miserable existence. I shot his picture around to some folks in Kansas City and St. Louis. They're going to check around and see if anybody knows him. He's tied to Shane, I know it."

"How?"

"Guy pulled into town last night and did donuts in the middle of Main Street. Had a bag of weed sitting on the dashboard and gave up without a fight. He wanted to get in the jail cell with Howie."

"How soon after the lawyer left did this guy show up?"

"Thirty minutes, maybe," Bear said. "You thinking what I'm thinking?"

"Yup. Old Shane got nervous. How'd he get the shiv into the cell?"

"That's what I'm trying to figure out. Could be half a dozen guys. Somebody in my crew is playing both sides of the fence. No doubt about it."

"Any idea who?" Jake asked. Bear shook his head. "Get anything from the house?"

"It was Royce Weather's place," Bear said. "Royce died and his wife left town a couple of years ago. My guys scoured the house and the woods around it. Verified somebody did a cook there recently. Pretty clean considering the usual shit we find. We're checking for prints. Didn't find anything in the woods other than Halle's iPod and the Devil Ice. The one lead we had tying this to Langston was Howie and he's stuck on a slab in the morgue."

"We can still use him as a lead," Jake said.

"Ayuh. Howie was in Willie Banks' crew. We're trying to find Willie, his brother and Bub Sievers. My guys are checking the usual places, but haven't found anything yet."

"Wish I could do something."

"You can," Bear said. "Come with me over to Willie's trailer. We'll toss it and see what we can come up with. The little taint jockey is tied up in this thing somehow. If we can link him to the cook house, we can link him to Halle."

Jake didn't want to ask the question, like it would be some kind of bad luck. But he needed Bear's opinion.

"Think she's still alive?"

Bear pressed his lips together. He peered through the front door at Maggie sitting on the couch with the phone pressed to her ear.

"I sure as hell hope so, partner. I sure as hell hope so. I got a bad feeling we're running out of time."

Keats' deadline loomed. If Bear only knew how short time really was.

*****

Willie paced the floor of the den, smoking and thinking. He couldn't stop his hands from shaking. The image of Shane beating on Bub while Antonio and some other mountain man held Bub down stuck in his brain, playing an unwelcome loop. Shane bombarded Bub with questions about his plans on skipping town, each question drawing another face strike whether Bub answered it or not. How the hell had Shane found out about that? Was his truck bugged? After twenty minutes, Bub's face held the consistency of raw hamburger, and he dipped in and out of consciousness.

The barrage of vicious swings should've worn Shane down, but with each punch he grew more agitated and ferocious. The last ripped Bub's three hundred pounds from the captor's hold and he crashed to the floor, his head bouncing off the hardwood.

"Fucking run on me, will you?" Shane screamed, lashing out a boot and cracking Bub in the side of the head. Shane's once slicked-back hair flapped over his brow, his eyes wide and mad. "I'll show you what happens to pieces of shit who run from me. Steal from me."

Shane scanned the room but couldn't seem to locate what he wanted. His eyes settled on Willie for a minute, but Willie turned away quickly. He wanted to get the hell out of there, but there was no telling what Shane would do if he ran. He forced himself to stay anchored to the wall, pressing into the paint. Shane locked in on something past Willie on the patio outside. He walked through the door and came back in moments later with an ax in hand.

"No," Bub groaned from the floor. His beaten eyes swollen to mere slits, but wide enough to grasp what was about to happen.

"Gag and drag this asshole outside." Shane removed his shirt and threw it on the couch. His bodyguards stuffed a rag in Bub's mouth and grabbed his arms, dragging him across the floor. Shane followed, his lean, ripped frame holding the ax like a Samurai warrior. Willie stayed at the wall, afraid to move. With each thunk, Willie's knees gave way a little at a time and he slid down the paneled wall. Bub's muffled screams forced their way through Willie's hands covering his ears. By the time the horror stopped, Willie sat on the floor, heart pounding and sick to his stomach.

Thirty minutes later, he paced, waiting for Shane to come back, his plan with Halle rolling through his head. It was a long shot and worthless if he was the next one to get the ax. As Willie crushed his cigarette into the ashtray on the coffee table, Shane returned, freshly showered and wearing a new set of jeans with his patented, tight gray T-shirt. He must have a dozen of those things. He crossed the room and poured a drink from the crystal carafe on the bar. Shane's cell rang while he poured.

"Yeah," Shane said, setting the bottle down, brow furrowed. "Who is it? What did he want? You get a plate? Okay, make the call and track it down. Call me when you find out." He hung up the phone and tossed it on the bar. "Want a drink, Willie?" This time Willie didn't refuse. Shane poured and handed it to him.

"Thanks." Willie took the glass, gripping it tight so his trembling hands didn't drop it. He sat on the couch and gulped the amber liquid, which burned all the way to his stomach.

"You see anyone poking around town asking about me?" Shane asked. Willie's cheeks tightened. Bub's bloody corpse made him worried about his omission to Shane about the stranger beating Bub and the Sterretts, and he shook his head.

Shane took a chair on the other side of the coffee table. "Sorry about that back there with Bub. Had to be done."

"Did it?" Willie asked, focusing on the ashtray on the table rather than face Shane's gaze. Bub may have been a dirtball, but he was Willie's friend all the same. In any case, no man should have to die that way. It was fucking medieval.

"I won't tolerate desertion or theft, Willie. Little Halle in there told me what Bub said and you confirmed it. I figure it had to be Bub who stole the money from the warehouse. Hell, even if he didn't, it was a matter of time before he did something stupid and exposed everything you and I have worked hard to build. The message had to be sent. You think anyone in my organization will dare question me after that?"

"No, sir," Willie said. Not if they like their legs attached. He sipped the Scotch, face scrunching as it worked its way down. "You could've just shot him, though."

Shane laughed. He took a swig of his drink. "You scared of me, Willie?"

"Most definitely," Willie replied, bobbing his head like a rooster. A little wood carving of a deer sat on the table. He pictured the deer in the woods with its legs chopped off, Shane bare-chested and holding a blood-dripping ax.

"You worried I'm going to hurt you?"

"A little."

"Don't. You've been straight with me and I know you'd never betray me. I'm not going to hurt you, I'm going to promote you."

Willie's eyes narrowed in confusion. What the hell? From worried Shane would take him out next to a light at the end of the tunnel. Where the light led remained to be seen.

"I want to expand your territory," Shane said. "I've got a new product line I'm delving into. Easier to make, more profitable, and nowhere near as high on the radar of local law enforcement as meth."

Shit. A new product line? So much for making a big score and fading into the sunset. Then again, something with high profitability and lower risk would still allow him to make his escape in a few years. "What is it?"

"Cannibinoids," Shane said.

"What the hell is that?"

"You hear of K2, Spice, synthetic marijuana?"

"Yeah, never tried it though."

"Don't," Shane said. "There's a reason they label the packages 'not for human consumption.' Doesn't mean we can't make a profit off it because there's plenty of idiots out there wanting to get high on the stuff."

"Why mess with dope?"

"It's not dope. You basically get the chemical, spray it on some natural herbs, bag it up in a colorful package which draws the kids' attention and bingo. Costs nothing to make and you sell it for ten bucks a gram."

Colorful packages selling for cheap that gets kids high? He had his doubts. "And the cops don't track it?"

"Oh, they're after it. The reason we're even talking about it is because of a big bust in Kansas City in October. Cops seized over twenty-four thousand packets of the stuff and a hundred grand in cash. Teddy Garrett got pinched and that leaves an opening for yours truly. Keats is bucking for the territory, but I'm going to wedge my way in before he gets the chance."

"How do I fit in?" Willie asked.

"I like you, Willie. You know how to maintain a low profile and you don't make stupid mistakes. I'm expanding into Kansas City and St. Louis with this. I've been in contact with some suppliers and I've got the lowdown on the distribution. You help me expand the web in Kansas City, hit both sides of the state line. We both make a shitload of money. You up for it?"

A change of scenery would be welcome. Get the hell out of Warsaw and Benton County. If he could save enough money over the next few years, he could get out of this violent world and do something legitimate, maybe open a bar or a liquor store. Still, there were loose ends.

"What about Howie and Bennett?"

"Howie's done. That leaves one of your crew, assuming Bennett isn't going to cause me any trouble about his brother."

He was afraid to ask what "done" meant after what Shane did to Bub. "You can't get Howie out of this?"

"He's dead, Willie. Got shanked in the eye in the jailhouse this morning."

Willie closed his eyes, trying not to react. He liked Howie and Shane just killed him. Two of his crew wiped out in one day. Play it cool, man. Never let 'em see you sweat.

"Bennett ain't gonna be happy," Willie said. "But random violence happens in this business, right?"

Shane winked. "You're going to need some additional help. I have a couple of guys I can move over from Sedalia while you're setting up in Kansas City. Bennett can handle the business here. Cool?"

Time to address the elephant in the room. "What about the girl?"

Shane held up his drink and swirled its contents, the light dancing in and out of the liquid.

"I'm not a monster, Willie. I don't want to kill a child. But she can't go home now. She's seen too much."

"I'll take her with me," Willie said, the perfect opening for his plan.

"She won't stay. She'll run to the cops the first chance she gets and you know it."

Willie fell silent. All the reasons he came up with to plead his case were stupid. He couldn't think of a logical argument. But maybe he could keep her contained until he made enough in Kansas City to run far, far away. Maybe she would run with him. Until then, he had to convince Shane keeping her alive wouldn't come back to bite him in the ass. He had to convince Shane he was tough and couldn't let him know of his love for Halle.

"I've got a plan," Willie said. "I'll keep the bitch drugged up and with me. I've been waiting to tap her ass for a couple years now. Either she comes to appreciate me or I'll deal with her."

Shane drained his drink and set the glass on the table. "Tap that ass all you want, but she isn't leaving this house. She's seen everything. She could take us all down and I can't risk it. Show me you're committed to the cause, Willie."

Willie's gut clenched, and he lowered his head, closing his eyes. Shane said he wasn't a monster and wouldn't kill a child, but he expected Willie to.

"You told me to bring her here," Willie said.

"Yeah, probably not my wisest decision ever," Shane said. He had the gall to laugh about it. "But it would've ended the same anyway. She saw me, you and your crew, the meth and my cook. She's gotta go."

Willie drained the rest of the Scotch. He shivered as it scorched its way down through his chest. He had to agree with Shane for now or he'd end up with a couple of bloody stumps for legs. Shane's phone rang, and Willie jumped.

Shane snatched up the phone on the bar. "Yeah?" His face crunched. "Who? Find him and find out what the hell he's doing here." He listened and poured another drink, the confusion turning to anger. "I don't want your excuses. You're getting paid to find that shit out. Do it."

Shane slammed the phone on the bar and threw the Scotch into the back of his throat. He sat on the couch and breathed out.

"Can I count on you to take care of this, Willie?"

"How long do I have?"

"I want you on the road to Kansas City by dark. That gives you a few hours to do what you need to do. You my man, Willie? I have to know if you're on board."

"I'm on board, Shane. You can count on me."

"That's what I want to hear. You got two hours to prove it to me. You take care of the girl and show me you have a stake in this game, or I'll kill you both."

There it was, the ultimatum. As much as it made his skin crawl, Willie shook Shane's outstretched hand and walked down the hall. Kill sweet little Halle. If he didn't, Shane or one of his crew would. Shane would kill both Willie and Bennett in the process and start over in Benton County. He stopped in the entry way and called Bennett on his cell, telling him to go to his trailer and bring his stash, his gun and his "hit the road in a hurry" duffel bag he stashed in his closet. He hung up and traced the shadows to Halle's closed door, feet like lead weights, wondering what in the hell he would do.

CHAPTER FORTY

Jake braced himself against the dash as Bear bounced his truck along the rutted dirt road leading to Willie's trailer off Poor Boy Road. A few black trash bags adorned the otherwise empty clearing around the mobile home. If not for the fresh bags, one could make the case someone abandoned the dump years ago.

Bear threw the truck in park. "No Shangri-La, is it?" Jake said.

"Hell, this is a pretty nice trailer compared to some of the ones in the back roads around here. He must have some money stashed somewhere because he sure as hell ain't spending his drug money here."

"What's the game plan?"

"I doubt we get this lucky, but let's make sure Halle isn't here," Bear said, opening the door. Jake followed him to the front of the trailer. An uncovered window in the front revealed a dark but neatly maintained living room with a chair, couch and lamp without a shade. Bear pounded on the front door. No answer. He tried the knob, locked.

"Shit," Bear said.

They split up, walking around either side of the trailer and meeting at the back door set above rotting wood steps. Ratty sheets covered the windows. Jake tried the latch, which was also locked.

"Too bad I'm a cop," Bear said, eyebrows raised. "Or I would kick the door in."

"Good thing I'm here." Jake leaned back and thrust his leg forward. The kick was strong, the door not so much. Jake's leg burrowed a hole through the center, the momentum propelling him forward, burying his leg to his crotch. Bear almost fell to the ground, doubled over with laughter, hands grasping his knees. Jake joined him.

"That shit never happens in the movies," Jake said, working his leg back through the hole.

Bear wiped the tears away. "Jesus God, if this wasn't illegal, I'd snap a picture with my phone."

"Good thing you're such a law-abiding officer of the court."

Jake cleared his leg and reached through the opening. He found the lock and seconds later they were inside Willie's trailer. A quick search found nothing helpful. The only thing of value was a collection of old vinyl records. Def Leppard, Iron Maiden, Black Sabbath. At least Willie had good taste in music.

"That would've been too easy, anyway," Bear said. "Let's hit the town and find the little douche weasel."

They started toward the back door when approaching tires crunched over gravel. Their eyes met and they ran to the living room. A beat-up Mazda pulled into the clearing. A young man with chopped, black hair and a few days stubble on his cheeks emerged from the car and stopped, his wary eyes darting between Bear's truck and the trailer.

"Who's that?" Jake asked.

"Bennett Skaggs. Dead Howie's brother and one of Willie's crew. Let's get out there before he puts two and two together and bolts. Go out the back. I don't want him to know we were inside."

They hustled out the door and trotted alongside the trailer. Jake had to admit Bear still moved pretty well for a big man. By the time they reached the front, Bennett had jumped back into his car and slammed the door shut.

Bear pulled out his pistol and pointed it at the car. "Stop right there, Bennett," he yelled. Bennett mouthed an expletive and raised his hands.

Seconds later, Bear had him against the car, frisking him. He threw a cell phone, wallet, a pack of smokes and a lighter on to the hood of the car.

"Damn, Bear," Bennett said. "What's this about?"

"Shut up," Bear growled. "Watch him."

Bear walked back to the open car door and rooted around inside. He paused in the middle of the search and stuck his head out the door.

"Bennett? I got your permission to search your car?"

"Hell, no," Bennett yelled. Bear looked at Jake who smacked Bennett upside the head.

"How about now?" Bear asked.

"Go to hell," Bennett said, scowling at Jake.

Jake bounced Bennett's head off the hood of the Mazda. "We can do this all day long, dickhead."

"Okay, okay," Bennett said, wobbling on his feet. "You got my permission."

"Why thank you for your cooperation. Much appreciated." Bear laughed and resumed the search.

"You look scared, man," Jake said.

Bennett's beady eyes narrowed. "Who the fuck are you?"

"Probably the only thing standing between you and an ass kicking of epic proportions."

"I didn't do shit," Bennett said. From the driver's seat, Bear raised a baggie of red crystals like the ones they found at the cook house. Jake crowded Bennett to keep his eyes away from his car. Bear climbed out empty handed. He walked to Bennett and sandwiched him between he and Jake.

"Where's Willie?" Bear asked.

"You tell me. I came by to have a beer and say hey."

"You better not be drinking. You're barely nineteen."

"Oh yeah," Bennett said. "I meant to say I stopped by to have a Coke."

Bear shot a hand forward and clamped a vise grip on the kid's face.

"I don't have time for games. Where's Willie?"

Bear released the kid's face, having grabbed his attention.

Bennett rubbed his reddened cheeks. "Don't know. Haven't seen him in a couple of days."

"You seen Halle Holden?" Bear asked.

Bennett's eyes darted between the two of them.

"Why?" he asked.

"I'm askin' the fuckin' questions. That okay with you?"

"Just around town, but not in the last couple of days," Bennett said, rolling his scrawny shoulders. "Definitely not as much as I'd like to."

Jake resisted the urge to backhand the little shit. Seemed different when the kid talked about his daughter, his personal stakes now totally raised.

"She's missing," Bear said.

"That's what I heard. But, like I said, I ain't seen her in a couple of days."

"What about Willie? He seen her?"

"Don't know that either," Bennett said. Good try by Bear to trip him up, but the kid didn't bite. "Like I said, I ain't seen him for a couple of days."

"You haven't seen much of anybody lately, Bennett."

"Nope, I've been a good boy, Sheriff."

"How about Howie?"

"I haven't, but I know you have. I heard he got pinched and is sittin' in your jail cells."

Bear leaned in close. The kid's cocky grin faltered and disappeared when Bear spoke again.

"I don't have Howie in my jail cell anymore. He's currently resting on a cold slab in the county morgue."

Bennett's dark eyes darted between Jake and Bear.

"Bullshit," he said, though without much conviction.

"No, that's true shit," Bear said. "Somebody, and I'm going to take a wild guess you know who, had a guy shove a steel pick into his brain. Howie was dead before he hit the floor."

"Bull...shit," Bennett repeated. His eyes took on a faraway gaze of disbelief. He squatted, rested his elbows on his knees and buried his face into his palms. After a moment, Bennett raised his head. The bravado was gone, leaving nothing but tears in the eyes of a scared kid. Jake could empathize and almost felt sorry for him.

"We're looking for Willie and for Halle. You hear from or see either one of them, you call me." He tossed a business card on the ground at Bennett's feet. "Remember, you know who did this. He's cleaning up loose ends. God help you if you're one of them."

Bennett remained by his car as Jake and Bear crossed the clearing and got back in the truck. Bear started it up and rolled back out the drive toward Poor Boy Road.

"I saw the baggie of Devil Ice you raised up," Jake said. "Better to let him lead you to Willie than to bust him for it."

"He's the last lead we got. Besides, Langston would kill him like his brother if I put him in a jail cell."

"So, are we going to follow him?"

"Nope. Stashed a GPS tracker under his seat. He went to the trailer for a reason. My guess is he's picking up something for Willie. He'll mill around town for a bit to make sure we're not following him, but he'll find Willie eventually."

"You're smarter than you look, you know?"

Bear grinned. "Don't tell anyone."

*****

At high noon, Willie knocked on the door to Halle's room, still

215

unsure what to tell her. He waited for an answer that didn't come and went in. Halle lay on the bed, facing away from the door. She looked so helpless. He could just crawl into bed with her and hold her, stroke that beautiful head and tell her everything would be okay. Then, she turned to look at him, and the fear in her eyes blew the fantasy away.

"We got a problem, Halle," he said.

"He's not going to let me leave, is he?"

Willie wanted to wipe away her pain. Just grab her hand and run like the wind, take her to safety, be her hero. "I'm sorry. I'm so sorry you're caught up in this."

"But you said you have a plan. You said you were going to get me out of this."

"I was gonna take you with me, but Shane said that ain't going to happen. God help me, I'm supposed to kill you."

Halle pushed away and rammed into the backboard of the bed. She braced herself with her muscular legs and held out a long, rusty nail between her fingers. Willie jumped back.

"Where'd you get that?"

"Never mind where," she said, voice wavering. "You get the hell away from me or I swear…I'll gouge your eyes out."

Willie held out his hands, eyes darting to the door. "Halle, please…"

"You let me go!" she screamed, tears rolling down her cheeks. "You let me go."

Willie's heart pounded; his stomach rolled and shoulders tensed. All the wrong turns he'd made, his stupid, wasteful life in pursuit of money, dealing poison to his friends and neighbors, cutting the legs off his future before he'd even given them a chance to take him anywhere. He traveled down a dead-end road to nowhere. The last twelve hours proved he'd rather be homeless than make another dime through Shane. He'd rather die than let anything happen to this innocent girl he loved.

"I'm not going to hurt you, Halle," he said in a low voice. "I'm going to find a way to get you out of here, but you have to trust me." He reached for the nail shaking in her clenched hands, her breathing heavy and desperate. He slowly moved his hand forward, maintaining reassuring eye contact to show her he cared. It worked. She handed it over.

"Why in the hell should I trust you?" she whispered.

"Because he wants you dead by nightfall and I'm the only one who can save you."

CHAPTER FORTY-ONE

Seconds after they pulled back on to Poor Boy, Jake's cell buzzed. Janey.

"Hey," he answered. "You still at Hospice?"

Janey's breath hitched over the phone. "It's time, Jake. I need you here."

"You sure? Thought we had a day."

"Doctor said he's almost gone," she said. She went through a bout of sniffles and sobs. "I can't do this by myself. Can you come?"

"I'm on my way," he said. "Hang in there." He pressed the cell to his mouth.

"It's time, huh?" Bear said as they rolled past Turkey Creek Cemetery. Jake looked back, catching a glimpse of his mother and brother's tombstones. Wouldn't be long until Stony would be lying next to them.

"What are the odds we'd be driving by there when I get the call?" Jake turned to Bear, shaking his head. Bear glanced over, but said nothing. "Can you take me to my truck? It's parked at Maggie's. I'll hook up with you as soon as I can."

"No problem. I'll keep an eye on Bennett and buzz you if he makes a move. I think we may have a couple hours until he tries to get to Willie. He'll be too worried I'm tailing him."

Bear parked under the large oak out front of Maggie's. Maggie emerged from the front door to greet him with a hug and an expectant stare.

"Anything?" she asked.

"Nothing on Halle. Janey called. Stony's close to going out and I'm heading up there."

"You want me to go with you? I'm going to go crazy if I sit in this house doing nothing."

"You sure?"

"I keep wandering the halls, staring at pictures, looking through her closet, wondering if I'm ever going to see her again. I have to get out of here. Let me come with you, okay?"

Jake nodded. "Yeah, I'd like that a lot, Mags."

A minute later they sped toward Sedalia, leaving Bear behind to track Bennett.

Thirty minutes later, Jake pushed through the double doors of Hospice House with Maggie at his side, the drone of the early afternoon trucks rolling along Highway 65 replaced with piped-in soothing music. He stopped, his skin crawling the closer they got to the room.

"You don't need to be here," he said. "Hell, I shouldn't be here. We should be out there looking for Halle."

Maggie put her cool hand in his and pulled him toward Stony's room. "Bear's on the case. He'll call you if something breaks. Come on."

Seconds later, they stood at Stony's room. Jake reached for the handle, but left his hand hanging in mid-air. Did he really have to do this?

Maggie put her hand on his shoulder. "I'm right here. You need to do this."

He opened the door. Janey sat in a chair facing the bed, holding Stony's fingers in one hand and a wadded up tissue in the other. She looked up when Jake entered, Maggie stopping at the door.

"I think this is it," Janey said, getting up. She wrapped Jake with her scrawny arms, heaved a few sobs and pulled back. She tried to wipe her tears from Jake's shirt. "Sorry."

"Don't be," Jake said. "What did the doc say?"

Janey moved to the foot of the bed. "Not much. That it wouldn't be long now."

"Stony say anything?"

"No. He's pretty drugged up. They're just trying to make sure he's comfortable at this point."

They spent the next couple of hours waiting, a few snippets of awkward conversation mixed in, but mostly silence. They munched on sandwiches brought in by volunteers, while nurses slinked in and out to check Stony's vitals. Jake checked in with Bear periodically, but Bennett hadn't made a move. Jumbled emotions pounded him. A thousand memories spinning around in a whirlwind. When he had a bead on them, he spoke.

"Can you give me a minute alone with him?"

Janey nodded, gave Maggie a quick hug and stepped outside.

"I'll be outside with Janey if you need me," Maggie said.

"No, stay. Please," Jake said. He needed her there.

Jake lowered himself in the chair stationed by the bed. Stony's cheeks were drawn, like he sucked them in. His mouth hung open and drew in labored gasps under closed, puffy eyes. Maggie rested her hands on Jake's shoulders. How should he begin? The words caught in his throat. He took a deep breath.

"I don't know what to say to you, Stony," Jake said at last. "I haven't said more than a handful of words to you in sixteen years. I sit here and look at you and all I feel is the fucking pain you've caused."

Maggie's hands tightened on his shoulders. Then she stroked his head and neck. The coolness of her soothing touch helped fight the anger like water on fire. Stony's ring hummed from Jake's front pocket.

"I haven't been a good person," he continued. "I've...hurt people using the tricks I learned from you. I sometimes lay awake at night and try to think back…try to figure out what I did to make you hate me so much. I've been running from your ghost for years even though you're not dead yet. I've been running from myself because of the man I was turning into. And I'm tired of running. I'm tired of hating you. I want to forgive you, but I don't know if I can."

Stony's eyes scrunched as if a wave of pain swept through his frail body. After a moment, dirty brown eyes creeped open and fixed on the popcorn ceiling before sweeping to Jake's face.

"Nicky," Stony whispered. "Oh my God, Nicky. It's you."

Stony's hand trembled upward from the bed, searching. Jake sat still as a stone until Maggie knelt by the chair, took Jake's hand and placed it in his father's outstretched palm. The old man's weak fingers closed around it.

"Nicky," Stony repeated. "I'm so sorry."

"It's okay, Pop," Jake said. "It's almost over."

"Tell Jake…tell Jake I'm sorry. I'm so damn sorry for what I did. So sorry."

Stony's voice trailed away and his eyes closed again. His breath hitched once, twice, and stopped. Jake waited for his chest to rise again, but it never did. A single tear rolled from the corner of Stony's eye and dropped on the white pillow. He was gone—now nothing but a shell. *Tell Jake I'm sorry.* Jake always wondered if Stony remembered what he did, if he even regretted it. Now Jake knew, but did the deathbed confession change anything? He pulled his hand back and stood. Maggie enveloped him in her arms.

"I'm sorry," she said. Jake kissed her forehead and opened the door. Janey leaned against the window in the hall, eyes cast wide like a miracle recovery was even a possibility. The somber expression on his face killed the idea and she began to cry. She'd wanted nothing more than to be there when Stony died and Jake robbed her of that. But he couldn't take on any more guilt. Instead, he hugged her tight.

"It's over, Janey," he said. She sobbed into his chest for a moment and pulled back. She reached up and stroked his stubbled cheek then went back into the room. Maggie hugged her and Jake's cell phone vibrated.

"How's Stony?" Bear asked.

"He's gone."

"Damn, Jake. I'm sorry. You okay?"

"I don't know," Jake said. "I suppose so."

"Look, I know my timing sucks, but Bennett is going to be on the move soon. He's been cooling his heels at the Turn It Loose for the last couple hours, but he's going to be hooking up with Willie soon and I know that little fucker has Halle. This might be our last shot."

"Who else is joining the cavalry?"

"Just you and me, partner. Somebody got the shank inside that killed Howie. Somebody has been feeding info to Langston. I don't know who I can trust in my department."

"Where do you want to meet?"

"Call me when you get close. We'll see where that little bastard is by then."

Jake hung up. Maggie waited in the hall.

"Bear?" she asked. "What did he say?"

"We might have a lead on Halle, but I gotta get back to Warsaw. I'll explain on the way."

He started walking then stopped. He should go back in the room and tell Janey he was leaving. But he didn't have time to explain everything. Instead, he grabbed Maggie, and they strode through Hospice House and into the late afternoon heat. As they headed south on Highway 65, the sun began its descent in the west and Jake had a sinking feeling their time ran short.

CHAPTER FORTY-TWO

Jake drove on to Maggie's drive and found Bear waiting for him. On the way, Maggie took the news about Willie, Shane and the death of Howie Skaggs better than he expected, considering known drug dealers and murderers had their daughter. Maybe the fact that Jake and Bear had a lead through Bennett helped her maintain her composure.

"Let's take your truck," Bear said. "They'll spot mine a mile away."

Bear slung a rifle case in the back along with a large, blue duffel bag. He hoisted his large frame into the passenger seat while Jake said goodbye to Maggie. He cupped her face in his hands, bending down so their foreheads touched.

She rose on her toes to kiss him. "Find her. Find her and bring her home."

Jake climbed into the truck and peered over Bear's shoulder, studying his partner's smartphone. A map of the area displayed on the screen along with a blue dot moving along the marked red line of the road in jerky spurts.

"How much does one of those GPS trackers cost?" Jake asked.

"Couple hundred bucks for a good one. Software is free. I can run it on my laptop or on my phone."

"Got many of them deployed amongst your shithead clientele?"

"A few." Bear grinned. "But it ain't exactly what you'd call legal.

But, I'm fightin' a war down here, and all's fair in love and war." He pointed to the dot on the screen. "Bennett left the Turn It Loose. He's headed this way."

They rolled down the driveway and stopped fifty feet back from Poor Boy Road. As Bear continued tracking the smartphone, Jake reached under the seat and pulled out the Glock. Bear raised his bushy eyebrows, but said nothing. Some serious shit could erupt before the night was through and he needed to come clean with Bear. He checked his loaded gun and set it on the seat.

"A few things you probably oughtta know," Jake said. "Keats put me on a contract to take down Shane Langston."

Bear's neck should have snapped given the speed he whipped his head around. "What?"

"Yeah, I told him I wanted out of the life. He knew I was coming here to see to the end of Stony and he came up with this brilliant idea to have me take out a potential rival. Shane's angling to step into the trade in Kansas City. Keats doesn't want that to happen."

"Why didn't you tell me this sooner?"

"Because you're a cop for one, and I didn't think you'd take well to my mission of killing the drug lord you've been looking to take down for the last several years. And two…I don't think I can do it. I may be a miserable leg breaker, but I'm not a murderer."

Bennett's Mazda sped past them along Poor Boy Road. Bear watched the smartphone for a few seconds before waving his hand forward for Jake to follow. Jake let off the brake.

"Stay back out of his rearview mirror," he said. "Damn, Jake. You can't whack this guy."

"I know. Taking Shane out is the only way Keats is going to let me go. Said if I don't, I'm the one who's going down for the dirt nap."

"How long did he give you?"

Jake checked the clock on the dash. "I've gotta call him in about four hours or he sends in a band of his merry goons."

"That ain't good."

Jake followed Bennett's car through the rises and falls of Poor Boy Road, past the Turkey Creek Cemetery. At Highway M, Bennett swerved north and Jake trailed behind, catching glimpses of his dusty tail lights.

"But I had another idea," Jake said. "Maybe I don't have to kill him. Maybe I have to help you take him out. Whether he's six feet under or in prison, it counts the same."

"That's true," Bear said. "I like the idea a hell of a lot better than trying to clear you of a murder rap. I wouldn't cry any tears over Langston eating a bullet, but I'd rather see the shitbird rot in jail for a while."

"Second thing, I'm the one who made the anonymous call about the warehouse." Might as well come clean.

Bear blew out. "And how did that come about?"

Jake told him about tracking Langston through the car dealership which gave him the address of the warehouse and the call to his hacker friend which tied it to Langston.

"Marion Holdings?" Bear said. "We heard whispers of that but could never track down anything definitive. Not sure how the hell you got what we couldn't with one phone call."

"It's all about knowing the right people."

"I was kidding before about hiring you. Maybe I should reconsider. You're Sherlock Holmes."

Open farm land on either side gave way to large clumps of towering trees as they neared the water. The road bent to the east and single family homes popped up. Bear kept his eye on the tracker.

"Stop," Bear said.

Jake hit the brakes past a gray farmhouse. A pit bull the size of a small horse eyed them suspiciously. The dog's ripped muscles tensed and he looked like he could snap the rope tying him to a nearby tree.

"What's Bennett doing?" Jake asked.

"Beats me. Stopped a hundred yards ahead. You've been a busy beaver, my friend. You got any other giant atom bombs you need to drop?"

"Yeah. Halle's my daughter."

Bear's jaw hung open. "Are you shittin' me?"

"Nope. Maggie told me last night."

"How in the hell did that happen?"

Jake narrowed his eyes. "You really need to have the birds and the bees talk? I know you aren't the sharpest crayon in the box, Bear, but I shouldn't have to explain it to you. Guess our last night together before I bailed town did the trick."

"Well, I'll be damned. I guess it makes sense, though."

"How so?"

"Kid's stubborn as a mule. If that ain't you, I don't know what is. Good thing she got her mother's looks."

Jake grinned, but the spinning calendar of all the time he'd missed forced the smile to fade. "I wish I'd known. I'd have been there for her."

"Let's get her out of this mess and you can do that." Bear pulled up his smartphone again. Bennett was on the move. He motioned for Jake to move forward.

Jake glanced to a paved drive twenty yards from the pavement marked by a fence post with a blue ribbon. A large security gate with a stand-alone keypad box in front closed in an arc, blocking the path. A man climbed back inside a black SUV hidden away behind a tree on the opposite side of the gate.

"Keep going, don't stop," Bear said, attempting to slide low in the truck seat to avoid being seen. His immense size made it an exercise in futility.

"What the hell are you doing?" Jake asked, resisting the urge to laugh.

"People know me around here. Trying to make my fat ass a little inconspicuous," Bear said, giving up when they passed the driveway. He checked his phone. "That's where Bennett went."

"What's up with the security?"

"Big property company came in years ago and bought up a ton of land to develop lakefront homes. You drive around Benton County and you'll see their signs all over the place along with these gated communities. Worked in some places but not as well in others."

"So that's the only way in?"

"Naw, we can slide in anywhere. It's not like the whole property is fenced off. The gate is just a deterrent. They have security trucks patrolling their properties, though. You can't wander in and cruise around for very long." Bear pointed across the cab. "Pull in this driveway."

Jake wheeled down a long, asphalt driveway. A well-maintained white rancher sprawled in front of them. There were no cars on the drive or lights on in the house. Bear directed him toward the back of the house and told him to park. A line of maples stood like sentries along the property line. A narrow footpath darted between them leading to the water.

"Nice place," Jake said.

"Belongs to my dipshit brother-in-law. Roy made a nice living selling insurance in St. Louis, and they retired here last year. My wife makes me drag his ass out on the lake fishing once a week. See that ramp by the door? Built it for him on one of my rare days off so he can wheel down to his dock. Smashed the crap outta my thumb with a hammer. Bitter old fart didn't say thank you or fuck you very much. Just handed me a warm can of Pabst Blue Ribbon and wheeled his crippled ass back inside."

"At least you got a beer," Jake offered.

"I'd rather drink your luke-warm piss than a PBR. We can park here without raising any suspicion. Come on."

Bear dropped out of the truck and Jake followed. Bear reached into the back and unzipped the rifle case. Out came a Savage 30.06 rifle with a scope attached to the stock; Bear slung it over his shoulder. He unzipped the duffel bag and pulled out a pair of binoculars, ammo for the rifle and a couple of magazines for the Beretta on his hip.

"You going to war?" Jake asked.

"Always be prepared. All hail the fucking Boy Scouts of America. You got extra ammo for the Glock?"

Jake went back to the driver's side and took the two extra mags he kept under the seat, shoving them into his back pocket. Without thinking, he reached into his front pocket and slid the gold ring on his finger. Bear leaned over the truck rail and retrieved a bulletproof vest. He tossed it over to Jake. Jake peeled off his shirt and donned the vest.

Bear rubbed his ample belly. "You coulda put it over your shirt. Show off."

"How the hell do I know? Haven't worn one of these things before."

"I think you just wanted to show off your six-pack."

"Get your eyes checked, old man," Jake said. "That's an eight-pack. Maybe we can rekindle our workout routine. I'll get you back into shape."

Bear huffed while Jake slid his T-shirt over the top of the vest. "Dragging my fat ass outta bed every day is my workout." He pointed back to the trees. "There's a big-ass house on the other side of these trees, a couple hundred yards through the woods."

"Whose house is it?"

"Don't know. Maybe your little buddy in Kansas City can tell us."

"Smart ass."

"I've just seen it from the other side of the river when I've cruised through Lakeview Heights on a few calls. We'll do a little reconnaissance through the trees here. See if there's anything interesting going on."

"And if there is?" Jake asked.

"We call in the dogs. I put some of my DEA task force guys on alert before you got back from Sedalia. Guys I can trust. If Halle's in there and Shane's got her, I don't want to spook him."

They entered the tree line, making their own path over brush and twigs. They moved at a quick pace before slowing as they caught glimpses of the house up ahead through the woodland. Bear moved like a cat. Just like their deer hunting days in the backwoods by the old house when they were teenagers.

Twenty minutes later, the day's dying sun made it nearly impossible to spot the path in front of them. Every twig they snapped sounded like a shotgun blast. Thankfully, rumbles of boat motors roaring by on the nearby water helped mask the sound of their approach. Thirty yards ahead, the house lit up like a Christmas tree. A spotlight blasted from the front door on to a driveway where a beat-up truck, a couple of black Lincoln Navigators and Bennett's Mazda were parked.

"Hail, hail, the gang's all here," Bear whispered. "That's Willie's truck and I'll bet dollars to donuts that's one of Shane's Navigators."

Jake took the binoculars from Bear and scanned the front of the house and the yard. A red ember flared on the far side of the house and faded, tendrils of smoke coiled across the floodlights. He scanned across the front of the house seeing nothing in the windows. Another dark figure hid in the shadows of the front porch, a rifle leaning against the house.

"Got two scumbags out front," Jake said, voice low. "One smoking on the far side and another sitting on the porch."

"Don't forget about the guy at the gate."

"So, that's three on the outside we can see."

A figure moved to the front window. Jake raised the binoculars. Long, dark hair, ratty jeans, your general scumbag appearance. He handed the glasses to Bear.

"There's Willie," Bear said. "And there's Antonio coming up behind him. Shane's bodyguard. Big, black sumbitch. I'd rather shoot him than fight him. Where Antonio goes, Shane goes."

They waited. Jake's knee ached from squatting, so he dropped to a sitting position. Though their eyes adjusted to the dark, it was still a shade short of pitch black in the woods, the only light now coming from the full moon. A snake slithered across his boot and Jake nearly gave away their location with a yelp.

"City boy," Bear said in the darkness. Jake hated snakes.

They alternated turns with the binoculars, quietly shifting up and down the tree line trying to get a different angle. On Jake's turn, a lean, but muscular guy with jet-black hair and a widow's peak spoke to the guy Bear identified as Antonio. Was that Shane? He looked like he could scrap and, if he was the one who took Halle, Jake hoped he had the chance to find out. Jake nudged Bear and handed him the glasses.

"Hell yes," Bear said. "Will the real Shane Langston please stand up?"

A minute later, Willie marched out to his truck. He rummaged around for a few seconds then came out carrying a couple of large, clear plastic bags. He said something to the guy on the porch and walked inside.

"Bingo," Bear said. "That was a shit ton of Devil Ice little Willie carried inside. We've got enough to bust in. Sit tight."

"Where you going?"

"I'm calling in the dogs. They can be here in thirty minutes. I'll go meet them back up the road a ways. We'll stage up and come back with guns drawn."

"What about Halle?" Jake asked. "I'm supposed to sit here with my thumb up my ass?"

"Yeah, that's exactly what you're supposed to do. Your keys in the truck?" Jake nodded. "Good. Stay here, out of sight. If you see anything to raise the alarm, call me on my cell. You're my eyes on the ground."

"This sucks," Jake said, legs twitching and hands clenching. He should be doing something.

Bear read his mind. "Don't do anything stupid. Sit tight and keep your head down."

Bear clapped him on the back and disappeared. He hoped Bear didn't unlock the toolbox on Jake's truck. Should've moved the money. Jake settled back and waited.

CHAPTER FORTY-THREE

Jake managed to follow Bear's order for a whole ten minutes. Fuck this. He worked his way toward the water to a spot where he could get a clear view of the back of the house. Following the trees, he crept to a large boathouse hanging out over the water and peered in a window at a white forty-two foot Regal Sport Coupé with a price tag of a half million dollars. Very nice. Did Keats have one of those? He made his way back toward the house, hugging the boathouse wall. He glanced at the bright lights on the back of the house and saw his daughter for the first time.

Her hands and forehead were pressed against the second-story window; what looked like a ceiling fan spun lazily in the background. He raised the binoculars. His breath caught, stunned by the beauty shining through the fear on her face, like she was the damsel in distress at the top of the bell tower waiting for her knight in shining armor. On a patio below, a bulky sentry with a bad mullet leaned against a stone column smoking, alternating his gaze between Halle at the window and the water behind the house.

Jake couldn't help but smile. He'd been in relationships over the years, some good, most bad. Some of the women had children with whom he'd become friendly. He never connected to the kids or really wanted one of his own. But now, marveling at something he created, he found that connection warm and inviting. She was scared, but he could see her strength, Maggie as she looked sixteen years ago but with the trademark Caldwell nose, narrow and hooked. His chest ached as he stared at her, at *his* daughter.

Jake opened his cell and shot Bear a text. *Halle in house—in back room on second floor.* A minute later, his cell vibrated. *How can you see back of house if ur sitting in woods? Don't move. Staging now. 10 minutes.* Jake stuck the phone back in his pocket. He dipped into the shadows of the boathouse to dutifully wait, when his foot knocked into a metal pail. He froze, imagining how the reverberating clang must have sounded to the man on the patio.

"Goddamn it," he muttered. He snuck a peek over his shoulder. The guy on the porch peered into the darkness and edged toward the stairs leading to the dock. Jake pressed himself against the wall and slid back. His hands found a door knob and twisted it open. The door creaked, the sound carrying over the August evening breeze. He slipped inside, leaving the door ajar.

A minute later, hard-heeled boots clomped across the wood deck surrounding the boat house.

"Emmit?" the man called. "If Shane catches you jacking around with his boat he's gonna skin your ass alive."

Scant light shined through the window from one of the nearby dock lights. Jake used it to inch deeper into the boathouse, ignoring the copper smell in the air and trying to find some measure of cover. With Halle held captive and Bear ten minutes out, sounding the alarm was the absolute last thing he wanted to do. With the area surrounding the boat providing no cover, he climbed on to the boat and crept to the captain's seat. Seconds later the boot falls reached the door and the guard pushed it open.

"Emmit?" The man hesitated before flipping the light switch. Overhead fluorescents blasted the boathouse and Jake felt as conspicuous as a naked whore in church. Thankfully, his perch placed him above the guard who slowly walked the length of the boat. Jake shifted slightly, and his knee popped. The boots paused, then circled the rest of the boat back to the door.

"Duane," a voice said from a radio.

"Yo," Duane replied, his voice dull and nasally.

"Where the hell are you?"

"Boathouse. Thought I heard something."

"Get your ass back to your post."

"Yes, sir."

The hinges creaked as the door shut. Jake silently counted five Mississippi and rose to jump to the deck.

Shit. Duane pointed a gun at him, the barrel wide and dark, like an open mouth waiting to swallow him whole.

"Oops," Jake said. Could he get to the Glock tucked into his waistband at his back? Doubtful. Even this dumb asshole could drop him before he would clear it. Duane motioned for Jake to climb down. Jake just had to stall long enough for Bear and company to arrive.

"Who the fuck are you?" Duane asked.

"Steve with Boats R Us. Shane said he had a leak on the bow."

"What?" Duane's brow furrowed in confusion. Jake didn't need Duane to believe him, but provide a moment of pause and an opening he could exploit.

Jake walked closer and ran his hand along the side of the boat. "Yeah, Shane called yesterday and said he had a leak in the bow he wanted us to look at."

"Bullshit, and don't take another step forward. You clamberin' around in the dark to find a leak?"

"I couldn't find the light switch."

"You mean the one by the door where every other light switch in the world is?" Duane asked. The gun never wavered. "I'll ask again. Who the fuck are you? You got five seconds to answer before I drop you like a bad habit."

Jake's mind raced. The guy stood too far away to make a move at him and the boat repair guy shtick hadn't given him the opening he wanted. The gun pointing at his chest didn't move a millimeter. He figured another five minutes until the cavalry arrived. The best course of action was to tell Duane the truth, in a way.

"I'm Jake Smith with the Drug Enforcement Administration. This whole place is going to be swarming with federal agents in less than five minutes. Give me the gun and you can walk out of here alive."

"Bullshit," Duane said. But, despite his statement of disbelief, Jake spotted a crack in his demeanor. He raised his radio to his lips.

"Don't do it," Jake said. "You raise the alarm and a whole lot of people are going to die here today, including you. Let my people swarm the house and take everyone there down. Hell, technically you haven't done anything yet. You could walk out of here alive and a free man, Duane."

"How do I know you're for real?"

"Inside the house is the drug dealer, Shane Langston, and his big black bodyguard, Antonio. Also inside is a drug dealer named Willie Banks and his errand boy Bennett. They brought in a new shipment of a new meth product they call Devil Ice. There's also a kidnapped girl named Halle Holden being held hostage here. Now how would I know that if I'm not who I say I am?"

"I don't know nothing about the girl," Duane said. Duane's gun dropped a hair as his brain chugged to process the information.

"My turn to call bullshit, Duane. You've been ogling her in the window from your little perch all day. We've had this place under watch by satellite for weeks now. Give it up and I'll make sure you get a walk."

Duane's mouse in the wheel worked overtime. "A full and complete walk?"

"Hand me the gun and you won't do a minute of time."

The mouse wheel finished spinning and Duane held out the gun out by the barrel. Jake stepped forward and gently took it from his hands. It had worked. "You made the right move, Duane. I gotta cuff you for now. Turn around."

When Duane turned, Jake slammed the piece into the back of his head. The body crumpled to the deck. Jake found a reel of fishing line, some duct tape and a knife on a workbench. After ensuring Duane still had a pulse, Jake wrapped Duane's hands behind his back with the line and did the same with his feet. He slapped a couple of strips of duct tape across his mouth and dragged him to the back of the boat, out of sight.

As he walked back toward the door, Jake noticed a bulging, blue tarp on the ground against the wall. He lifted the tarp and jumped back. He'd seen some crazy shit in his time, but nothing like this.

The remains of Bub, the guy he pounded by the Community Center downtown, lay under the tarp, a horrified expression pasted under his glassy, dead eyes. Clutched in either one of his fat, dead hands were his legs stumps, a macabre mess of crimson and bone. Jake suppressed the urge to puke before backing away. When he reached the door, he killed the light and stared up the hill toward the house. Langston mutilated his own guy. What kind of psycho were they about to deal with?

*****

The guard posted below Halle's window stood at the edge of the patio and peered toward the water. He yelled out something Halle couldn't make out, waited a moment and walked down the steps. The light in the boathouse had turned on when the door to her room opened. Willie entered, his complexion a whiter shade than normal, like he was about to vomit. He closed the door behind him. Not good news.

"Willie? What is it? What's wrong?"

Willie didn't answer. He sat on the bed and patted the space next to him. As much as it made her skin crawl, Halle obliged. Muffled laughs and shouts came from down the hall. Willie's gaze locked on his feet, as if he couldn't raise his greasy head to look her in the eye.

"I stalled as long as I could and racked my brain trying to figure out another way, but I'm supposed to kill you now," he said, his voice flat and monotone, like a shock victim telling someone about their traumatic experience.

Her optimistic thoughts of surviving this ordeal fell away. The panic she'd managed to hold in check leapt forward and she slammed her back into the headboard of the bed, pressing into the wood as far from Willie as she could get.

"Shane said for me to rape you first. He said it the way someone would say you should try a new restaurant or you should go check out the new George Clooney movie. Like it was a friendly little suggestion."

"What did you say?" Halle whispered, her voice trembling. Images flooded her brain of Willie raping her, Shane over his shoulder cheering. Shane with his knife, running it up and down her leg again before plunging it into her.

"I told him I didn't think I could do it. I was happy to run his meth for him, but Bub's the muscle of my operation and when Shane killed him, he cut the legs out from under me. Shane started laughing his ass off telling me what a great pun that was, but I don't know what the hell a pun is so I didn't laugh. Next thing I know, Shane has the big knife out and he's pointing it at me and prodding my chest with the tip of it."

Willie pulled the collar of his shirt low. Half a dozen bloody little slits cut into Willie's skin. Not the first time she'd seen him hurt. When she was younger, he'd show up in town with cuts and bruises all over him. Mom said he used to be a sweet kid. Halle almost felt sorry for him. Almost.

"Then," Willie continued, "he said if I didn't do it, he would be the one doing the raping and the cutting. He said, 'Better if it comes from you, Willie. She might take it better coming from you.' What a mess."

Halle got up from the bed, full blown panic surging through her. Escape. She had to. She ran her eyes over the window panes to the ground below. Maybe if she flung herself through the glass she'd break her neck on the patio. If not, maybe she could slash her wrists with the broken glass. Both options sounded better than what Shane planned for her.

"This isn't how it was supposed to be, Halle," Willie continued. "I wasn't plannin' on making a career out of selling meth and being stuck in this town. Just tryin' to make a little cash and get the hell out of dodge. Make a legit life somewhere. I even thought for a bit I could do it with you. Pretty stupid, huh?"

A figure came up the steps from the dock, and it wasn't the mullet-head that had been there all day leering at her. The new guy limped a bit, big with cropped hair, jeans and a plain dark T-shirt. He slowed as he approached the patio, scanning for anyone nearby, a pistol aimed, ready to shoot. When he broke the plane of the patio's light, he looked up to her. His face broke into a smile, not a creepy one like the mullet-head's, but a genuine one. She recognized something familiar about it even though she'd never seen him before.

"Tried to get Shane to let you come with me to Kansas City. I said I'd keep you under control, but he knew that wasn't gonna work."

The man outside checked his watch, pointed to it and raised two fingers in the air. He mouthed the words "two minutes," exaggerating so she saw it. This guy wasn't part of Shane's crew, but there to help her. He disappeared below. Two minutes. She didn't know what in the hell would happen in two minutes, but for the first time since those animals grabbed her, optimism flashed.

"So, I don't know what the hell to do. I don't see any way out of this, Halle."

Halle spun from the window, trying to suppress the smile cropping up on her face. It disappeared at the sight of Willie moving toward her with a knife in his hand.

*****

The back door slid open, and Jake crept into a rec room. A long hallway led to several rooms with closed doors. A wet-bar held several half-empty bottles of Crown Royal and Jack Daniels along with a smattering of crushed beer cans. A long leather couch lay empty in front of a big screen, ironically playing one of his favorite movies of all time: *Unforgiven.* On the screen, the Schofield Kid sat on the ground, knees drawn up in front of him, drinking whiskey from a bottle, contemplating the man he assassinated. As Jake passed the pool table heading for a stairway leading up, the Schofield Kid tried to justify his actions, saying to Clint Eastwood, *"Well, I guess he had it comin'."* Jake whispered the comeback line along with old Iron Clint. "We all got it comin', kid." That's goddamn right.

He snaked up the stairs, the Glock raised in front of him, afraid of what would happen if someone came bounding down. If he fired a shot, it would raise hell and put Halle in danger. If Bear kept to his timetable, he and his crew would be storming the castle any minute now. He'd rather be in the room with Halle keeping her safe than wondering about her when the bullets started flying.

After a moment of contemplation, he continued his ascent. Halle's room sat above the rec room. With any luck, he'd be able to slip in undetected and protect her. At the top of the stairs he paused. Voices murmured from the closed door to Halle's room twenty feet away. With his gun trained in the direction of the voices, Jake crept with his free hand running along the wall. Through the door, Halle spoke and relief washed over him. His hand gripped the doorknob when the cold steel of a gun barrel pressed against his temple. A large black mass moved out of the darkness of a hallway he hadn't noticed. Antonio.

"Drop the gun," Antonio said. He pushed the barrel harder into Jake's temple, shoving his head into the wall. He should've listened to Bear and waited. Jake dropped the gun.

CHAPTER FORTY-FOUR

Willie advanced with the knife in hand. Halle backed up against the dresser, reaching for anything she could use as a weapon, but came up with nothing but a doily, like the ones her grandmother used to knit. Not helpful.

"I'm sorry, Halle," Willie said. "I don't wanna do this, but if I don't Shane is going to kill us both."

"You don't want to do this, Willie. You're not a killer." Where the hell was the stranger on the porch? Outside the door, something clunked on the floor. "Listen to me, people are coming here to rescue me. I saw one of them coming through the back. It's not too late to stop this."

Willie stepped closer, raising the knife. "Nice try. I got two minutes. That's all. Nobody's coming."

Two minutes. The clock on the dresser. Halle spun, grabbed the cord and yanked it from the wall. She held the cord in both hands and swung the clock in an ever vicious circle. Willie took a cautious step back, holding the knife and his free hand in front of his chest.

"What the hell..." he said before Halle lunged. The clock caught him square in the temple. Willie crashed backward into the door and bounced to the ground. The knife flew from his hand, and Halle dove for it.

*****

"So who the fuck are you?" Antonio asked, the barrel of the gun biting into Jake's forehead.

"The Schwan's man," Jake said. "Didn't you guys place an order?"

"Comedian, huh?" Antonio kicked Jake's Glock down the hall. Apparently the man had no sense of humor. "Let's go talk to the boss."

He grasped Jake's shoulder as something smashed into the door behind them. Halle's room. Antonio startled and Jake rammed his elbow back with all his might, connecting with Antonio's nose. Before the bones could stop crunching, Jake buried his shoulder into the man's chest, driving him backward. They both hit the wall at the end of the hall and crashed to the floor. Jake swung his knee up as hard as he could, landing so solidly with the man's chin that his leg went numb.

He crawled down the hall, dragging his numb leg behind him, going for his gun. He reached for it. A pair of black cowboy boots stopped in front of him, the right one resting squarely on his Glock. He rolled over on to his back. Shane Langston regarded him with his black, marble eyes and a gun big enough to make Dirty Harry cry with jealousy.

"Who the fuck are you?" Shane asked. The question of the day.

*****

The Drug Enforcement Tactical Strike Team leading the charge on Langston's house was short a few men. Bear surmised the eight they had would have to do.

By flashlights on the hood of Jake's truck, Bear drew a rough map of the house and surrounding land. Three agents would enter from the left side and back. Two others on the right side through the woods. Bear, Team Leader James Rouse and Agent Lonnie Hashagen would tear through the front gate. They planned a synchronized hit on the house with a mix of flash bangs and tear gas. Bear described Jake so the team wouldn't take him out.

Agent Hashagen led the charge, floating through the woods like a ghost and tasering the guard at the gate. He reached into the guard's SUV and found a button opening the gate. As he secured the guard with thick zip ties, Bear rolled the truck forward with the lights dark, using the scarce moonlight to navigate the quick drive to the house. Hashagen hopped on the tailgate and rode the truck.

"So far, so good," Rouse called into his collar mic. "Team A approaching the front of the house." He got call backs saying the other two teams were in place and ready.

"We've been waiting a long time for this, Jimmy," Bear said.

"Let's not mess it up. Everyone gets out alive."

They climbed out of the truck. Hashagen grabbed the ram to bust through the front door and took his position. Bear and Rouse crouched ready.

Rouse hit his collar mic again. "Move in."

*****

Hashagen busted the front door wide open with the ram. Rouse tossed in a couple of flash bang grenades, which erupted in sound and blinding light. Following the toss, Bear and Rouse charged through. The next sixty seconds were a chaotic mass of screams and gunfire. Bear tackled one of Langston's staggering men in the living room. Rouse dropped another with two well-placed shots to the chest when the man grabbed a shotgun off the dining room table. Bear quickly zip-tied his man and scrambled to his feet, moving room to room to find Jake and Halle.

*****

Jake opened his mouth to provide a smart-ass answer to Shane's question when the front door exploded. Shane whirled at the sound in time to catch a face full of light from the flash bang. He collapsed against the wall, hands on his eyes. Quickly gaining his composure, he darted for the stairwell. With bulbs of light dancing in his eyes, Jake rolled over and grabbed his gun, swinging it toward the stairwell in time to glimpse the back of Shane's shirt. Shaking the cobwebs, he started to climb to his feet when Antonio tackled him from behind. He crashed to the ground under Antonio's immense weight, the behemoth raining blows on the back of his head. The next punch bounced Jake's forehead off the hardwood floor and black spots of looming unconsciousness appeared. Jake bucked, gaining some room and tried to get to his feet, sweeping the floor with his hands to find his gun. Antonio slammed him back to the ground, straddled him and pointed the Glock at Jake's head.

"You a dead motherfu…" Antonio said before his face exploded. One minute a triumphant snarl, the next a crimson wreckage. The giant swayed and toppled off to the side. Jake pulled his legs out and craned his neck to see Bear in a shooter's stance in the hallway holding a smoking gun.

"Thanks," Jake managed. Bear ran over and helped Jake to his feet. Jake grabbed his Glock from Antonio's dead hand.

"Halle?"

"In here," Jake replied. They flung the door wide. Halle hovered over Willie wielding a large knife. Willie cowered in the corner, his legs drawn to his chest and hands raised in the air, blood oozing from the side of his face.

"Halle?" Jake asked.

Tears sprang forth from her baby blue eyes. The knife shaking in her hand.

"He was going to kill me," she said. Jake slid the Glock into his waistband and gently took the knife from her.

Bear yanked Willie to his feet and cuffed him. "You're under arrest, needle dick."

"He was going to kill me," Halle repeated, in shock. At last, the tears flowed and her shoulders shook. She moved to Jake and he held his daughter for the first time. Pangs of regret filled him that he'd missed sixteen years of doing this. Now wasn't the time. He focused on the moment. After a minute, she seemed to calm down.

"It's okay, Halle," Jake said.

She pulled back, her eyebrows furrowed. "Who are you?"

"It's a long story."

Agent Rouse entered the room, a bloody hole in his shoulder, leaning against the wall for support. "House is clear, but I can't find Pater and there's no sign of Langston."

"Pater on the rear entry team?" Bear asked. Rouse nodded.

Out the back window by the dock, a muzzle sparked twice in the darkness along with the distinctive pops of a handgun.

"Langston went down the stairs," Jake said.

"Come on." Bear bolted out the door.

"Stay with this man, Halle," Jake said, nodding to Agent Rouse. "I'll be back."

He followed Bear out the door and down the stairs. They'd no sooner hit the patio before a boat motor roared to life from the boathouse. Seconds later, the Regal Sport Coupe shot on to the lake speeding northeast across the black water. Langston was gone.

CHAPTER FORTY-FIVE

"Son of a bitch!" Bear screamed as Shane tore away across the lake. A form lay crumpled on the ground by the boathouse. Jake tugged Bear by the sleeve and ran down the steps. The black-clad agent was dead—shot once in the chest and once in the throat. His gun missing.

"Pater," Bear said, baring his teeth. "Had a wife and two kids."

"What now?"

"I'm going to get that little fucker," Bear said, the anger radiating off him in a red wave.

"How? You swimming after him?"

Bear's eyes darted around for a moment, then smacked Jake on the arm. "My brother-in-law. Roy's got a boat. Come on."

They ran up the hill and into Jake's truck, Bear behind the wheel since he knew where they were going. Jake pulled out his phone and groaned at the spiderweb of cracks in the glass face. Probably happened when Antonio landed on top of him. He worked his way around the cracks and tried to call Maggie to let her know Halle was safe, but she didn't answer her phone. He redialed the number and got her voicemail again. Jake wanted nothing more than to take Halle there himself, but they had to take Langston down.

Back on M, they headed east, Bear gunning the truck too hard and spinning them out on the blacktop. He flew a couple hundred yards to the east and swung into the Dell's driveway where they'd made their original entry hours earlier. Bear jumped out and ran to the house with Jake close behind.

"What the hell are we doing? Bear?"

"We're taking Roy's boat and going after Langston. I know where he keeps the boat keys in the house."

Bear tried the back door. Locked. He pulled out a flashlight and the two of them quickly scanned the ground around the porch for anything that might house a hideaway key. They came up empty. Shane got farther away with every second they wasted here.

"Screw it." Bear returned to the door. He reared back then threw his shoulder into the door, which flew open. "I'll reimburse him."

Inside, Bear flipped on the lights revealing a spacious kitchen with stainless steel appliances, and decorated with country-quaint wall paper. Bear darted to the pantry and disappeared inside. A second later he emerged with a key on a green plastic fob.

"Now we're cookin' with gas," Bear said.

He ran out the back door. Jake followed, and tried for a few fruitless seconds to close the door Bear bashed in, but his friend had trashed it beyond redemption. He left it. Thirty seconds later they managed to navigate the stone path through the trees and reached the covered dock. The only sounds from the dark lake were water lapping against the boat, buzzing cicadas and the distant hum of a high horsepower motor. Jake hopped in the thirty-foot Watercraft after Bear who made a call on his cell organizing roadblocks.

"You know how to drive this thing?" Jake asked.

Bear huffed. "I've lived on a lake my entire life. I drive a boat better than I drive a car." He fired up the engine while Jake cast off the lines holding the boat to the dock.

"Like that's any accomplishment," Jake said. "I've seen how you drive."

Bear put the boat in reverse and backed out of the dock.

"How in the hell are we going to find him? There's miles of shoreline."

"I think I know where he's going." Bear wheeled the boat around, flipped on the headlights and put it in drive. He gunned the motor and Jake flew back into a thankfully cushioned seat. "Shane has another house off Grover's Cove by Cooney Creek Road. We tracked it through a real estate front and had it under surveillance for months, but got nothing useful. Think I can find it in the dark. If he's not there, I don't know what the hell we're gonna do."

The Watercraft sliced through the dark water and Jake kept a wary eye out for other boaters. They crossed the lake at an angle and hugged the far shore line running southeast for a couple of miles. The lake took a sharp curve to the northeast and Bear slowed, scanning for the cove entrance.

"Gotta be here somewhere," Bear said. "Me and Roy hit this up a couple of weeks ago. Caught a helluva catfish that morning."

Along the bank, lake houses lit up the shoreline as the weekend folks arrived for some last days of summer fun. People sat on the docks drinking beer and listening to music while their kids jumped off the wood structures into the warm lake water. Bear idled toward one of the docks with a group of men and women hanging out. A stocky, pot-bellied man with no shirt and a Santa Claus beard rose from a folding chair and waved as Bear approached.

"Hey, Bear," the man said as they idled up. "Steal Roy's boat for the evening?"

"You could say that, Professor. Looking for a guy in an expensive-ass power boat who might've come ripping through here a few minutes ago."

The Professor cast a wary glance at Jake then back at Bear. "You're wearing a bullet-proof vest. Anything I need to be worried about?"

"Depends. You see anything?"

"Yeah," the Professor said. "Guy came tearin' through here a few minutes ago. Yelled at his dumb ass to slow down, but he buzzed past. Think he turned into Grover's Cove."

Bear thanked him and threw down the throttle. A few hundred yards on, the houses grew farther apart. Bear found the entrance to the cove and spun the wheel. They split the gap in the shore measuring fifty feet across. The lights of the boat caught a glint of the eyes of an animal that darted back into the thick woods. After another hundred yards, Bear killed the spotlight and trolled forward.

An illuminated house loomed atop a jagged bluff, connected to the water by a long, wooden staircase. Shane's getaway boat bobbed in the water at the bottom. Jake and Bear drew their guns as they approached the dock, but lowered them at the sight of the empty boat. Jake hopped out and quickly tied Roy's boat to a cleat bolted to the dock. They stared up the long staircase.

"You ready for this?" Jake asked.

"That's a lot of fuckin' stairs. I might have a heart attack before I reach the top."

"I was gonna mention something about your weight, but I didn't want to get my ass kicked."

"Tell you what. You help me take this dickhead out and you can make all the fat jokes you want."

"Deal."

They climbed the stairs to the house, keeping a wary eye out for Shane as they ascended.

*****

Shane darted around the lake house collecting last minute things before getting the hell out of Benton County. He'd already loaded the Navigator in the garage with several days' worth of clothes and a stash of cash hidden in the spare tire in the back. Just needed some extra guns he kept around the house along with bags of product before he hit the road. He called in his backup on the way over, but didn't know if they'd have time to navigate the dark, winding roads before his internal escape clock ticked to zero. At least he put his insurance provision in place. He'd have to give Brad at the dealership a little bonus for his vigilance.

Bear closed the noose around his neck the second he nabbed Howie and found the cook house. With the coke found at his warehouse, it was a matter of time before Bear looped in the Feds and had him in a bind he couldn't get out of. Should have killed that fat Boy Scout long ago. But how in the hell had the cops found the blue house? He'd bought it through a double-blind realty association a year ago and only a handful of people knew the location. Had to be Willie or someone from his dumbass crew who either rolled over for the Feds or led them there.

His stupid decision to bring the girl unnecessarily raised the stakes. He didn't make stupid decisions. He should've ordered Dexter to whack the girl at the cook house and burn the place to the ground. Mistake number one. Number two? Trusting Willie and his incompetent hillbilly crew with the Devil Ice. When Shane got out of this, Willie would die a horrible fucking death. He hoped his plan of adding extra insurance to the mix wasn't a mistake as well.

Shane grabbed his Winchester hunting rifle and a 9 millimeter from the den, and paused at the rumbling of an approaching boat. He killed the lights and looked out the window to the cove. The bright moon reflected off the water, revealing a Watercraft angling into the dock and two figures climbing out. He couldn't make out features, but from the size of the first guy it had to be Bear. The second character must be the stranger he was about to drop when the Feds busted through the front door. A second later, it clicked. Caldwell. Matched the description Brad gave him from the dealership and the subsequent plate search on his truck. But why in the hell would Caldwell be after him? Did he know about Nicky?

Shane made his way across the darkened den to the sliding glass door leading to a large, wood deck overlooking the water. The door opened noiselessly. Shane went to the railing closest to the staircase, laid his arms across the top board and trained the rifle on the approaching men. He lined up Bear, clicked the safety off and fingered the trigger, grinning at the prospect of shooting the long-time thorn in his side. Unfortunately for Bear, Shane was a good shot.

CHAPTER FORTY-SIX

"Jesus God." Bear hung on to the railing like it was a lifeline as they reached the halfway point. Jake trailed behind, amped up and ready to storm the house despite the oncoming headache from getting his head pummeled and bounced against the hardwood floor by Antonio. Still, his powerful leg muscles burned with the adrenaline to run.

"Keep going," Jake whispered. "Almost there."

The house lights went out the second they pulled to the dock; someone knew they were there. Jake kept an eye on the deck as he patted Bear on the shoulder for encouragement. By the light of the moon, a figure crossed over to the railing and leveled something in their direction.

"Move!" Jake yelled, pushing Bear forward. The crack of a rifle blast echoed through the cove sending sleeping birds flying and squawking. Bear cried out and spun around, falling to the steps. Jake raised his Glock and fired six rapid shots in the direction of the deck. The figure darted back inside. Jake dropped to a knee on the stairs.

"I'm okay. Get his ass," Bear said, groaning in between words.

"You sure?"

"Yeah, he just caught me in the shoulder. Sumbitch, that hurts."

Jake patted Bear on the leg and ran up the stairs towards the house, slapping a fresh mag into the Glock.

*****

Shane darted through the house toward the garage, heart racing with adrenaline and anger. He missed his head shot. The way Bear spun around, he'd at least hit him. That should at least slow the pursuit long enough for him to get away. His cell phone vibrated as he got to the garage. Shane hit the door opener. He checked the number on the display and answered his phone as he hopped into the black Navigator.

"Where the hell are you?" Shane asked, cranking the engine.

"Almost there. They're organizing roadblocks. If you want to get out, it has to be now."

Shane yanked the gear shift into drive and burned rubber out of the garage. He scraped the front of the Nav on the sharply ascending driveway. He hit the edge of the road when the driver's side window exploded and pings of bullets rained into the side of the SUV. He lost control, mashed the gas, and crashed head first into a tree on the opposite side of the road. The airbag deployed and he fought his way around it as he climbed out the door. The shooter ran up the darkened driveway, loading another magazine into his pistol. Caldwell.

Shane's vision shimmered as he tried to shake off the crash. As he staggered up the road, a Benton County Sheriff's patrol screeched to a halt in a blazing display of flashing blue and white lights. Shane pulled out his pistol. The cop jumped from the car as Caldwell hit the top of the driveway with his gun trained on Shane.

"Drop the gun," the cop yelled. "Drop it now or you're done."

Shane swayed unsteadily on his feet. He dropped the pistol on the ground and Caldwell drew closer. The cop's footsteps pounded down the hill on the asphalt.

"Gotcha, dickhead," Caldwell said. The cop clipped two shots from behind Shane, and Caldwell dropped like a stone on to his back and didn't move. Shane reeled toward the cop.

"Took you long enough." He bent over and picked up his gun.

"You got me running all over the county chasing license plate numbers and kidnapping people," the cop said, heading back toward the squad car. "You're lucky I got here at all. We gotta move."

Shane walked the twenty yards to the car. The cop opened the back door and Shane slid in beside the woman and pointed his pistol at her.

"Maggie Holden, I presume?" The terrified woman leaned back against the window with her hands cuffed in her lap.

"Where to now?" the cop asked.

"One last stop," Shane said. "Back to Poor Boy Road, Sad Dog. To the red house."

Deputy Randy Daniels spun the car around and sped off into the night.

*****

Jake clawed his way through the fog clouding his brain and tried to sit up. Pain erupted in his chest, and he settled back on the warm asphalt. His breath came in quick hitches; the bullets that struck the vest knocked the wind out of him. He turned his head to the right, the squad car was gone. Slow footsteps sounded to the left. Bear hobbled up the driveway, his shot shoulder drooped low and face crumpled in a mask of pain and concern.

"You okay?" Bear asked, dropping to a knee.

"Just thought I'd take a rest after this excitement," Jake gasped, drawing in pain laden breaths. Man that hurt.

"You always were lazy," Bear said. Jake started to laugh but it hurt too much. Bear reached with his good arm and helped Jake to a sitting position. Jake growled with pain.

Bear pointed to the crashed SUV across the road. "Please tell me the douche bag flew through the windshield and impaled himself on a fence post."

"I had him in my sights. He pulled his gun out and I was about to drop him when one of your squad cars came barreling up. Cop gets out with his piece drawn, starts walking toward us. Tells Shane to drop the gun. Shane does and I lower mine. Cop turns the gun on me and fires off two rounds."

"What the hell..." Bear whispered.

"Not quite the words running through my head, but about the same sentiment. Impact knocked me back and I cracked my noggin on the ground. Pretty sure I have a concussion."

"It was one of mine? You sure?"

Jake climbed to his feet slowly, like a football player who got his bell rung. "Said Benton County Sheriff on the side. Didn't see exactly what the cop looked like. I was focused on Shane."

"How long ago?"

"No tellin' how long I was out. However long it took you to get your fat ass up here."

"I'd punch you but it'd hurt too much. I was still on the steps when I heard the gunshots. Took me a few minutes to get up the rest of the steps through the house. I ain't feelin' too good about now."

"That makes two of us," Jake said. "You were worried you had an insider. Looks like you were right."

"I'd rather be wrong. Just got to figure out who it was."

Bear opened the GPS tracking app on his phone and scrolled through a couple of screens.

"You got that on your squad cars too?"

"Yup. They don't know it though. Helps me keep tabs on whether they're out doing what they're supposed to be. Let's see...four cars are out. Howard is parked at the Casey's. Go figure. Smajda is by Fristoe. Kuhlmann out at the dam. And...damn it."

Bear dropped the phone to his side. He took a few steps up the road and stopped, shoulders slumped and head dropped. Rubbing his forehead as he turned, Jake's heart sunk at the anguish pasted on his friend's face.

"Randy Daniels is moving west. About five miles from here at a high rate of speed. Sad Dog, you piece of shit."

Jake hadn't met the man. Bear's scowl told him it was about the worst possible news he could receive.

"I don't believe this," Bear said. "I vouched for him, trained him, brought him up through the ranks. Our fucking kids play Little League together on the weekends. What in the holy hell is he thinking?"

"Call it in," Jake said. "The other cops or the Feds can nab him up."

"Can't do it. Sad Dog would hear the call and they'd abandon ship. We'd never find 'em. And the Feds are tied up at Shane's house."

Jake hobbled over to the Nav. He struggled into the driver's seat, moved the deflated air bag out of the way and put the still running SUV in reverse. Metal screeched and resisted the mold it formed around the tree, but came free. He backed it up to Bear.

"Climb in," he said. "Let's go catch us some bad guys and end this thing."

CHAPTER FORTY-SEVEN

Deputy Daniels drove into Fraction Point Estates, a well-to-do subdivision off Poor Boy Road. The lights glowing through the broad windows of the multi-story family homes made them shine in comparison to the tiny ranch he crammed his wife and two boys into, a giant reminder of the life he'd never be able to provide. At least working for Shane gave him a sniff of that life, a flicker of what pleasures life could hold with a little infusion of cold, hard cash.

They rolled down the asphalt to what Shane titled the "Red House," no more red in color than Shane's blue house was blue. Shane thought it clever to name them by need. He chilled at the blue house, reserving the red house for emergencies. In the two years since he'd been on Shane's payroll, they'd never needed to use it before tonight.

"What are we doing here?" Maggie asked, the first words she'd spoken since Shane got in the car.

"Ah, she does speak with that pretty mouth," Shane said, his voice carrying through the partition opening. "We're picking up a few things I'm going to need before we leave town."

"We?" Daniels asked, checking Shane in the rearview mirror.

"I meant Maggie and me. Since I shot the big bad Bear and you shot Halle's would-be rescuer dead in the street, there's nobody to chase you, Randy. Relax."

"Halle? Is she…" Maggie asked.

"She's fine," Daniels said. "DEA has her at Shane's house."

Maggie heaved a cry of relief, leaning forward and resting her head against the protective glass. "What about Bear?"

"Probably okay," Shane said. "I tried to kill him, don't get me wrong, but the other guy, Caldwell, he jerked Bear out of the way when he saw me aiming at them from the porch. I missed. Lucky for Bear because it doesn't happen often."

"But Jake?"

"Dead in the street on Cooney Creek Road with two bullets in the chest courtesy of your local law enforcement."

They pulled to the end of the lane in front of a lone house hiding among a grove of trees. Daniels stopped in front of a detached garage and killed the lights. In the rearview mirror Maggie closed her eyes and bowed her head. Daniels got out and opened the door for Shane. He shut the door, trapping Maggie inside, the beautiful design feature of a police cruiser. The two walked toward the garage.

"I still don't get why you had me nab her," Daniels said. Maggie added complications they didn't need and things were pretty complicated already.

"Insurance, Sad Dog. We already had her daughter. I knew Bear would make the connection between the cook house, the missing girl and eventually me. How'd she know Caldwell's first name?"

"Think they were high school sweethearts or something. His sister works at the Sheriff's office for Bear."

"Well, the plot thickens, doesn't it?"

They reached the garage and Shane opened the door with a key, raising it overhead.

"I still don't get it," Daniels said. "We had the drugs, we had the money. All you had to do was take care of the kid and there was enough for us to go our separate ways."

Shane flipped on a light switch. A dark blue van, covered with a thin film of dust waited inside.

"So I wanted two in case something happened to the other one. I needed leverage against Bear and you told me he looked after Maggie and the girl. You'd already picked her up when everything went down at the blue house. You see the beauty of it? I lost one and I still have one. Leverage, Sad Dog."

"She knows me, Shane. She knows I'm involved with you."

"And she won't see the light of day again. Trust me. As soon as I'm clear of your little town, I'm going to take care of her. Don't worry, you're going to be a rich man soon."

Shane told Daniels to wait outside and keep an eye on Maggie, then he disappeared into the house. Daniels spent the time pacing and smoking. He could shoot Shane and Maggie and end this whole thing. He knew where Shane kept his money stashes. He could be the hero who took down the bad guy. Shit. There were a million ways this could go wrong and put his ass in a sling. When a good ten minutes passed, Shane came out with two large black leather bags and threw them into the back of the van. He told Daniels to get Maggie out of the squad car.

Daniels was unconvinced he would get out of this unscathed. All he wanted was a little extra cash to help pay the bills and get his kids' college funds started. Maybe pay off the house a little early and get a boat. But, in a short time, Shane's requests grew from running plate numbers of suspicious cars cruising around his property to more nefarious acts. As the risk rose, so did the payoffs. Trapped by the money with no way out. He didn't sign up for kidnapping, drugs and murder, though. If he got out of this mess, he'd have to figure out a way to get out from under Shane's thumb. He opened the back door to the car and hauled Maggie out by the chain of the handcuffs. Guilt sagged his features. He liked her.

"I'm sorry, Maggie," he said. "This isn't what I planned."

"What about Becky and the kids?" she spat. "How are you going to look them in the eyes after this? Think what you're doing, Randy."

"I know what I'm doing. So, shut up and come on." He led her back toward the garage like a dog on a leash. Shane emerged and met them at the entrance. He opened his mouth to speak, then stopped and squinted into the darkness up the road. Impossible. Jake Caldwell emerged from behind the squad car with a gun trained on them.

*****

Bear tracked Daniels' squad car with his smart phone while Jake drove the Navigator. They were both surprised to be back at Poor Boy Road. Jake figured Langston would hightail it out of town and they'd be chasing him to Kansas City or St. Louis, somewhere where it would be harder to find him. But he'd need a car. Must have one stashed somewhere close. Bear was familiar with the subdivision. Based on where the GPS unit read on the screen, he even described the house where the squad car was parked long before they reached it.

"Sits at the end of the road. Small, brown house. Detached garage. Never seen anybody in it or really wondered much about it. We're almost in the line of sight. Kill the lights."

Jake fumbled along the dash and found the switch for the headlights and a dimmer knob for the electronic displays. Thank God, because the crash lit the dashboard up like a pinball machine of warning lights. Now, the sole illumination came from Bear's phone, which he held low by his knees. Jake eased off the gas and they coasted forward until a light shined in the distance. In seconds, the outline of the house and the garage developed in the darkness. The light came from the detached garage where a lone figure milled in front of it. Bear raised the binoculars.

"There's the miserable turd sniffer," he said.

"Which one?"

"Mine. Where the hell is Langston?"

Bear scanned the area, contemplating the best course of action. Jake's head thumped from his repeated head trauma of the evening and his chest still viciously ached from the gun shots. He twirled the gold ring on his finger, ready for some measure of retribution.

"How good a shot are you with that rifle?" Jake asked.

"With this scope on it? I could shoot the ass out of a fly at a hundred yards. What do you have in mind?"

Sixty seconds later with a makeshift plan in place, Jake left the vehicle and crept forward on foot, using the scarce trees and the squad car to block Daniels' line of sight. He would move in to take Daniels. Bear would cover him with the rifle. If Shane emerged, Bear would shift his target to Shane. If he could eliminate Daniels first, it would be one less gun to deal with, but Shane was their priority.

With Jake thirty yards from the car, Shane came out of the house with two large, black bags and carried them to the garage. He placed them in the back of a van parked back-end first. He said something to Daniels who headed toward the squad car. Jake dropped behind a thin sapling, feeling completely exposed. But Daniels cast his attention to the car, not at him. Jake raised his gun and drew a line on Daniels' head. He could take the miserable prick out right now. He stopped and lowered the gun when Daniels pulled Maggie out of the car and shoved her toward the garage.

He looked back to the Navigator, almost invisible from this distance. No doubt Bear spotted the fly in their ointment.

"Damn it," he muttered through gritted teeth.

Staying low and using the car for cover, Jake crept forward and covered the remaining ground in less than a minute, his limited options flying through his head. Maggie would die if she got in the van with Shane. He'd either wriggle away or there would be a chase or shootout. Jake didn't like the odds of Maggie making it through either scenario. If he moved now, he could take Daniels out and Bear could take out Shane with the rifle. Even if they missed one, they weren't likely to kill their hostage. It was more risky, but had a chance since neither of the men had guns drawn. Better odds.

Jake stepped out from behind the squad car, gun trained on the men in front of him. The shock on Shane's face was almost worth the price of admission.

"Don't fucking move," Jake ordered, moving forward. Fifteen yards and closing. Maggie stood equidistant between Daniels and Shane. He didn't want to kill either of them, but if it came down to them or Maggie, he wouldn't hesitate a second.

Daniels glanced at Shane then went for his gun. Jake squeezed the trigger three times in rapid succession striking Daniels in the chest. Daniels flew back, bouncing off the front of the van and collapsing in a bloody heap on the ground. The rifle cracked behind Jake as Shane darted behind Maggie. The bullet ripped into the front of the van. Shane grabbed her by the hair and whipped out a knife, holding it at her throat. Jake froze, not ten yards from the two of them.

"Give it up, Langston," he said. "You got no way out of this. I got you covered and Bear's up the road with a rifle trained on your pea brain. Let Maggie go and you'll get out of this alive."

Shane shrunk behind Maggie. "I got a better idea. You take one step closer and I'll gut her like a deer. So, drop your gun and get the hell out of here and we'll live to see another day."

"That ain't gonna happen. I let you go with her and you'll kill her anyway."

"It's always possible," Shane said. "No need to lie about it now. But you won't risk the shot here and old Bear up there certainly won't try it. So, how about you let me get in the van with pretty Maggie here, I take her up the road and drop her at the end of the lane. At least gives me a fighting chance. Maybe a chance for an exciting car chase."

"Car chases are overrated."

Shane poked his head around the back of Maggie's, like a boxer bobbing and weaving. Son of a bitch. He had no shot and every second that went by with the knife at Maggie's throat gave one more chance for Shane to slit it.

"Well, it seems we're at a stalemate," Shane said. "I'm not sticking my head out far enough for you to get a shot. I'm not dropping the knife and letting go of the one thing keeping me alive."

Maggie's wide and desperate eyes darted about. Was she trying to tell him something? Her eyes dropped sharply to her legs and she shifted her left one to the side. He couldn't hit Shane in the head, but he could take his leg out, which would give Maggie an opening to get away. But with that leg, the impact of the slug would swing the knife toward her throat, not away.

"The other one," Jake said.

"What?" Shane asked. Maggie didn't get it either. Jake darted his eyes to her legs.

"The other one, Mags."

She got the message and moved her right leg giving Jake a clear shot of Shane's thigh. Jake dropped the sight and fired, the bullet crashing into Shane's quad. He screamed, and the impact drove him sideways, the knife falling away from Maggie's throat. She threw her elbow back into Shane's gut and spun away. Shane staggered back, and Jake held the gun on him while Maggie ran clear.

Shane fell to the ground with a guttural groan, releasing the knife and clutching his leg. Jake took a couple steps forward with the gun trained on Shane's head. The Navigator roared up behind them.

"I won't go to prison," Shane said. "Might as well kill me now."

"The old 'you'll never take me alive' dupe? You don't have a choice, pal," Jake said. "A little jail time will do you good. Clear your head."

"I should die and you know it. You just don't have the balls to do it."

"I got the balls. But I like the thought of you playing house bitch to a big-dicked inmate named Bubba for the next thirty years. Sounds more appealing. In the meantime, I'll just think about how I'm going to spend the fifty grand I took from your warehouse."

Shane's eyes widened, then he grinned. "That was you, huh? Guess I killed the wrong guy for it. You should shoot me now, or you'll pay me back someday with your blood."

"No chance, asshole."

"Still no? Maybe I can up the ante for you. I've been thinking about your name. Caldwell. Now seeing your face has me wondering. Did you happen to have a brother named Nicky?"

Jake stiffened.

"I thought so," Shane continued. "I can see the family resemblance. He overdosed, right? Got a little bad heroin?"

Bear parked the Nav next to them and climbed out.

"Who do you think Nicky was dealing for, Caldwell? Who do you think supplied Nicky with the drugs that killed him?"

"He's baiting you, Jake," Bear said, his own 9 millimeter pointed at Langston. "I called it in. Squad's on the way."

Jake pictured Nicky on the dock, the needle sticking out of his arm like his sister described, dull and vacant eyes. A hint of a smile that it was all over. He flashed to the times he took Stony's punishment for Nicky because that was his job, to protect, to watch out for him because they were brothers. A job he failed because of the piece of human garbage on the ground in front of him.

"You know he tried to go straight, Jake?" Shane asked. "He tried to kick the habit."

"Shut up," Jake warned.

"Said he owed it to his family. But I was the devil on his shoulder who put the needle in his hand."

Jake's grip on the gun tightened.

Langston grinned. "I gave him the needle because a good junkie is a loyal customer for life. Your brother was weak and a coward. Just like you it appears."

Bear took a few tentative steps forward. "Jake...don't."

"You son of a..." Jake said, the gun trembling. He wanted to shoot him. Oh God, how he wanted to put a bullet hole through the middle of that smug face.

"But Nicky was a loose end and I hate loose ends. He knew too much about my operation and I couldn't let him live. I gave him a nice, extra uncut dose to put him out of his miserable existence. On the house."

Jake took another half-step forward, his finger tightening on the trigger. He never wanted to hurt someone more badly in his life. The desire to shoot Langston and cut his face with the gold ring flooded his every cell. Snaps of breaking bones and echoes of screams.

"You're not the only one who wants to put someone out of their miserable existence," Jake said. "You know who wants you dead and buried? You know who is paying me...paying me to end your miserable fucking life? Jason Keats. And you know what? I might just do it for free."

The smile dropped from Shane's face, his bravado gone.

"Jake..." Maggie said, but it was too late.

Jake fired the gun. Again and again and again until it clicked empty and tendrils of smoke wisped from the barrel.

He lowered the weapon and took a step back. Shane lay huddled on the ground, his eyes as wide open as Jake imagined Nicky's were in those waning moments. But, instead of a lifeless gaze to the sky, Shane focused on the ground in front of him riddled with bullets. Other than the growing wet patch in the front of his slacks, Shane Langston was otherwise unharmed.

With Bear guarding their foe with a pistol, wrapped his arm around Maggie. As they walked away, he pulled out his cell to give Keats the news.

EPILOGUE

Tears leaked into both Bear and Jake's eyes as Halle and Maggie reunited an hour after Bear's men hauled Langston off to jail. Maggie had picked up their daughter and swung her around. Halle's strong arms wrapped such a choke hold around her mother's neck Jake was surprised Maggie didn't pass out. Bear was carted away soon after at the insistence of the volunteer paramedics. They transported him to Sedalia to get the bullet out of his shoulder. Jake, Maggie and Halle were completely exhausted from the day's traumatic events and everyone crashed out early with Jake not making it past Maggie's couch, Maggie and Halle together in Maggie's bed.

The next morning, Jake lay awake on the couch considering his future. Being fifty thousand dollars richer with Langston's stash made the process a whole lot easier, even if it was blood money. Jake thought of it as spoils of war. It took him a minute to work his way to a sitting position. He stood and made his way back to Stony's house, his truck parked outside. Bear must've had it brought from the shootout at Shane's, the damage minimal given the war it had been through. He unlocked the tool box and breathed out. The money bag waited untouched.

Inside the house, he grabbed his last change of clothes and went to the bathroom to take a shower. He let the hot water beat on him until he emptied the tank and his skin turned red. He got out, dressed and went to the kitchen. As he waited for the coffee to brew, he looked out the back window to the pond. Heavy algae covered the surface of the water, but the old dock on the far bank floated unchanged. For the first time in years, the image of the two of them fishing for crappie replaced the nightmare of Nicky lying there. Good times instead of bad.

He poured the finished coffee into a large mug. His stomach growled, but the coffee was the only consumable thing in the house besides a half empty bottle of ketchup and a jar of dill pickles. He walked out the front door into the morning sun. Not much of a breeze, the humid air already sticky. Minutes later, he gazed from the top of the world at the swaying tree tops that would soon explode into a rainbow of colors. Maybe he'd stick around to see it if Maggie would have him.

"Hey." Jake turned to see Halle walking up the hill from home. Her hair pulled back in a ponytail. She wore a pink T-shirt and cut off sweats with the Warsaw Wildcat logo on them.

"Hey, yourself," he said. "How are you feeling?"

"Still tired." She dropped next to him and admired the beauty of the valley below.

"Me too. It'll take a few days to catch up. Doing okay otherwise?"

"I had a nightmare about Shane and his knife last night. Scared the hell out of me. Woke up in a pool of sweat."

"Most nightmares fade with time," Jake said.

"Most?"

"Best I can do."

"How are you feelin'?"

He rubbed his chest. "Sore. I don't recommend getting shot. Even with a bulletproof vest."

She laughed. "I'll try and remember that. So, this was your spot, huh? You and my mom?"

Jake looked over. Halle looked so much like her mother at that age it gave him chills.

"Yeah, this is where we came to get away from it all, even if it was just for a short while. I didn't have what you would call a...satisfying home life."

"Mom told me a little. Sorry about your dad, even though it doesn't sound like he was much of a good person."

"Thanks. He wasn't. But we'll bury him tomorrow and life will go on."

She picked up a few blades of grass, peeling them in half lengthwise, one at a time. Jake remembered Maggie used to do that before she broached a difficult topic.

"So, my mom dropped the bombshell on me. You're my dad."

Jake exhaled deeply. "She did, huh? How do you feel about it?"

"I don't know," she said, eyes narrowed and contemplative. "Kind of weird. I always thought it was some random guy. I'd see strangers around who kind of looked like me and I would wonder if he was the guy or not. After a while, I gave up thinking about it. I guess it's nice to put a face with the name. You know what's funny, though?" She peeled another blade in half and tossed the remainders, watching them drift away in the wind. "She's always telling me to not get swallowed up by any boy. That none of them are worth it. But I don't think she believed it. I could tell she was waiting for that boy who left her behind back in high school. She always believed you'd come back someday whether she would admit it or not."

"Halle," Jake started before faltering. He didn't know what to say.

"It's also pretty cool," she said, rescuing him, "to know I have the kind of dad who would risk his life to protect me."

She leaned over and kissed Jake on the cheek. Before he could respond, she ran down the hill back to her house. His daughter's lips tingled his skin, a pretty good feeling. It had been a long time since he felt good.

*****

They buried Stony in the Turkey Creek Cemetery next to his wife and son. Two plots remained to one day hold Janey and Jake. Maggie and Halle waited under the tree, next to Janey, Luther and the boys. Jake barely recognized his nephews. Earlier, Luther tried to make polite conversation. Jake cut him off and informed his brother-in-law if he hurt Janey again, he'd spread Luther's remains over ten different counties.

The service was quick and generic. Stony had few friends and none bothered to come. Jake and Bear helped carry the coffin from the hearse and placed it on skids that would lower the casket. The preacher talked, but Jake processed little. Instead, he played back the Stony movie one last time. The coffin lowered in the ground and the crowd dispersed, but Maggie and Halle remained, waiting for him. If he wanted it, they would be there for the rest of his life. Maybe he could handle that.

Two workers leaned on old shovels, waiting patiently for Jake to make his exit. He hadn't been able to say the words at Stony's death bed. They'd likely bring peace and allow him to let go of the anger driving him down the wrong path for far too long. He had the perfect opportunity multiple times over the last few days, but couldn't bring himself to do it.

Jake walked to the edge of the grave, snaking trails of rich, brown dirt rolling off the top of the plain casket. He reached into his pocket for the ring. He ran his fingers over the rough, pain-laden surface. The ring caused scars. Scars were reminders of how life went wrong. But scars were also reminders that despite them, one could make the choice to live.

He stretched out his hand and released the ring. It clinked off the surface of the casket and settled into the loose dirt, the scarred side down. Ashes to ashes, dust to dust.

"I forgive you," he said.

THE END

About the Author

James L Weaver is the author of the Jake Caldwell series featuring IAN Thriller of the Year finalist *Poor Boy Road* and the IAN Thriller of the Year Finalist and New Apple Thriller Official Selection *Ares Road*. He makes his home in Olathe, Kansas with his wife and two children. His previous publishing credits include a six-part story called "The Nuts" and his 5-star rated debut novel *Jack & Diane*.

His limited free time is spent writing into the wee hours, running, binge-watching Netflix, and futilely trying to coax his teenagers to hang out with their parents.

You can follow him on Twitter @jlweaverbooks

or visit his website at www.jameslweaver.net

ACKNOWLEDGMENTS

Major thanks to Kate Foster and the wonderful people at Lakewater Press. Your unwavering belief in Poor Boy Road carried me through the dark times of doubt. Thank you for pushing me along the way and not killing me for my repetitive word choices.

Thanks to my dad for always being there for me, for being such an amazing role model of what a father should be and for being absolutely nothing like Stony Caldwell. Love you, Pop.

Thanks to my mom who always encouraged me to write. I wish more than anything that you were still with us to celebrate this novel.

Thanks to Brenda Drake whose Pitch Wars and Pitch Madness competitions provided a ray of hope through the onslaught of rejection letters and connected me with people who loved Poor Boy Road every bit as much as I did. If we should ever meet, the first drink is on me, Brenda!

Finally, thanks to my cheerleaders and fellow authors Barry Brakeville, E.L. Wicker, Aften Szymanski and Sarah Henning. Your writing and encouragement helped me more than you know and mean the world to me.

CONTINUE THE JAKE CALDWELL SERIES...

ARES ROAD OUT NOW!

"A tense plot, tight writing!"

"Weaver is getting better and better!"

"Loved this book more than the first!"

With his days as a mob enforcer behind him,
Jake Caldwell's trying to go straight.

But it seems his past won't let him go.

His first job working as a private investigator turns up a teenage girl
screaming down a dead man's cell phone, and Logan, his mentor
and the only man with answers, beaten into a coma.

Now Jake's taking it personally.

The only clues Jake has to unravel the mystery are a Russian with a
stolen silver briefcase and three names: Snell, Parley and Ares.

Teaming up with his best friend Bear, the sheriff of his home town,
and an attractive FBI agent, Jake quickly discovers they're not the
only ones looking for the briefcase and its deadly contents.

It's no longer about seeking revenge.

The thrilling second book in the Jake Caldwell series
is a heart-stopping ride that won't disappoint fans.

information can be obtained
ICGtesting.com
n the USA
3114329O919
0BV00001B/47/P

9 780994 451132